BABY DADDY

LAUREN LANDISH

D1311108

Edited by
VALORIE CLIFTON
Edited by
STACI ETHERIDGE

BABY DADDY

BY LAUREN LANDISH

A single night changes everything.

I go from town to town, never staying in one place for long. I'm always chasing the next deal, the next adrenaline rush and thriving in the great outdoors.

Until one fateful trip, one chance encounter. When I meet her... my beautiful Rose.

It was only supposed to be one night. No strings attached. Our chemistry was off the charts and we didn't fight it.

But ever since then, she's all I think about. Replaying the perfect night over and over and thinking about what could've been.

Now I'm back in her town, and it could be my one chance to claim what should have been mine forever and not for just one night.

I've got it all figured out. But as soon as I see her, I come to a screeching halt. What's with the anger in her eyes? And whose baby is she carrying?

Am I too late to make her mine?

Join my mailing list and receive 2 FREE ebooks! You'll also be the first to know of new releases, sales, and giveaways. If you're on Facebook, come join my Reader Group!

Irresistible Bachelor **Series (Interconnecting standalones):**
Anaconda || Mr. Fiance || Heartstopper
Stud Muffin || Mr. Fixit || Matchmaker
Motorhead || Baby Daddy

CHAPTER 1

ROSE

I flip through the rack of dresses, looking for the sparkly black one I know will be perfect. My boutique has a lot of things, but one item that I do better than anyone in town is dresses. Proms, weddings, engagements, whatever . . . you want something unique for that special day, I'm the woman you see.

The problem is, I think to myself as I go through the next rack, *I'm running out of space to keep everything on the floor.* Prom dresses aren't exactly like selling lingerie. They take up a lot of space.

Just when I'm about to grunt in frustration, I see it. I've got a sorting system for all of my dresses . . . I just have a problem remembering what, exactly, that system is at times. "A-ha!"

"Find it, dear?" asks my customer, a lovely middle-aged woman who's been trying on dresses for an hour now in preparation for her twentieth anniversary. She wants something special, and as I pull out the hanger, I know she's going to be happy. Slinky but not skintight, with a spray of jewels on the left side of the top, it's perfect for a woman who wants to look sexy without showing too much skin.

"Found it, Mrs. Alameda! You'll have to pick your husband's jaw up off the floor if you wear this on your night out."

I slip the dress past the dressing room curtain, a smile taking over my face as I hear her gasp in delight. It's a good dress, one I picked up online for a lot less than it should have been from a designer who sells one-of-a-kind pieces on Etsy. I'm not one to care about names, but if the dress looks great, I'll snatch it up for myself or for the store.

"It's perfect! Thanks, Rose!"

She comes out of the dressing room, and I'm impressed. She's rocking that dress like nobody's business. "Whoo-whee, you wear that and you're going to be getting the attention of more than your husband. Hope you know you're going to be causing whiplash."

Mrs. Alameda blushes, running her hand through her long, thick black hair, and she shrugs a little. "Well, as long as John enjoys it . . . but I feel like—"

"Like we need some accessories," I finish for her before she can start the negative self-talk. Sure, retail therapy isn't as good as a shrink, but I try my best without screwing my customers. "I know just what'll go with this."

A little more rummaging around, and I find a long necklace with pearl accents that goes great with the dress, and a pair of peep-toe booties too. "What do you think?"

"I think," she says, grinning, "that I'm going to have a really good anniversary."

Ten minutes later, Mrs. Alameda is on her way to knock her

man's socks off, or maybe his shorts, if things go according to plan.

"Another happy customer," I say to myself, warm with the satisfaction of a job well done as I lock the door behind her to close for the day. Totaling out the register for the day, I'm thrilled to see the daily receipts match the running sum I always keep in my head.

I quickly export the info into my accounting software and do a little wiggling shake of celebration as I realize my sales are on track to make this my best month yet.

At least I'm a rousing success in this area of my life. I've worked incredibly hard since graduating college with both business and marketing degrees, making my dream of owning my own boutique a reality.

I hadn't known a single person when I moved to Great Falls, a sleepy little suburb nestled in the shadow of the surrounding mountains. With a university just to the south and the promise of a growing ski and mountain resort trend, all things had pointed to it being an up-and-coming destination spot. What sealed the deal for me was the throwback Main Street vibe to keep that small-town feel for visiting tourists.

It was perfect for me and my new venture, the Mountain Rose boutique. I don't know if it's magic or not, but since the new Mountain Spirit Resort went in and my friends McKayla and Brad opened their salon down the street from me, my customer base has definitely grown. I've turned the corner, and I'm kicking ass and taking names.

Every day, I help people create fashionable looks that represent who they are, or sometimes who they *want* to be. I scour fashion magazines and decide which trends will sell to my demographic, and I order thoughtfully to make sure the profit margin stays well into the positives.

I think my main strength is that I give each customer what I think is best for them and work to make sure they walk out looking their most awesome, whether it's tight pants, long or short cuffs, high waists, low waists, whatever.

So yeah, I'm a Boss Bitch. I love every facet of owning my own business . . . the people, the clothes, the marketing, the strategy, all of it.

It's definitely a good thing I love it so much, because it's basically all I have. The boutique's been my whole focus for years now, taking up every minute of my days and nights, overwhelming my mind with swirling ideas and requiring every drop of my spirit. At first, it was because I couldn't afford to do it any other way. I had plenty of weeks where I ate cheap ramen noodles for dinner because that was all I could afford. I'm not quite at the level of eating filet mignon or fresh Atlantic salmon nightly, but that's okay. It's been worth it. Until now.

Something about achieving a level of success I'd barely dared to dream of has me thinking, *now what?*. I'm satisfied with my life, I guess, but I really thought by now I'd have a husband, a couple of kids, and a white picket fence. Hell, maybe even a dog or a cat.

But none of that has happened. Seriously, who gives a damn if I've sold a ton of dresses that made women look fabulous? I don't want my headstone to read *Here Lies Rose Samuelson. She Really Knew How to Make a Bitch Look Her Best.*

I'd like to have more than that, but no man has walked into my women's clothing boutique to sweep me off my feet. The closest I've gotten is Brad, who co-owns the salon down the street with my friend McKayla. And while he's basically my new bestie, he's definitely not the type to sweep me off my feet. More likely, Brad would swish about until his boyfriend Trey swept him off his feet, and neither would even notice me with all of my girliness.

So no Mr. Right for me yet. Which is understandable. He'd have to come in here because it's basically the only place I go besides home. And if he's looking for women's clothing, he's probably either married or a cross-dresser.

And while there's nothing wrong with cross-dressing, I really don't share my clothes well, so that's out, and a married guy is definitely on the no-go list. I've joked about getting a cat, something to keep me company at home and curl up under the desk at the boutique, but Brad says that's a surefire way to run off customers.

"Especially with the amount of silky fabrics you have here, honey," he'd said the last time the conversation came up two months ago, fingering a slip set I had on display. "The claws and fur would turn this into a tufted ball of fuzz in two days."

I'd laughed when he'd fake-hissed and scratched the air like a bitchy kitty, but I realized he was right. A cat in a clothing store does sound like a match made in hell.

"Great," I grumbled as he did a full Z-snap of victory when I admitted he was right. "But you know my biological clock is ticking. *Tick-tock-tick-tock*. Besides, it's not the cat I really want. It's the husband and kids."

"Yeah, well, I'm not gonna string you along. You're my bitch and all, but even as cute as you are, I just can't help you with that little issue," he says with a grimace as he gestures to my crotch. "I don't swing that way for any woman. Trey would kick my ass, and not in the fun way like at the gym where I get treats afterward."

I laugh now at the memory as I finish sweeping the floor. But the laughter seems forced. My biological clock never seems to stop its annoying little song deep in my core. I'm only thirty, but it's so damn loud sometimes. I'll see women walking along Main Street with squishy little babies bundled up tight in soft blankets, all cozy in their strollers. The ones that really pierce my heart like an arrow are the moms kissing their baby's heads as they bounce along in a sling across the mom's body, heart to heart with each other.

That sight is always a bittersweet moment for me . . . so sweet and so not me. I sometimes wonder what my baby might look like. I imagine fluffy tufts of hair the color of silk like my blonde locks, maybe even blue eyes?

Somehow, the dad's coloring never plays into my fantasy since he's an unknown and it's my dream. I mean, when I've had fantasies, they've run the gamut, and are all equally impossible. Jason Momoa hasn't walked into my store anytime recently, and neither has Ryan Phillippe. I'd take either one. I'm not choosy. Shaking my head to let the imaginary baby drift away, I gather up my things and head home. To my empty house. Again.

CHAPTER 2

ROSE

*C*urled up on the couch, halfway through my takeout fettuccine Alfredo, I sigh. There's a rerun of some old sitcom on, although I have no clue what it is or even what the episode's about. One of the dangers of cable, I guess. You can easily veg out, and the box isn't going to stop pumping sound and video into your living room.

"What the . . .?" I wonder, setting down my fork. The fettuccine is cold. I'll probably have to nuke the stuff to make it halfway palatable again, but that's not what's roused me from my stupor. Looking around my small living room, I blink for a moment before there's another knock at the door. "Oh . . . just a second!"

I climb off the couch and hurry over, opening up to find Brad leaning against the frame. Before I can say anything, he looks me up and down and starts *tsk*ing me. "Girl, you own the premier fashion institute in town. The one and only person I trust to find me accessories, yet currently, you look homeless, and not in the distressed chic scissor-slashed way."

After completing his head-to-toe summary of my disheveled appearance, he sashays in, not bothering to wait for an invitation.

The brassy bitch. I stare after him, knowing that if anyone else barged in on my downtime, I'd be pissed. But Brad is allowed certain privileges since he's my nearest and dearest in Great Falls. But that doesn't mean he gets a free walk. "It's called comfort home wear, Brad. You should try it sometime. Unclench your nuts from those skinny pants."

"Mmm-hmm . . ." he says, not disturbed at all. "Trust me, honey, I get plenty of chances to free-ball in my free time."

I groan, closing my door as Brad heads to the kitchen. "Well, then I get plenty of dress-up time too. And now it's my dress-down time . . . but please, no free-ballin' now."

"Touché. Fine, I'll stay dressed appropriately and you can stay . . . like that." I can hear the smirk in his voice as he roots around in the cabinets. As his head pops up, he lifts a green bottle. "All right, I hereby call this night to order. Initiate wine and dinner. I brought chicken and feta salads, but I see you've jumped the gun and started in on the pasta. Thankfully, this Chardonnay goes well with both."

I laugh at how comfortable he is, taking over the evening without so much as a second thought. "Fine," I reply, elbowing my way past his thin frame to head over to my cabinet. I grab him a plate and pull down two wine glasses. "I brought home enough pasta for us to split if we share the salad too."

Shaking his head sadly, Brad starts putting salad on one plate, leaving a good chunk of it in the bowl he brought it in. "No pasta for me. Trey has me counting my carbs, and pasta in cream sauce would be my allowance for days. Salad only."

Looking back down at my previously delicious plate with a frown, I sigh and stick the rest of it in the fridge. "Yeah, going over to Casa de Rosseti is probably not the best choice, but it was fresh and hot, and the best part . . . I didn't have to cook it."

Brad laughs and uncorks the bottle. "I know just what you mean, girl. And if I could, I would, but considering my trainer also sees me naked, it serves me well to follow his nutrition plan. Otherwise, I hear it from both my trainer and my boyfriend. Hell no on that."

Grinning, I think of Brad's boyfriend. They met at the gym. Where else, I guess. What started out as a 'free trial trainer consultation' progressed to Brad asking Trey out a few days later. They hit it off pretty quickly and have been inseparable and adorable ever since. Yeah . . . I'm a little jealous. "Where is Trey tonight? Figured y'all would be out?"

Brad shrugs and does little air quotes with his fingers. "He had a 'work emergency' down at the gym."

"He's a personal trainer," I note, confused. "How the hell does he have a work emergency at nine on a Friday night?"

Brad sighs and takes a sip of his wine before he continues. "It's fine. One of his high-paying clients had a schedule change this week, so their regular time had to move too."

I look down my nose at Brad for a moment, considering what he said for a moment before airing my worries. "Does that, uh . . . concern you? *Late-night impromptu training session* sounds like a cover if ever I heard one. No offense, Brad, but Trey is hot as fuck and you two did hook up at the gym."

Brad smirks, draining about half of his glass before getting a refill. "Not in the least. His client is a cougar . . . of the human female variety. She's a professor at the university who's got a conference in Italy next week, and I think she wants to sample more than the local cannoli. So I'm thinking my hottie is just fine. Maybe not as fine as me," he says as he pops his ass out in his signature move, "but for reals, have you seen his ass? My man is fi-i-ine. Mmmhmm."

I bust out laughing because while Brad might be over the top, he is right about Trey. He's a good-looking guy, all muscle and skin so smooth I might consider killing for it. And a bubble butt that no man should ever, ever have naturally.

Settling on the couch with our plates and glasses of wine, we catch up on work. "So, how's the Triple B?"

"Oh, salon's going well. We're rollin' for the winter formal season. I bet that's a good time for you too."

"Not too bad," I admit. "Most of the stuff for the next few months is rentals. High school kids can't afford to buy, but that still means a lot of good money in the register. And let's face it, being able to dry clean and then sell some of those dresses later is sweet."

"I remember my prom," Brad says, giggling. "I ended up giving the captain of the football team a blowjob in the locker room. Ten minutes later, he and his girlfriend were elected King and Queen. What about you?"

"Me?" I reply with a small sigh. "I've actually never been to a dance. Like, ever. I went to a high school that thought proms were too old-fashioned for modern times. So, no dance, no King and Queen. Although they did have *Student Leaders* take a lap around the track at the homecoming football game. The winners my senior year were two girls who were the farthest thing from leaders as you could get unless you wanted to be led to the liquor aisle at the Pick 'n Go. After high school, I buckled down in college, just studied and never went to a single party. And now, in the blink of an eye, here I am. Never been danced, although I've definitely been kissed." I laugh at my own bad joke, but it's halfhearted.

Brad catches a hint of wistfulness in my tone and sets his glass down, leaning forward. "What's wrong?"

I shrug and drain my first glass of wine before holding it out for a refill. "Same as always, nothing to get your panties in a twist. I'm thrilled with everything I've accomplished at the boutique, but there's just a big void where I thought my personal life would be by now. All I do is work, work, work, and while I love that song, as a description of my life, it sucks."

Brad hums and refills my glass. "All right, so you want the whole hubby and two point five kids deal? Hit Tinder, hit eHarmony. Find a guy who's after the same things and go for it. They can't be that hard to find."

If only. "Ugh . . . blind dates, swiping left and right, and matching all just sound like heartbreak. Finding a guy is the hard part! You know what I sort of miss, Brad?"

"You mean besides a man?" he asks, and I nod. "What?"

"I've never done anything really out there. I mean, I was serious in high school, even more serious in college, and then I jumped into the boutique and I've been basically living there ever since. I've accomplished my to-do list, but maybe I didn't realize that I should've had things like do something wild, meet Mr. Wrong *and* Mr. Right, get married, and have babies on the list too." As I list things out, I make checkmarks in the air.

Brad shakes his head, sipping his wine again. "So do something crazy! You don't need a guy to have a baby. Tackle both goals at once. Have a whole 'I am woman . . . hear me roar' moment and do it the turkey baster way. You'd be a great mom."

My jaw drops in shock, and I double-check my glass just to make sure I have downed only one. "Turkey baster way? What the hell are you talking about? Like get inseminated? I don't think I could do that."

Brad lifts an eyebrow and drains his first glass. "Of course you can. Single moms are all the rage now . . . well, really, I think they've always been a thing, considering my mom raised me alone, and look how fabulous I turned out. But there's no stigma these days, just one of many ways families are made. You could totally do it."

Brad judges my reaction, his grin widening. "You're thinking about it! You are! Where's your laptop . . . give it to me, bitch!"

"Well . . . I guess there's no harm in just looking. But that's all it is, okay? I don't think wine and artificial insemination mix."

"Nope," Brad says while doing a quick Google search. "Wine tends to help with the natural way though. That's been going on for thousands of years."

The dry humor helps, and in moments, we're on a website full of the dos and don'ts of artificial insemination. It's not trashy or desperate, as I thought it could be, and Brad nods.

A few more clicks and he's in a database of sperm donors, all available for purchase for artificial insemination. "Okay, hocus pocus, tell me your dream baby daddy and we'll cook him up right here."

There's a series of drop-down fields, and I answer them in turn. "Tall, over six foot for sure . . . dark hair, brown or black. I don't care about his eyes. Teeth . . . well, I don't want anyone snaggletoothed, I guess, but I mean, who cares, right?"

"You'd be surprised," Brad says, clicking away. "Education level?"

I think, but it's really not that hard. "I don't care if he's a doctor or anything, but I want him to be smart."

Brad nods and clicks a few times. "And here . . . we . . . go."

Admittedly, I'm shocked when multiple options come back for my criteria. I mean seriously, where are all these tall, dark, handsome, smart guys in my life? There *have* to be some around here if I actually got out a little, but here I am, looking at a website full of men who match all of my boxes. We click around at the different listings, some with pictures and some anonymous.

As we start going through the profiles, Brad chuckles. "What about Tyler here? Says he makes soap."

"Does not!" I giggle. "It says he's a plastic surgeon."

"Which means those dimples for damn sure aren't natural." Brad laughs. "Hmm . . . Michael?"

"Looks like he'd be a lumberjack," I protest. "Beards might be in fashion with some guys, but he most certainly needs a trim."

"Good point. What about Rex?"

I pretend to gag, shaking my head. "Oh, hell to the no. He looks like Pee Wee Herman!"

Brad throws up a hand and gives me a look. "Fine, you tell me. Who's your type here?"

I look up and down the list and point out one with piercing green eyes and a clean-shaven jaw that looks strong enough to slice through steel. "Here's one. Whoa, that Superman could save me any day!"

Brad hums, nodding as we pull up the profile. "Six-four, two twenty-five? Too bad for me he's straight."

"How can you tell?" I ask. "It's just a picture."

"Trust me," Brad says. "I've got an eye for it. Now Don, here . . . just no," Brad hisses, shaking his head with distaste. "Jesus, girl, he looks like Jeffrey Dahmer and Charles Manson had a baby!"

"Lord have mercy," I say with a laugh, almost thinking the same thing as I see one scary-looking dude with a mullet.

Brad lets out a harrumph, turning the picture to the side. "Well . . . I don't know, girl, from this angle he does look kinda cute . . ."

"Don't even start," I say dangerously, cutting my eyes.

We both stare at each other for a moment before erupting into gales of laughter.

After an hour of looking and the rest of the bottle of wine, Brad leaves, but not before one last parting shot. "Figure out what you really want and go get it. If it's a man, you've gotta get out there. But if it's the baby, just get yourself some baby batter and call it done."

I know he's right, but I'm not really sure which of those options is what I want. Instead, I crawl into bed, not even bothering to clean up the dishes or brush my teeth.

It can wait.

CHAPTER 3

ROSE

"*P*sst!"

I look up from my laptop to see Hillary Young-man, one of my youngest customers even if she's normally just in for costume jewelry, giving me huge eyes.

"Yeah, Hillary?" I ask, minimizing my browser where I'm shopping for some new dresses to stock. "Why are you whispering?"

"Is that . . . you know?" she says, tilting her head slightly to her left. I glance over to the tall, leggy raven-haired woman who's currently looking through racks of coats. "From *Westworld*?"

I nod. "She's staying up at the resort," I comment. "Just taking a break from filming."

"You mean," Hillary says, her eyes going wild, "she *talked* to you?"

My celebrity customer glances over at Hillary, whose voice went up a bit too high at the last comment, and smirks. I get it. I've had enough celebrity customers in the boutique over the past six months that I've gotten used to it. Some want to *live* the celebrity lifestyle. They want their asses kissed, but only in the ways they want them kissed.

Thankfully, most of *those* avoid my boutique. I get the others, who are either normal people who work a rather unique job, or better yet, those who understand that their public persona means people might go nuts like Hillary is and are happy to interact with fans.

In this case, my customer is the best kind. "Excuse me," she says in that lilting British accent that I find charming, "I could use some help."

"I'd be happy to," I reply, but I see her shake her head slightly. I get the message. "But . . . Hillary, would you mind helping me out? I think you might understand what she needs more than I do."

Hillary goes over, and I know I should be excited. She's going to have a great story to tell, and probably a little bit of gossip to share later. Win-win for the boutique. Instead, my brain has swirled on Brad's parting words last night over and over, and I've been perusing the sperm donor site every time there's a lull in the shop. Thank God for multiple tabs in a browser.

I've been looking at it so much that I'm actually starting to think it might be a good idea.

God help me.

I've picked out a couple, but one is really the front-runner. The guy that Brad and I both agreed looked like Superman just keeps popping up in my mind, and I checked the website. They'll deliver nationwide. During lunch today, I even went down the rabbit hole of a few recipient forums where they talk about the whole process.

"Hey, Rose?" Hillary calls, submerging herself fully into her role as 'assistant'. "What's the price on this one? The tag fell off."

I glance over to see her holding up a faux leather jacket that I think is way too thin for when we get into deep winter, but right now, it should look chic and sexy up at the resort in the evenings. "Hundred and seventy-five, but it's faux leather."

"Perfect for me. I'll take it. And that should be all for now."

Hillary brings up the jacket, and I ring up the total—nine hundred dollars. I offered to give a discount because she volunteered to take a selfie with me and Hillary to post on her Instagram and Facebook pages, but she wasn't having it.

After they leave, I go back to my browsing, biting my bottom lip. *Time to fish or cut bait,* I think.

Closing my eyes as I take a big breath, I make my choice. I'm doing this. I'm really going to do this. Tick-tock away, you bastard clock. I'm taking the bull by the horns, controlling my own destiny, and fate had better watch the fuck out because I'm in charge.

I go to the front door of the boutique, flipping a sign to say *Back in Ten Minutes* and grab my phone, dialing my doctor. "Dr. Eldrich's office," the nurse, Melina, greets me. "How can I help you?"

"Melina, it's Rose Samuelson. How're you doing?"

"Oh, it's a good day, Rose. How's the boutique? Got anything especially cute in?"

"Check my Facebook later and you'll see a great selfie I just took," I reply. "But in the meantime, think Dr. Eldrich can fit me in for a checkup?"

"Just a checkup?" Melina asks, and I feel a flutter of nervousness. Dammit, Melina, it's not your business! If I want to do a checkup because I want to do mail-order baby making, that's my business.

I swallow back my biting reply, knowing she's just doing her job. "Yeah, if you don't mind."

Melina hums, and I tap my foot impatiently. A few seconds later, though, she comes back. "Okay, Rose. I looked through Dr. Eldrich's schedule, but he's going on vacation next week, so for just a checkup, it might be a little bit. But we'll see you soon and I can call you if he has any cancellations."

"That's fine," I reply, knowing that I could sweet talk Brad into covering for me last-minute if they do get a cancellation. "I'll see you in a few weeks, and if I get a cute outfit in that I think you'll like, I'll show you some pics."

I hang up, feeling a new lightness. Step one of *Project Have My Baby* complete.

This calls for a celebration. To hell with it. The Mountain Rose is closing a bit early today.

Knowing that Brad and Trey are probably going to be busy making up for their missed date last night, I decide to celebrate on my own. A toast, if you will, to single motherhood.

Grabbing one of my just-in sexy new dresses off the rack—and enjoying the hell out the employee discount—I slip into the dressing room and change. A glance in the mirror tells me all I need to know. My spun-silk hair hangs sleekly down my back, my not too bad curves are banging in this slim-fitting dress, and my eyes are alight with joy. Sure, I might look a little better with some of Brad's makeup artistry on my face, but I think I could turn a head or two tonight.

Grabbing my purse from under the counter, I'm ready to celebrate. I head out to my car, and twenty minutes later, I pull up in front of the Mountain Spirit Resort Hotel, the biggest key in the success of my boutique. Really, I didn't plan the similarities in our names, and the management here is totally cool with it, especially considering I'd been here for a couple of years before they even laid the resort's foundation.

A single woman walking into the bar at the local resort would usually seem like the start to a tasteless joke, but this place is really a gathering spot for locals and tourists alike. Besides, it's got the best views of the whole valley and great music. While the old Grand Waterways south of us might have a better spread of buffet food, I'm not looking to stuff my face. I'm here to celebrate.

I perch on a barstool near the wall, ordering a Michelada with an extra twist of lime. Sure, beer and bloody Mary mix might be weird to some people, but it's good shit and it's my 'thing'. When the bartender delivers, I lift it up slightly, closing my eyes momentarily in a silent toast to my future.

Relaxing as the spicy goodness creeps down my throat, I sigh happily. The music's just right, real bluesy rock that isn't quite roadhouse but certainly isn't pop-rock. Just right for getting my damn groove on, and after finishing off half my drink, I wonder which should come first, dancing or food.

My question is quickly answered a moment later as a guy approaches and pulls out the stool beside me, resting on the edge of it but facing me.

"Hey, gorgeous, how're you doing tonight?" he asks, all

swagger and cockiness in his designer jeans and shirt that's a clear Ralph Lauren knock-off. He's not too bad, but all of my switches are saying *nope*.

"Doing okay," I reply politely, trying to say with body language that I'm not interested.

"So . . . you lookin' for some company? Because I gotta tell you, I would love to see if our companies could merge for the night."

Ugh. Really? That's like nerdy and creepy at the same time. Still, I shake my head and don't throw my glass at his chest. "Sorry, I'm here to celebrate myself tonight. But thanks for the offer."

Luckily, he takes the hint and meanders off, leaving me to enjoy the rest of my drink.

I'm debating whether to get a second glass when I see a man among men walk around me toward the bar. Tall, dark, and handsome . . . check to the check. He turns, glancing to the side, and I nearly have a heart attack when I see that he's got a jawline that makes Mr. Superman Sperm Donor look like a total softie.

He's been sitting a bit behind me, in my blind spot, so I hadn't noticed him, but I'm sure noticing him now. I surreptitiously try to look him over more thoroughly, but it's difficult in the 'mood lighting' of the bar. Dark waves flop down over his light olive complexion, just in line with my eyesight, so I can't even see much more than his fine aquiline nose. But I can see his broad shoulders and a swell to his chest that nearly leaps off his torso in thick slabs of muscle. He's gotta be ripped as tight as that waistline looks. I can even see the ripple of muscle under his thermal shirt.

He must feel my eyes on him because he drops his hand after ordering a drink and turns, his eyes meeting mine as soon as he turns. They widen just slightly, and I get to see his face completely.

He's even got piercing eyes, a dramatic golden hazel that glimmers in the light. I smile at him, a little flirty but not too forward, and I'm rewarded by a flash of white teeth and a set of dimples deep enough to swim in. I watch, enthralled as he picks up his beer and a yellow tablet from the bar and strides toward me.

I follow him with my eyes until he's standing right beside me. His deep voice is smooth as silk as he asks, "Mind if I sit down?"

My tongue feels thick in my mouth and I'm not sure I can speak just yet, so I make an offering motion with my open hand, my smile growing wider. To hell with it. Celebrating by myself is lame. I can certainly celebrate with a fine looking man like this without any problems.

He offers a hand, and as soon as I take it, I feel a spark shoot from my hand through my whole body. "I'm Nicolas Broad-moor, Nic for short. And you are . . .?"

"Rose," I say, my heart hammering in my chest. I feel like I've just dropped into a movie where there should be music playing in the background to tell everyone watching, *'Hey, big shit's going down!'* "Rose Samuelson."

Nic smiles and sits down. "I would love to say 'a beautiful name for a beautiful lady' but I know that sounds like a pretty lame pickup line. It's not. It's just the truth."

He shrugs as if I'll never believe him, but he wanted to say it anyway. I laugh a little, caught off-guard that this gorgeous man could possibly be calling me beautiful.

I mean, I'm pretty enough, I guess. I even thought that about myself when I put on this dress back at the boutique. But it's not something I hear from a man often, if at all, especially not one like this fine specimen here. Something about the way he calls me beautiful feels like the best compliment I'll ever receive.

I decide right here and now to order another drink and see where this goes. "Well, Nic, I suppose everyone's allowed one bit of corn in a first conversation," I reply. "So, what brings you to the resort?"

"Work and pleasure," Nic admits. "I'm a Vice President of Sales for ADRENALIN Sports."

"ADRENALIN?" I ask. They're not the biggest sporting goods name in our part of the country, but they're up there, and I've checked out their site a time or two. "Thinking of opening a store in town?"

"No. I handle direct sales," Nic says. "We don't have too many traditional stores. They're a remnant of a merger we did a while back. The resort's looking at stocking some stuff they'd rent to guests."

I nod, impressed. "You must be into sports yourself."

Nic grins, looking boyish as well as handsome as hell. "I've done outdoor sports for a long time. Hiking, mountain biking, skiing, kayaking, ATVs. Hell, if I could do it outside, I've done it. Of course, they don't make a lot of college scholarships for being able to do Spartan Races, so I got my MBA and turned my passion into my job. So far, it's worked out. How about you? What do you do?"

I blush. I hate trying to talk about myself, but I know it's part of the dance. "I have a boutique in town. It's a small place, but I get to be my own boss, which is nice."

"That's very true," Nic admits. "Except you don't have anyone to bitch to when the boss makes you work overtime."

I laugh, nodding. "I haven't really thought about it that way."

Nic laughs. "So what do you like to do besides work?"

"I wouldn't know," I admit with a laugh. "I mean, years ago, I liked doing outdoor stuff, but I've been spending almost all of my time indoors. I'm just glad the local gym downtown is open until midnight and has a good set of rowing machines."

Nic hums, looking me over again and making my skin tingle. "I'd say your gym deserves credit then. You too."

I feel my heart start hammering again. The way he's looking at me makes me feel like I haven't felt in a very long time. "So, how did the meeting go?"

Nic chuckles ruefully and sips his drink. "Not as good as I'd hoped. Let's just say that I need to talk with the head office to make sure this isn't just a great tax write-off trip."

I laugh. He's not cocky but confident. "So, drowning your sorrows?"

"Nope, not that kind of guy," Nic admits. "I'm going to step back, reformulate my plans, and meet again with the general manager tomorrow afternoon. This time, I'm not going to walk out without a handshake at the least."

His go-getter attitude and willingness to use his brain impress me. He's the kind who knows what he's going after and is going to get it. "Sounds like a good plan."

"Do you do business with the resort here?" he asks.

"I offer dress rentals, but they've got their own shop," I admit. "When they need something new and hot, they check in with me. To be honest, though, it's after work, and I promised myself this would be a relax and let loose night. How long are you going to be in town?"

Nic smiles. He catches the point, but a hint of regret touches his sparkling eyes. "If you'd asked me this morning, I'd have said until tomorrow and been glad about it. Now . . . well, *regretfully*, tomorrow."

His answer disappoints me. I just met him and he's leaving town in just twenty-four hours? Just my fucking luck. I meet the first guy in a long time who's not only hot as hell but he clicks with me. "I'm sorry to hear that."

He reaches out, laying a fingertip on the back of my hand, moving it in little circles that leaves me biting my lip. I can easily imagine him circling my clit the same way, and by the look in his eye, that's exactly what he's thinking. "You know," he says in a deep, commanding voice, "there's nothing wrong with making the most of every moment."

Inside, I'm mentally telling myself to go for it. *Do it,* the little devil who sounds remarkably like Brad on my shoulder says. *Fuck him. Suck that huge cock you know he's got and get him begging to fuck you. Why the hell not?*

I've never had a one-night stand before.

And? Everyone's got a first time for everything. Maybe I'll mark 'do something crazy' off my to-do list after all.

Before I can answer, Nic leans forward, taking the decision out of my hands. There's a half-second of anticipation as he hesitates a breath's width away before our lips meet, and I know exactly what's going to happen.

The blood rushes in my ears as Nic's lips caress mine. Damn, he's an awesome kisser. I wonder what else he's good at. Hell, I'm going to find out, one way or another.

Maybe a little different than planned, but I'm celebrating big tonight. One last hurrah before I happily tie myself down with a baby from Donor X377A.

CHAPTER 4

I feel half-hypnotized following Rose down the hallway to my room. My mind is focused on the sway of her ass in front of me, teasing me along like the Pied Piper of booty. I know I should be focused on how logically, this makes no damn sense, and I should be doing anything *but* bringing her to my room. But I can't deny that I want her, and I can't deny this amazing, almost instant connection we have.

When I left the General Manager's office here at the resort, I certainly hadn't planned on meeting anyone tonight. I'd gone back up to my room, changed out of my suit and into some exercise clothes, and ran a four-mile trail run just because I needed to get my damn head right to think of my next strategy. Nothing gets my brain working better than the smell of fresh pine, and by the time I got back and showered up, I threw on a t-shirt and jeans to work in the bar over a few relaxing drinks.

I mean, what's wrong with a nice highball before dinner? I never thought I'd meet a fucking angel in a dress that sends my hormones into overdrive and my brain into spasms of laughter.

But Rose has kept me engaged, laughing, and enjoying myself as we talked through work and life and nothing at all. It's like talking to her has been as soothing as a long, hot shower and as exciting as white water kayaking. She's smart and funny with a quick, warm laugh that sends tingles down my spine.

Still, regardless of how perfect she is, I never dreamed of getting laid. I'm not going to be in town past tomorrow afternoon. As it is, I'm going to have to squeeze in the meeting with the GM before catching the redeye back home. One-night stands? Totally not my style. Whether I've been in a relationship at the time or not, I'm not the sort to take 'road comfort'. I get the feeling it's not hers either, so what the fuck is it about tonight that's making both of us go a little wild?

Maybe it's a full moon? I remember seeing the moon just crest over the mountains as I ran, but I can't remember if it was full. All I can remember right now is the flush on Rose's cheeks.

Whatever it is, I'm damn thankful because I think we're about to rock each other's world. I can feel it when she glances over her shoulder and in the magnetic tension between our bodies when I walked her up the stairs, my hand resting just on the upper curve of her hip.

We get to my room, and I wasn't lying in that the company paid well for the tax write-off. My bosses thought that by renting a suite rather than a single room, it'd make that sort of unconscious good impression that could help me seal the deal. Whatever. I'm doubly glad for it as Rose stands aside and lets me insert the key card, the glow of the green light seeming to signal both the opening of the door and that we're actually doing this. Not a word passes our lips as I turn the handle and push it open, holding it open for her.

We step into the still darkness, and as the door slowly closes on its pneumatic arm, there's a breath where I think she's changed her mind. Hell, maybe I've changed my mind. The part of me that puts on a tie Monday through Friday says this could be the worst decision of my life. I mean, I don't know this woman. She could be carrying everything between her legs under the damn sun. But I know that's not true the moment our eyes meet and I can see the heated need in her big blue eyes.

She's like me, someone who's worked to make their mark in the world. Someone who's sacrificed hours and hours, sacrificed relationships, maybe even sacrificed a part of ourselves that we didn't even realize was missing until we woke up one morning, looked in the mirror, and wondered *what the fuck is going on?*

No, Rose is pure and clean . . . and like me, she needs this. So I move closer, slowly so as not to startle her, and lift a hand up to cup her cheek. She turns into my touch, a soft sigh escaping as her lips part. "Nic . . ."

"I know," I whisper as the need to taste her sweet lips overtakes me. I cover her mouth with mine, kissing her softly at first. But the sparks ignite, and quickly, our kisses are passionate, her tongue dipping in to tangle with mine.

Moaning deep in my chest at the velvety feeling of her mouth against mine, I nibble at her bottom lip, pulling her body flush with mine and wrapping my arms tightly around her waist to hold her to me. Rose lets out a little whimper and tilts her head back, and I take the invitation, kissing down her neck to the line of cleavage pressed upward by her tight-fitting dress. She even tastes good, her skin lightly spicy and smelling almost like cinnamon as I bury my nose in the dark valley of her cleavage.

She pulls away from me, sliding along the wall to gain a little separation from me, and I'm disappointed for a moment, thinking she's changed her mind about . . . whatever craziness this is.

But instead, she turns in front of me, giving me her back. "My zipper?"

My heart and my cock leap, one pushing only slightly more painfully within its restraints, and with surprisingly steady hands, I reach up and slide the zipper down, exposing more and more of her back with every inch. Her skin is flawless, and as I ease the dress over her shoulders, my fingertips whisper that they've found perfection and no woman could ever compare to what they're feeling. The interplay of soft skin and an undeniable feminine essence combines to weave a magic spell that captures part of me that'll never be the same again.

My cock pulses achingly in my pants, heavy and nearly oozing precum already, and we've barely started. Desperate for another taste of the angel in front of me, I lean forward to press a soft kiss to her bare shoulder, grinding against her ass a little. "Do you feel that, sweet Rose? That's what you do to me. And tonight, it's all yours."

She presses back, humming in appreciation as she swirls her hips against me. Her ass presses against my cock with a deep cleft that awakens a desire within me. Could she be truly perfect for me? I reach around, pulling her tighter, and she whimpers. "Mmm . . . is that what you like?"

"Maybe," I rumble in her ear. "You think you could take me?"

"I'd try," she says in a voice that tells me while she might have fantasies of what I'm talking about, she has no idea what the reality's like. I loosen my grip, letting her spin back around to lower the top of her dress. She smiles, reaching behind her to undo the clasp, dropping her bra away.

"Perfection," I rasp as everything but her panties falls toward the floor. Her nipples are already hard, and they're calling to me. With a soft growl, I bend my knees and cup her tits in my hands, burying my head so low that my words are almost lost in her chest. "Rose, fuck, you're gorgeous. I want to lick these little pink nipples, suck them deep into my mouth, bite them till they stay hard for me. Tell me you want that, Rose."

Her eyes sparkle with desire as I tell her what I want, and she arches, hissing out a breathy "Yes."

Needing no more invitation, I dive in, layering kisses with long, swirling licks around her breasts before focusing on what we both want. I tease and suckle on her nipples, flicking them with the tip of my tongue until they're hard, like twin pencil erasers chewing between my teeth.

Rose wraps her fingers through my hair, holding me to her, and I add a slight pinch to her other nipple, making her gasp in delight. "Nic . . . oh, fuck, yes . . . more . . . don't stop."

Eager to bring this beautiful angel to ultimate satisfaction, I drop to my knees, kissing down her belly while tracing her curves with my hands to reach the remnant of her dress that's clinging to her right hip, caught between her natural curves and the wall behind her. Pushing it down, I offer Rose my hand, and she takes it, another spark jumping between us as she daintily steps out of the dress. I look up at her, my breath hot on her soaked panties, and she bites her lip in invitation, spreading her thighs as best she can without moving her feet.

I kiss just on the edge of her panties and run my hands up from her ankles to her hips, learning her amazing legs. The feel of her ass under my hands is amazing, and I stroke a slow fingertip up and down her crack, making her gasp and tremble. Yes, my sweet angel, you've got a dirty side . . . but not this time. I need something else tonight.

Reaching around, I encourage her to spread her legs a little more so I can cup her pussy. Resting my palm against the hot, damp silk, my throat goes parched, and I look up into her huge blue eyes. "Mmm, Rose, you're so wet for me," I murmur, smiling. "I need to taste you."

"Please," she whispers desperately. "I need you."

She trembles at my words until she's nearly like a plucked guitar string, and I help slip her panties down to her knees, leaving them there to lock her legs a little bit as she leans back against the wall to give me unfettered access.

My eyes lock onto the coral pink lips of her succulent pussy, bare and shining. Cupping her ass, I lean forward and dip the tip of my tongue to her clit, making small circles around it. She shudders, unintelligible soft sounds of pleasure erupting from between her lips with every stroke.

Wrapping my arms around her, I hold her still, keeping her upright, and I start licking and sucking her pussy with one mission in mind. "Do you like that, Rose? Fuck, I know I do. You taste so sweet, I could eat you all night. I want to taste your honey on my tongue."

I flicker my tongue over her clit, teasing it with feather-light licks that make her shake from head to toe. Rose reaches down, clutching at my hair and pulling me in tighter, giving herself over to the dangerous desire pounding through our veins. "Oh, fuck . . . Nico—"

Before she even gets my full name out, she shatters in my hands, her orgasm overtaking her and making her grind her pussy against my hungry lips, filling my mouth and coating me from my nose to my chin in shiny deliciousness. Before her legs give way, I prop her up, lifting her with my hands on her ass, never stopping the delightful torture to her hard little clit.

"Nic, please, I—" Rose begs, and I pull back, looking up at her eyes, her pupils so dilated they barely show any of her baby blues. She's shattered, rocked to her very core, and I know that any more would take her from pleasure to pain.

That's not what I want, so I wipe my mouth with the back of my hand, nodding reassuringly. I stand up and pull her close, covering her mouth with mine, kissing her deeply and letting her taste herself on my tongue. "See how sweet you are?"

She nods shyly, and I lead her toward the bed, her panties falling off as she follows my lead. Her knees hit the edge of the bed, and I ease her back, the soft bedding catching her fall as she rests on her elbows.

I virtually rip my shirt off, the clingy fabric peeling from my skin so quickly I feel static crackling in the light hairs on my chest. My pants join my shirt just as fast, and I suspect that I've popped a button on my fly from the sound. To hell with it. I don't need them anymore. I pause before I drop my boxer briefs, feeling her eyes roving my body appreciatively.

"Like what you see?"

She nods in awe, her eyes tracing every muscle. Her eyes lock onto my groin as she holds her breath in anticipation. I smirk, hooking my thumbs into the waistband of my underpants and pushing them down, letting her see what she's getting tonight. Before they even hit the ground, a smile breaks out across her face. "Holy shit, Nic. That is . . . wow."

I notice she called me Nic again, and somehow, from her, I like it. Most people in my life are colleagues or casual acquaintances, and they insist on calling me by my full name. She's not a colleague. She's something different, something special.

"In my purse, I've got a condom," she says. I reach for her purse, handing it to her to retrieve the condom. I learned a long time and a puncture wound ago to never, *ever* go digging around in a woman's purse. You don't know what might be lurking in those clasped depths.

She pulls the square package out triumphantly and rips it open with her teeth, sliding the tight rubber over my length. My head falls back, a moan escaping my chest as I feel her light touch along my cock, giving me a few strokes.

I growl and pull her up, taking a second to make sure the condom is all the way down before kissing her again. She strokes me lightly and nibbles at my throat. "Nic, please . . . fuck me."

I feel that same strange sense of destiny, of never having this opportunity again take over, and I nod. I climb over her, caging her in with an arm on either side as I cover her with my body. We kiss, our bodies pressing together, warm in the cool room's air, as I stroke her skin, feeling her legs rub against my hips. She shifts, and I feel the hot length of my stiff cock slide over her lips, the underside rubbing against her clit and making her moan thickly into my mouth.

"Put me inside you, Rose," I growl into her ear. "You want it this way? Then take my cock in your soft hands and guide me in."

I feel her reach down, the silky whisper of her fingers lightly grasping my cock, adding a couple more strokes down my shaft and rubbing my tip along her lips and clit a few times. She's so wet I know she doesn't need it, but there's something in her eyes that says she's feeling the same way I do. This is perfection, and perfection only comes once in your lifetime unless you're incredibly lucky. She's going to enjoy this as much as she can. Eventually, she lines me up, the head of my cock pressed against her entrance, and she lets go, giving me total control.

I can feel her already pulsing with need, her pussy trying to draw me in, and I brace my hands on each side of her head, looking into her eyes. I see my need mirrored in her eyes, and slowly and steadily, I press inside. She's tight, vibrating with need, to the point that I can feel her heartbeat through my cock as she squeezes me. I can see fear in her eyes, and I reach up, stroking a wisp of hair out of her eyes. "Relax, I've got you."

She nods, taking a deep breath as I pull back a bit, thrusting in a little farther in the next moment, giving her slow strokes to let her adjust to me. I take my time, relishing the nearly virginal feeling of her body underneath me. This will be a fuck we'll both remember for the rest of our lives.

It feels like an eternity of delicious torment until I'm fully engulfed in her hot, slick pussy, and I pause just a moment to memorize the feeling of being completely inside her. Our eyes meet and she nods. The time for slow is over. Time to see how much we can explode.

Passion takes over, and we pound into each other, hips driving harder and faster as I lift her up off the bed with every hammering thrust.

Rose reaches down to grab my ass, pulling me into her, wanting more. I push her legs up higher, nearly rolling her in half as my hips slap into hers, my cock hammering her body into total ecstasy. She gives it back, squeezing me each time I thrust and clutching at my arms.

Needing to feel more of her, I let her legs down to the bed, driving into her as I press her into the bed with the weight of my body. I bury my face in her neck, her hair splayed all over me, but I don't care because I want to be surrounded by her in every way and I want to engulf her with my body.

I grab her hands, entwining our fingers and pressing them to the bed above her head as I continue pumping into her. Our lips meet in a searing kiss that seems to join our very souls, and I tighten my grip, desperate in this instant to get a lifetime's worth of memories from our moment of passion.

Her cries get louder, and I know she's on the edge, right there alongside me. Pulling back, I press my forehead to hers, panting. "Come with me, Rose. Fuck, come with me."

Rose gasps something in reply, and I feel all the tension shoot out of my body, coming fiercely as I pump into her until I can't anymore, wishing I could have this feeling for the rest of my life.

In the same instant, Rose screams out, falling into her own release. "Nic . . . oh, God!"

I hold deep inside her through her orgasm before my arms lose all strength, and I collapse onto her, shifting my weight off to the side a bit so I don't squash her. Rose cuddles against me, kissing my chin playfully. "Mmm . . . that was amazing."

I cover her with kisses as I agree, humming as she giggles. "Amazing."

We lie there for several minutes, and I pull her close, wondering if we could enjoy the full evening like this. "Rose . . . you want to stay the night?"

She turns, pressing her ass against my cock and humming. "Think you can take care of business one more time before we both need sleep?"

I kiss the back of her neck and reach around, cupping her soft breast and tugging lightly at an already hardening nipple. "I'm pretty sure."

Rose uses her toes to tug a blanket halfway up our legs, giggling lightly. "Good. Because I'm not ready to be done with you yet."

I smile against the soft cloud of hair and wiggle my cock against her ass. "Neither am I."

CHAPTER 5

ROSE - TWO MONTHS LATER . . .

*W*alking up to the table late, I relish the heat from the diner's heater compared to the cold outside. Winter's really set her damn teeth in, and I'm bundled up pretty tightly.

I pull down my hood to see that Brad and Trey are already seated along one side of the booth, and Trey's little sister, Ana, is sitting on the other side. I smile. It's good to see the girl again. I've hung out with Ana a few times as we're both third wheels for Brad and Trey's dates.

Yeah, I know if there's two of us, we're not technically third wheels, but I definitely get that awkward 'I shouldn't be here while these two are thirty seconds from going at it' feeling at times. Still, we put up with it because Brad and Trey are always adorable. Somehow, Trey is just this calm, stabilizing normalcy for Brad's crazy, drama-filled life.

I sit down beside Ana, giving her a side hug as I apologize. "Sorry for being late, as usual. These silver-hair special early dinners are just a little early for me with closing time at the boutique."

Ana waves it off. "No worries. We ordered you a drink and a salad. I knew that much and figured you could order the rest when you got here."

"Thanks!" I reply happily, pulling off my scarf. Ana is always sweet like that, thinking of other people first and herself last, but she's got a touch of spitfire in her too. She's just sweet and sassy, virtually unflappable like Trey, whose blood pressure never ticks up a single point in response to Brad's melodrama. "It has to be sub-zero out there. I swear I'm about to feel my fingernails freeze and drop off."

"Not with that mani I gave you last week," Brad says tartly. "You drop your fingernails, I'm going to have to put on some gel extensions, and if I do that, I'm going full fab."

"Oh, hell no, not with Valentine's shopping coming up," I protest. "You know how much lingerie I'd get snagged on one of your full fab sets? I saw the last one you did . . . didn't know you could put actual sequins on someone's nails."

I sip my water with lemon, realizing as it washes down that I was parched. I need to keep better habits or Trey will have me on the same macro diet deal he's got Brad on. No, thank you. I like having comfort food once in awhile, and frankly, for the past two months, Ben and Jerry have been my best boyfriends.

I drain my water and raise the glass for the waitress to come around and refill, turning to Ana. "How's the job? New place?"

Ana moved to town a month ago, following her big brother after wrapping up her nursing degree at the nearby university. She recently started a new job in the local hospital's ER as a trauma nurse and got a new apartment close to the hospital so that she can easily commute for her odd hours, which I'm sure helps. After four years of dorm life, I'm thinking solo apartment life is heaven for her.

Ana grins and adjusts the sleeve of her scrubs. She's the sort of girl who looks great in the casual hygienic outfits, and I'm sure more than one doctor has wondered if she's a 'naughty nurse'. "Everything's going great! You know me, saving lives everyday."

She says it jokingly, but it's pretty close to the truth. She's already helped on two life-saving resuscitations, and from some of the tales she tells, I'm glad I live closer to the resort side of town. Down around the university has some shady areas.

The waitress comes, and in deference to Trey, I order a grilled chicken and veggie plate, knowing full well that I'm gonna scarf down the pint of Truffle Kerfluffle I've got sitting in my freezer back home.

Everything in moderation, I guess. Besides, recently, my appetite's been through the roof, and while I've been working hard and still hitting the gym, I'm just rolling with it. Hell, body positivity and all. Not everyone needs to have a six-pack.

We're chatting, unwinding after a long day of work, and Brad has us all roaring with laughter about a bridezilla he did makeup for last weekend. "So I get one eye done when suddenly, she decides that cerulean blue isn't the color she wants. Instead, she starts throwing a damn tantrum that she wants ice blue."

"There's a difference?" Ana asks.

"Hardly, and considering it was the third damn change, I just told her I could take care of it," Brad says. "Turned around, did a little bit of hocus-pocus with my hands, pretending I was making an adjustment, and went right back to work with the same stuff I had before. She lies back, I do a light dusting of glitter on top of what I'd already done, and she's happy."

"Happy?" I ask, and Brad snickers.

"Well, she didn't try to claw anyone's eyes out and she said I did an 'okay' job," Brad admits. "Her poor overstressed daddy slipped me an extra fifty on the credit card tip for the trouble."

"I'll drink to that—" I start to reply before a buzzing in my purse alerts me that I've got a phone call. I pull it out to silence it but freeze at the number on the display. "Sorry, guys, it's my doctor. I need to take this real quick."

They all quiet down, using the opportunity to stuff their faces with dinner while I answer. For someone who talks about macros and 'staying shredded', Trey sure can get down and devour food like a starving Rottweiler sometimes. "Hello?"

"Rose, this is Dr. Eldrich," the warm but concerned voice on the other end of the line says. I've been going to him since I got to town, and he's the definition of country doc in terms of his patient interaction, but with a twenty-first-century level of care. "I wanted to check in with you about your bloodwork. I just got the results back."

"Okaaaay . . ." the word is drawn out because while what he's saying sounds reasonable, I can hear an inflection in his voice that's setting me on edge. Besides, who the hell calls at early-bird special time?

"If I'm remembering correctly," Dr. Eldrich continues, "we did a full physical and bloodwork in preparation for you to begin a donor insemination cycle."

"That's right, sir. I kind of have a donor in mind. I just wanted to make sure I'm healthy," I reply. "I was thinking of coordinating with your office about that as soon as everything gets signed off. I figured on taking my time getting prepped for the cycle."

At my quiet words, the table is totally silent, every eye on me. All three of them know about my plans and have been super supportive, but still . . . one simply doesn't talk about sperm donations in the middle of a diner.

But my friends all know. Once I finally decided, Brad even joked that he might consider using a donor womb one day to have a mini-Brad, so it was kinda the same thing. It's really not, but I appreciated his support.

I shake my head, my memories interrupted by Dr. Eldrich's comment. "I figured you wanted to make sure, Rose. Well, your blood counts all came back good—cholesterol and blood pressure are healthy. There's just one thing."

In an instant of almost precognition, my life flashes before my eyes. Something's wrong. I've got bad hormones, cysts inside me, or just flat out can't have a baby. My dream crashes in the span of a heartbeat.

Holding my breath, I bury my chin in my chest, trying to hide from the world. "What's wrong?"

I feel Ana place a friendly hand on my thigh, grounding me for whatever I'm about to hear. Dr. Eldrich replies quickly. I guess he heard the worry in my voice. "Rose, part of the standard workup is that we run a pregnancy test. And good news

—you're already pregnant. So it looks like you won't need the insemination cycle after all."

What? Did he just say what I think he did? I'm stunned, my jaw hanging slack and my eyes wide, as I stumble over his words, trying to make sense of what Doc just said. "Pregnant? Already . . . pregnant?"

Vaguely, I hear him telling me to schedule another appointment and congratulations. He hangs up, and I drop the phone to my lap in shock, my eyes scanning the expectant faces around me. "I'm uh . . . pregnant."

With an overwhelming roar, time starts moving again and everyone's faces light up, nobody's brighter than Brad's. Trey throws his hands in the air, fists pumping. "Congratulations!"

"Oh, my gosh!" Ana adds, throwing her arms around me and squeezing so tightly I think I feel my ribs start to rub together. I guess all that nursing work makes you stronger than you look.

"I think I'll be Auntie Brad," Brad says, signaling for the waitress. "And in the meantime, get this woman a chicken fried steak!"

As they all start to celebrate, talking fast and animated, it takes them a minute to recognize I haven't said anything. I feel frozen, the world rushing past me without my even being able to interact with it as realization crashes over me. "It's not . . . I didn't . . ."

"Didn't what, honey?" Brad asks.

Finally breaking through my paralysis, I grit out between clenched teeth, "I didn't do the cycle yet. It's not a donor. It's . . . it's . . . Nic's."

That gets through to Brad, who whistles slowly. I'd told him about my celebration night and how it was quite a bit hotter than my usual two-drink and home alone party. He teased me for days about getting my freak on and high-fived me when I told him about the little devil Brad telling me to go for it, claiming sagely that it totally sounded like him. "Rose, that's so you that I can't even begin to wrap my pretty little head around it. Only you could have a one-night stand to celebrate deciding to get inseminated and end up pregnant. I thought you were safe?"

"Well," I say, "we were safe. But we were so into it, I don't know, maybe it slipped off a little or tore."

"Lucky bitch," Ana mutters under her breath before jerking as Trey kicks her under the table. "What? An orgasm and a dream baby in one night? That's gotta be fate—"

Trey interrupts. "Wait, so the one-night stand guy? You're really sure the baby is his? I mean, I don't want to say you might be mistaken but . . . are you sure?"

I glare at him. I know he's not trying to say I've been slutting it up, but still, it's hard not to read that between the lines. "Yes, I'm sure. He's the only man I've been with in longer than I care to admit."

Ana looks at me, takes my hand, and gives me a determined nod. "Okay, then. Well, you wanted a baby, you've got a baby. Maybe the old-fashioned way, but the result is the same. And you saved yourself baby batter fees? Congrats, girl!"

Brad looks serious and sips at his water. "So, you gonna tell your baby daddy about the little one?"

I groan, putting my head to my arms on the table. "Guys . . . I don't even remember his last name. First name, the company he works for, and the fact that he's in sales. That's it."

Brad hums, tapping his lips with his index finger. "Hmm, maybe we can do a little check-around, but you were prepared to be a single mom. So if you can't find him, are you going to sweat it? You've got family right here, and we're gonna support you and the little one. Safest, most spoiled rotten wee tyke in the whole country."

His simple words reassure me, and I place my hands on my belly, a huge smile taking over my face. Brad's right. I need to take joy in this. "I'm going to be a mom. I'm pregnant."

Just like that, almost all of my dreams come true. I've got the business, I've got a great circle of friends, and now I'm having my baby.

So what if I'm missing the husband piece of the puzzle? I'm so damn grateful for what I do have.

CHAPTER 6

NICOLAS

"Sorry Nicolas," Wesley, my friend and boss, says as I sit across the desk from him. "They're still a no-go, but I appreciate your going above and beyond. I'll remember that, and so will they."

"What's the problem?" I ask, wondering what happened. It was a pretty standard meeting with a sporting goods manufacturer. "The distribution network?"

Wesley nods. "They said our online network's fine, but with Dick's, Big 5, and a bunch of others out there being so much bigger with brick and mortar shopfronts, they can't handcuff themselves to an exclusive contract."

Shit. This sucks.

I was so certain that my proposal additions would get that manufacturer to choose ADRENALIN Sports. I'd been unsuccessful in person, sure, but I left the company headquarters with a handshake and a smile. I was certain the supplementary information should've had them choosing us.

They are new on the market, and our company is tailored toward the outdoors 'extreme' sportsman.

Apparently, our market overlap doesn't matter though. Thinking back to the initial vendor meeting, I wonder about the rough two-month streak I've been running on. My contract negotiations have gone to shit since that resort declined to sign with ADRENALIN, and my brain sidetracks to the night with Rose. I'd run into her that very night in the hotel bar, my brain initially focused on fixing the contract issue because that's what I do. But we'd had amazing chemistry from the get-go and she'd been a welcome distraction from my fruitless strategizing.

We spent a fantastically hot night together, but when I woke in the soft morning light, it was to cold sheets and a *Thank You* note on the bedside table written on hotel stationery.

Not what I was expecting, honestly. I mean, I wasn't expecting breakfast and warm goodbye kisses while Whitney Houston sings her ass off in the background, but then again, I'm not sure what I was expecting considering she lived in that area. I barely live anywhere since I'm always traveling, and we both have jobs that are time consuming.

Still, from that moment, I've run into bad luck after bad luck. I know half of it is my fault. I'm not focused. Rose was an angel, something never to be enjoyed again . . . and it's tearing me up.

Wesley clears his throat, and I realize he's waiting for a reply to his comment. Blinking, I try to quickly refocus. "Thanks, Wesley. I wish we'd landed that contract, but I'll check in with the guys in the bullpen and see what else is on the horizon."

Wesley waves it off, sliding a piece of paper across his desk to me. "No, I think we need to get you to clear your head some, break the bad luck you seem to have picked up. So I've got a mission for you. There's a new upstart out in Oregon that's doing well, especially considering there are so many adventure tour services there. It's pretty far out, but that's their niche . . . totally off-grid. They take their customers out, and the only way you know they fucking survive is when they come back. I'd love for you to go up and be our initial contact, see what we can place in their hands to get our name on their tours because they're getting some hot publicity. The official supplier for these guys? That's the sort of shit ADRENALIN can use right now. Ironic that an off-grid company is buzzing all over social media, but that's the nature of the beast, I guess, and it's getting customers to them in droves."

I lean back, thinking that Wes's idea is exactly what I need, away from the norm. "Sounds interesting. I might even take a day or two off-grid myself, see what exactly they do, pitch it to them as a way to make sure we can tailor our stuff to meet their needs."

Honestly, I'm just spouting bullshit because I just want to get out for a while. But this project sounds like my idea of heaven. While I usually have to wear a suit and tie for work, my heart lies outdoors in the woods, in the wild, roughing it up and living off the land. My favorite fantasy would be to head out with a good knife, a bow, and a tiny backpack of supplies. All I need for a week of utter bliss.

Wesley smiles and raps his knuckles on his desk. "I'd say that's why you've always been my best sales guy, but I know you're not doing it out of the goodness of your heart for the company. You're out for a nature walkabout, aren't you?"

I shrug, grinning sheepishly. "Yeah, a little time outdoors

always does the spirit good. And you're right, I'll be able to shake off this bad luck. I've just been a little off my game since that meeting with the people at the ski resort."

Wesley smirks. "I still think it's because you can't shake the girl."

I feel heat creep up my neck, but I don't really have a sharp comeback for him. The week after coming back, I told him about my night with Rose—not all of the dirty details of course, but that I met someone sexy and brilliant and talking through the proposal with her had actually resulted in a few of the additions I'd made.

The contract for the Mountain Spirit resort might not have gone through, but her input was invaluable to me, and Rose has been on my mind ever since.

Trying to brush off his comment, I give Wes the finger. "Fuck you, man. Yeah, that was a good night, but you know how life is. Still, not everyday I meet a woman that smart and gorgeous."

Wesley, who married his college sweetheart and has been happy about it every day since, shrugs. "Maybe your walkabout can give you a few ideas for your upcoming vacation? Hell, you could head out there for a repeat performance."

I smile, shaking my head. "While that could be fun, I'm not sure I want to risk ruining a great memory when she obviously left the next morning with no intention of seeing me again. It's just that sort of night that you can never, ever live up to again. It was just that, a night to remember forever."

Wesley shakes his head. For a man who's an executive, I swear he's a lot more idealistic than I am. "Then maybe you'll meet some little Earth-loving lady out in the wilds on your trip. Can I give you a hint?"

I look at him expectantly, ready for the joke because I know him and that's where this is going. When ideas don't work, resort to humor, usually the closer to frat house humor, the better. He's just lucky everyone working directly for him is a guy who isn't going to get offended at his occasional comments. "What?"

"If she doesn't shave her pits, there's no lady garden tending either. Full 70s bush, guaranteed."

There's a half-beat of silence and then we both burst out laughing. "Thanks for the tip, man. But I'm not looking for anything right now, bare or hair. Just some work, some relaxation, and then I'll be back, hopefully with a new deal with our off-grid tour company."

CHAPTER 7

I don't know if I've ever felt this vulnerable before, sitting in the doctor's office waiting for my first prenatal exam. I'm wearing a barely-there sanitary gown that peekaboos my ass no matter how many times I wrap and rewrap it around myself. To top it off, the cold is making my nipples ache they're so goddamn tight, and my ass and thighs seem to be coated in superglue as much as they're sticking to this paper-lined bed. Examination? More like the goddamn Spanish Inquisition.

Finally, there's a soft knock and Dr. Stevens walks in. While Dr. Eldritch is going to monitor me and still be my main physician, he referred me to his friend for the baby itself. He's young, and I wonder how someone his age could have finished all of his training already. He looks like he should barely be old enough to shave, and if it wasn't that the hair's way too light, he'd be a perfect stand-in for Sheldon Cooper. "Uh, Dr. Stevens? How old are you?"

He chuckles as he sets his clipboard aside. "I'm thirty-four. I know, I know. My mother kept getting carded for drinks up until I was in junior high school. Even now, she gets men half her age giving her compliments. Hope I get that when I'm sixty."

I nod, relaxing a micrometer. "Okay. Sorry if I offended you."

"Not at all. Now let me go get Julie, and you get yourself arranged for the exam." He leaves, returning a moment later with one of the nurses I saw up front, a pleasant motherly-looking woman who puts me at ease with her seen-it-all demeanor. "All right, Rose. Let's check you out, see how everything's going."

I scoot down, letting my ass hang off the table, and lift my heels to the stirrups for the exam. Dr. Stevens wants to do a full workup, make sure I don't have anything brewing down-stairs that might give rise to complications later. I feel the chilly air between my legs and shiver. *Okay, I was wrong . . . forget five minutes ago. This is the most vulnerable I've ever felt.*

"Relax," Dr. Stevens says as he pulls on rubber gloves. "This part only takes about two minutes . . . and then we can do the ultrasound to see if we can get a view of your baby."

At the mention of the sonogram, my heart starts pounding, excited to see the baby. My baby. I'm still in shock, have been since I got the phone call a few weeks ago, but the reality is starting to sink in. "O–okay."

"So have you started following the advice Dr. Eldrich gave you?" Stevens asks as he swabs me. I know what he's doing, trying to distract me, but it still helps.

"I went right to the store and started the vitamins he suggested, and I'm getting forty-five minutes of exercise in every day," I reply, shifting my butt a little. "How much can you tell on the ultrasound?"

"Depends on your date of conception," he replies in between giving orders to Julie the nurse. "If you're more than six or seven weeks pregnant, we might be able to detect a heartbeat. We'll see what we can see."

I relax as best I can as Dr. Stevens begins the sonogram and starts scanning for my baby.

My eyes lock on the monitor screen as Dr. Stevens takes measurements, but all I see are swatches of grey static and an occasional black orb. He makes a few comments to Julie, but nothing I can understand. "Uhh . . . doctor?" I ask nervously. "So does everything look okay?"

Dr. Stevens smiles and looks me in the eye. "Yep, perfectly fine. I'd make an estimate that from the size of your baby and some of the other things I'm seeing, you're about two months along now. Now let's see if I can get an audio for you on the heartbeat."

He clicks a few buttons on the machine, maneuvering his sensor around some more, and a few moments later, I hear the most glorious music I've ever heard as the sound of my baby's heartbeat fills the room. My eyes fill with tears of joy, overflowing down my cheeks as I sniffle. Just like that, in a simple pulsing sound that sounds like an electronic bass drum beat, it's real.

I'm a mom, just like I wanted.

Maybe not how I'd planned, but Ana was right, the result is the same. "Okay, Rose, I'll leave you to it to clean up and get dressed. Meanwhile, I'm going to get you some printouts of the pictures we took."

Five minutes later, I'm cleaned up with my casual clothes back on, and Dr. Stevens hands me a few tiny pictures. I can feel the smile overwhelming my face as I look at the pictures in one hand and rub my belly with the other. "Wow."

Dr. Stevens nods in appreciation. "Congratulations again, Rose. Your blood levels look great and sonogram looks great, so we'll get your labs done and set up all your routine appointments for the next few months. If you need to wait to check your schedule or the father's schedule for the appointments, that's fine, of course. We just want to get them on the books ASAP."

At his mention of *'the father'*, my smile falters a bit. Julie catches it and looks like she's about to say something when I take the bull by the horns. "Uhm, Dr. Stevens . . . this is kinda embarrassing to say, but does it matter if I don't know who the father is? Does that make a difference in the tests you need to run? I had an encounter and we used protection, but—"

His face doesn't even flinch. He's a consummate professional and I'm suddenly glad that Dr. Eldrich referred me to him. "But stuff happens and very few things in life are 100%. Unknown father . . . okay. Just in case, we'll add some extra screenings to your labs, but it shouldn't matter medically. Dr. Eldrich already ran a full screen with the blood he took when you found out you were pregnant, and you're clear. If you can get some health information from the dad, that'd be helpful but not really necessary."

"Okay," I stammer, my mind whirling at 'helpful but not really necessary'. What the hell sort of 'helpful but not really necessary' information could he be thinking of? "I just wanted to make sure. I mean, I know who the father is. I just don't know him all that well. You know?"

Dr. Stevens smiles at me and makes a note on his clipboard.

"Rose, it's fine. While I might look like I just stepped off the high school cross-country team, I've been running a practice on my own for going on six years, and you're not the first single mom who doesn't want the father notified. My job is to keep you and the baby safe and healthy. No judgment here whatsoever."

I sigh with relief, just now realizing that I'm kinda nervous about what people will think about a single mother who got knocked up from a one-night stand.

But he's right, people shouldn't judge, and I'm just so excited to be a mother. Seems like fate stepped in to help me out with my dream, and I'm not going to question that for even a second. I've got good friends and what seems like a good doctor. I'll be fine. Who needs a baby daddy when my baby's gonna have a whole crew supporting him or her?

Walking outside, I lift my face to the sun, letting it wash over me. I'm already floating with happiness and it feels like even the world around me is celebrating as the birds sing and the wind blows softly around me.

Now that I know everything is okay with the pregnancy, I really should make an attempt to let Nic know. I really should. I don't actually want anything from him because he certainly didn't ask for or expect this, but he deserves to know.

What if he thinks I did this on purpose? While I certainly wanted a baby, I didn't mean for it to happen like this.

What if he gets mad? That's definitely possible, but if he's a jerk about it, he can just leave us alone. That wouldn't change anything for me.

What if he wants to be involved? That actually gives me pause, because I don't really know Nic. Maybe he'd be an awful father? I dismiss that thought, knowing that he was so sweet with me that surely, if he chose to be an active parent, he'd be that good with a baby.

My thoughts keep swirling, question after question. But the result is the same. I need to let him know and see how the cards fall.

I sit in my car, pulling up a Google search on my phone. Typing into the search bar, I put in what I know. Sales. Nicolas. ADRENALIN. I get pages of results back and also realize that there's like four different ways to spell Nicolas and I don't know how he spelled it since we didn't write anything down besides my *Thank You* note.

I click and search for almost an hour before I find the right number.

There . . . just ten little numbers and I can tell Nicolas that, well, I've got a memento of our night of passion that lasts a hell of a lot longer than a left behind handkerchief or pair of panties. I take a big breath, looking skyward for a moment searching for strength, and dial the number.

The phone rings three times before a crisp female voice answers. "ADRENALIN Sports, Nicolas Broadmoor's office. How can I help you?"

I gulp. Shit's hit the fan now. "Yes, can I please speak to Nic . . . I mean, Nicolas?"

"May I ask who's calling?"

"My name is Rose Samuelson. I met Nicolas on his trip to the Mountain Spirit resort recently. I wanted to follow up about our meeting."

My words are stilted, trying to make a hook-up sound like a professional encounter. God, I'm such a terrible liar. I'm sure this woman is seeing straight through my bullshit.

"I'm so sorry, Ms. Samuelson. Mr. Broadmoor is out of state right now, but I'd be happy to pass along a message."

I feel the disappointment flood through me. I was ready to get this over with, but I don't really have a choice.

"Sure. Rose Samuelson. My number is 324-952-8156, regarding our meeting." There, that sounds reasonable and not suspect at all. She repeats the number back to me with another promise of passing the message along, and I hang up. My car's suddenly way too warm, and I crank the engine, lowering a window to let in a drift of cool air.

Well, I might not have gotten to tell him, but this will at least be a barometer of whether he wants to talk to me again. If he doesn't call, I guess I'll know that he doesn't want anything to do with me, and he certainly wouldn't want anything to do with a baby.

CHAPTER 8

NICOLAS

*T*he sound of birds singing wakes me up, and I roll over in my sleeping bag, feeling the long-missed tingle of cool air on the tip of my nose and the freshness of sleeping outside again. Taking a big breath of crisp air, I slide out of my tent and stretch my arms high and wide.

Looking around, I'm stunned as I look around at the scenery. I'm deep in the forest, surrounded by tall redwoods that rise toward the sky all around me. It's both grand and knocks you down a peg. There's no way to think you mean all that much in the world when you're surrounded by thousands of trees that were standing tall and proud a hundred years before your family even came to this country.

I zip up my tent, heading up the narrow trail that winds through the trees toward the headquarters of this little camp that I'm staying in tonight. Reaching my rental ATV, one of the few vehicles that can reach this place, I quickly brush my teeth with peroxide before spitting into the dirt. That done, I approach the little cabin nestled in a small clearing just as the front door opens.

A huge, grizzly looking guy comes out, unkempt beard hanging wildly down to his round gut that's covered with a classic lumberjack plaid flannel. I don't think I've ever seen a more obvious stereotype of a 'mountain man' in my life.

There's a moment where I hope that he remembers we have an appointment because I have no doubt that he could easily kill me with an axe and hide my body somewhere out here, and I'd never be seen again. There are good and bad things about making a sales pitch fifty miles from the nearest town . . . axe-wielding maniacs definitely fall into the bad things category.

My initial fears immediately soften when he smiles, lightly yellowed buck teeth peeking out through the unruly facial hair, and offers me his callused working man's hand. "My boys said you checked in last night. How was your sleep?"

"Best I've had in weeks," I admit honestly. "Thank you for letting me pitch a tent on your land."

"Not a problem," the big man says. "By the way, I'm Sam Sampson, owner-operator of this outfit. Come on in the house. I'm sure my wife Susan will have a glass of tea ready for you. If I'm lucky, maybe she'll let me have one too." He says it with a wink, so I smile back.

"Yes sir, Mr. Sampson. I'm Nicolas Broadmoor of ADREN-ALIN Sports. Looking forward to seeing if we can be of assistance with your equipment needs out here," I reply, following him. I know I should feel strange about doing a sales pitch out here dressed in rags . . . but hell, I'd feel stranger wearing a suit right now.

"Just call me Sam. Everybody does," he says. "Not sure if that's short for Samuel or Sampson, but that's what they call me."

As we walk in the house, I hear a laughing voice, mocking Sam's deep speech. "I don't know what my ma was thinking when she called me Samuel Sampson, but story goes she lost a bet to my dad."

A petite grey-haired woman comes out of the kitchen carrying a tray with a pitcher of tea and two glasses. I can't help but smile as her twinkling eyes take in her husband and she sets the two glasses down on the rough-hewn wooden table. I vaguely wonder if they're for me and Sam or me and her. "Sorry, Sam, but I hear that same damn line every time you meet someone new. You need new material."

He laughs and growls at her, waiting for her set the tray down before grabbing her in a big bear hug and shaking her silly as her giggles bubble out like champagne. It's cute . . . adorable, really. I mean, both of these people are well into their sixties. They might even be in their seventies. But it's totally obvious they're both still crazy in love for one another.

There's a twinge in my heart, a quiet hope that I'll have a love like that someday. I have a momentary flashback to Rose but dismiss it just as fast considering we barely knew each other. But damn, I wish I'd gotten to know her a little better. Just a chance, an exchange of phone numbers, something . . . but now all I have are memories.

Smirking at my own internal monologue, I tune back in. The tiny woman offers her hand, and while she looks like a strong wind might blow her over, her hand is work-worn and her handshake solid. "Welcome to our place. I'm Susan Sampson, charged with keeping this old coot in line. And let me tell you, that's a full-time job. Sit down and let me pour you two boys a glass of tea."

I catch Sam giving me another wink that he got a glass after all as he takes it from Susan with a hearty smack on her cheek. "Thanks, honey. You know I love it when you give me some sugar . . . in my tea."

She shakes her head, but there's a slight flush in her cheeks when she slaps him lightly on the shoulder. "Behave."

She leaves, and Sam turns to me. "So, Nic, what exactly do you think ADRENALIN Sports can do for me and mine? No offense, I know you're a good man by the way you came out of those woods feeling right at home . . . but military surplus has done right by me for a while now. What can you guys do different?"

"Well, let me break it down tour by tour that you offer. First, your adventure tours. I know ADRENALIN sounds like we're all extreme sports, and there's a kernel of truth to that. We got started with extreme outdoor sports. But we cover all forms of outdoor sports. Right now, the big buzz about you guys is your ATV and hiking trips, everything loaded onto backpacks."

"That's my son's gig," Sam admits. "While I got no problem riding an ATV anywhere, the idea of walking up the side of a mountain anymore just gets my knees aching something terrible. Then again, half the folks who come here end up aching too."

"Sure, and I know that a lot of those folks show up . . . less than prepared," I reply. "And you rent out equipment to them, which I think is a smart idea. No worries about fussing around with replacement parts, no problem with substandard equipment. And surplus, it's usually good stuff, I'm not gonna put it down. But I can guarantee you that ADREN-ALIN can provide you with equipment that's been tested from the Rockies to the summit of Everest. You need clothes, packs, boots, whatever, we can get it for you. What about your other programs?"

"Well, I like to take folks to do some fly fishing when the season is right, and occasional hunting trips for recommended guests," Sam says. "I gotta admit, that's the trickiest. I don't just take any old Joe out hunting around here. I've gotta know you're good with a gun, safe and able, because I'm not running a lesson range out there. Most of the folks I do allow, they bring their own kits, although I will provide ammo if they need it."

I nod, laughing lightly. "Makes sense. Personally, I can't imagine that teaching someone to shoot on sight is going to result in a satisfied customer with a big game trophy. And professionally, there's reasonable risk and there's stupid. Good to know that you know the difference."

He gives me a nod. "Come on, let me show you the garage."

Sam takes me out back to their garage, which is more like a good-sized country barn filled with ATVs and snowmobiles where there used to be horse stalls. Along the other side, arranged with all the neatness and efficiency of a good storeroom, is the rest. Fishing gear, snowshoes, cross-country skis, packs, tents, and all the needed accessories, all neatly arranged and obviously well-cared for.

"My shooting bench, along with equipment and my lending gun safe, is in the back corner," Sam says, flipping a switch. Another light switches on, and I see two military-style weapons racks with locks. "They're not as good as my old Winchester I keep in the house, but I keep them all in good condition. Also in the locker there, I've got the archery equipment, not too much since most of my bow hunters treat their bows better than most men treat their women. But I got the accessories if they need it."

"Very nice," I reply, making a mental note to add archery to my proposal. Knowing that our primary placement is going to be the larger pieces of equipment, I head directly to the ATVs, which are maintained and seem to be in great working condition, but they're dated, and well, not ours. "Let's get a start here, if you don't mind. Now, it's very obvious you take pride in caring for your gear, but I think we can do better."

We spend the next two days going through our catalog item by item, and the contract line by line. I have to give and play some, but I use a sales tactic that I'd picked up long ago. By giving some more in the 'big' items, like the price of an ATV, I can gain ground in other areas. A six months' supply of gunpowder, primers, and rifle cleaning materials runs quite a pretty penny, and ultimately, Sam can pass that along to his customers as a convenience fee for onsite supplies. Win-win for everyone.

In the end, all the office sales time isn't the same as the real deal, so we decide a test drive is in order. I call the head office after the first night, and that weekend, a trailer pulls up in town, delivering a couple of ATVs for us to take out on one of their usual adventure tour tracks, along with all the accessories we'd pack. Sam and one of his sons even agree to take along a 'customer pack' for comparison.

Side by side with their older models, the difference is immediately obvious. The ADRENALIN packs are lighter and easier to carry, and by the first night of our tour, it's just a matter of getting names on papers and setting it aside for lawyers. That lets us spend the bulk of our time enjoying some time outdoors with no pressure, and Sam offers to sidetrack to show me his favorite fishing spot. He has a passion for living off the land, being outdoors, and I can appreciate that.

Over the next few days, I thoroughly enjoy rising with the sun and exploring the forest all day as we hike, fish for our dinner, and camp under a canopy of stars. I brought along one of our bows, one that works for both fishing and hunting with minimal adjustments, and I'm thrilled when Sam seems impressed with my prowess and the equipment.

On our last night deep in the forest, Sam stares into the small fire we'd started to cook the trout we'd caught. It's after dinner, the trout eaten, and we're just enjoying the last of the warmth. "So tell me about your life back home, Nicolas."

I lean back, enjoying the warmth of the flames as the night chill starts to come on. "Well, not much to tell, I guess. I grew up loving the outdoors, but at the time, I didn't think it'd pay well. So, I went to school for business, did sales after graduation. But I kept up doing a lot of outdoor adventure stuff as much as I could. Every weekend, every holiday, every vacation I get, I'm going somewhere and seeing new things, experiencing a different world, learning something. Hiking, skiing, parasailing, hang-gliding, bungee jumping, skydiving, you name it, I've done it. If there's a rush involved and it's outside, I'm in. But I also love the rush of seeing the world in an uncommon way and the peace I get in the quiet, far from the city where I mostly work. Started working with the guy who owns ADRENALIN as a sales rep and worked my way up. What about you? How did you and Susan decide to start doing adventure tours?"

Sam pokes around in the fire to distribute the coals before answering. "This has been my family land for generations, but Susan and I used to only come here for weekend getaways. We lived in town when the kids were little, but when they'd all grown and gone, we just felt empty. They send us pictures of them in the mail, and everyone came out for Christmas—made Susan so damn happy. Anyway, we all came out to the cabin for Christmas one year, and after the kids went home, we stayed to clean up the house, do a few projects, and ended up snowed in for a couple of weeks. By the time we could get out, we didn't want to leave. Sounds crazy, but locked up in a cabin with that woman for two weeks is my idea of heaven and we just didn't want to go back. So we didn't. One of my boys had a friend who wanted to go hiking so he asked if I'd show him around a bit, so I did. I guess he posted some stuff on the Internet and all the sudden, I'm getting letters asking if I'd take them out too."

"That's quite a story you have there," I reply honestly, feeling slightly jealous.

Sam nods. "We get to stay busy, be alone when we want to be, and share this beautiful Earth with folks who recognize they need a little time with Mother Nature."

"I definitely needed this recharge myself. I haven't been getting out as much as I'd like with the busy work of business taking me here and there. I travel—hell, all I do is travel, it seems, but it's all work, no play."

Sam hums knowingly. "You know what they say about that? Makes Nicolas a dull boy. Hell, before this, I was like you. Worked a job just like you . . . then I realized something. All a man really needs is a woman he loves and some time in the sunshine. That's all we could ask for."

He smiles, lifting his face up to the night sky speckled with bright stars as if they're the sunshine he's talking about. "Think I'll turn in. Gonna see my Susan in the morning, and she's gonna have missed me something fierce these last few days, if you catch my drift. I'm gonna need my Zs to keep up with her."

Laughing, I lie back, staring at the stars too, catching a flash of light streak across the sky.

I have a moment of childhood innocence and make a wish on the shooting star. "A good woman and sunshine . . . sounds like a great life if you can make that happen."

With a smile, I head over to my sleeping bag, curl up, and nod off.

CHAPTER 9

ROSE

*J*uggling my bag, my coffee, and my keys, I try to get the door to the Mountain Rose open. It's a lot harder than it was three months ago when my tummy was flat-ish, I wasn't having weird food cravings, and I didn't spend half of my mornings chucking into the toilet.

That's okay, I'm halfway through my pregnancy, and despite the difficulties, every day is a new adventure and I'm looking forward more and more to what's to come. Still . . . "God-damn lock," I mutter, hissing.

Finally, it clicks, and I push the door open, setting everything on the counter and hustling back to flip the lights on and the sign to *Open*. Hustling is getting to be a little bit relative since I've already started to get a little waddle to my gait even though I'm barely showing. What with winter still in full effect, when I wear loose, warm clothes, almost nobody notices unless I tell them.

Brad says my little baby bump looks like maybe I just had a

big lunch, just a little food baby. But at five months along, this is definitely not just some burritos, although I could go for some breakfast burritos right about now. Mmm . . . warm eggs with some spicy sausage, cheese, and maybe some rice in there . . . yeah, baby, that's what I want.

I've been fortunate that while I've had some morning sickness, I've been able to eat just fine. Actually, I think Brad's a little jealous. Every time I stop by the salon, he's drinking something that looks like it was mixed up for the Toxic Crusader while I'm rocking something covered in cheese.

I grab my morning coffee from the K-Cup machine, a birthday gift from Ana last year that I've come to love. I inhale deeply, breathing in its steamy goodness as I boot up the computer and check emails. "Enjoy it while it lasts," I remind myself. "These eight ounces of liquid sanity are a precious commodity."

Everything electronic looks good today, just some spam, a few bills that I click *Pay* on immediately before I forget, and then my weekly pregnancy newsletter. These are my favorites, reading about how big my little Jelly Bean is, what's developing, and what I'm likely to be experiencing.

That one is tough because while some women are already feeling movement, I'm one of the few who haven't yet. It worries me, even as I tell myself that everything is fine.

The range is 16–25 weeks, and I'm smack in the middle at 20 but just ridiculously impatient for what I think will be a monumental moment in my pregnancy.

I've tried a few of the 'recommendations' to trigger squirming like drinking orange juice, and last weekend, Brad gently poked my belly to see if that'd get some movement going. But no luck so far. He's declared me defective, though he was only kidding. I still threatened to not let him be an auntie, so he's piped down after that. But I'm still trying to feel something, anything.

Sighing, I close down my emails and get the store ready for customers. About five minutes later, the door opens and my new assistant walks in. "Devon, so great to see you this morning."

Knowing that I was going to need some help as the pregnancy progressed and for some maternity leave, I hired help. Today's her first day, and I'm excited that the Mountain Rose and I have reached the level where I can hire some help, and Devon seems like a really sweet girl, ready to learn and happy to help.

"Thanks, Rose! Great to see you too. Where do you want me and what can I do?"

Good start, girl. Very good start. "Let's unload the new order that arrived yesterday afternoon, get it all hung and set out. I'll show you the system and how I like to tag things. Then I'll go over the register with you."

Without another word, she's off and running, going into the back of the store and grabbing the box and moving it closer to the rack. We get to work, and within twenty minutes, I'm already in love with this girl. It would've been impossible for me to move that box and I would've spent too much time and energy walking the clothes back and forth from the box to the rack. But Devon's got wiry strength and energy for days, and we get the racking going in half the time it would normally take.

We move over to the register, and I quickly go through ringing up a sale, making change, and doing a return or exchange as we see customers all morning. It's not too busy, but enough that Devon is able to train.

"You're a fast learner," I tell her during a small lull in foot traffic. "You're going to do fine."

Devon smiles and gives me a thumbs up. "Thanks, Rose. It's not too different from the other registers I've worked so it's an easy pickup. And this is a lot more glamorous than doing shifts down at the supermarket."

"Glamorous?" I laugh. "Oh, hell, Brad's gonna love you! He's a friend from down the street, part-owner of the salon. He stops in from time to time. You don't mind being called bitch, I hope? It's said in love, I promise."

Suddenly, my tummy lets out a loud rumble and we both freeze for a second before bursting into laughter. "Well, apparently, that's my alarm clock for lunch. Did you bring something?"

Devon shakes her head. "No, I figured I could grab something from the diner if we weren't too busy, or later if we were. I mean, I could afford to skip a meal or two."

I don't know if it's the soon-to-be mother in me or just hearing that sort of bullshit too often, but I grab her hand. "No. Get rid of that thinking right now. You're gorgeous, Devon . . . and the diner sounds great. So here's the deal. Your boss is buying and you're it picking up. Have any idea what you want?"

She's already nodding, grabbing a notepad off the desk to write down the order, when I change my mind. "Actually, this would be a great test. I'll go grab our lunch—the walk will do me good—and you stay here. There shouldn't be too many customers coming in right now, but if they do, you know how to ring them up. Call me if you need anything. I'll be right back."

I rip the top sheet off the notepad and head out with a wave. Outside, I check what she wrote down. A garden salad? Hell no, this girl's getting at least a turkey sandwich to go with it. Stepping into the sunshine, I tilt my chin up and close my eyes, appreciating the bracing chill that rolls through my body after being in the heat all morning. My cardigan is just right for the chilled air considering my Jelly Bean has my body temperature rolling a little warmer than usual with the bonus insulation and hormones.

As I walk, I'm mentally debating if it's a cheeseburger day or a club sandwich day, finally negotiating myself into a compromise of a burger with extra lettuce and tomato. That's basically a salad, right?

Vaguely, behind me, I hear someone calling out my name. Thinking for a moment that maybe Devon had a question after all, I look back and see the last person I expected to ever see again. Nicolas, my baby daddy, is jogging toward me, a wide smile on his face as he waves.

I turn and he screeches to a halt, his eyes tracking from my face to my obviously rounded belly, then locking onto my eyes.

I see the confusion, the questions written all over his face.

CHAPTER 10

NICOLAS

*I*t's been a tremendous couple of months. I signed Sam and Susan to a generous contract with ADRENALIN and even inked a few more. I should be ecstatic, but there's something missing, maybe exactly what Sam and I were talking about.

I was surprised and maybe a little vindicated when Wesley told me the Mountain Spirit Resort had called back. Apparently, they want me to come back out to rehash possible options.

I sort of feel like this is my chance to right some wrongs. Wes hasn't said anything, but I know that my nearly three-month-long funk before getting the sale with Sam was tough on the company. We can't keep depending on an online presence. There are too many rip-off companies flooding the online marketplaces that result in blowback on us all.

So yeah, I'm feeling the pressure still. Not only was my funk hurting the company, but I'm supposed to be the sales leader, the guy who goes out and shows the rest of the team how to get shit done.

Having the chance to come back to Great Falls and sort of close that circle and nail the contract that really set me off on my short-term downward spiral is awesome.

Admittedly, while some of my delight is professional, there's also a part of this that is personal, hoping that I might be able to track Rose down while in town again. I'm sure someone can help me out. I mean, a town this size can't have too many women looking like her running around.

In the months since I saw her, no one has called out to me like she did. I'm not bitter, but I'm sure that at least some of my funk was that I've been unable to focus on doing my damn job because I've been thinking of her. I know when I wished on that star, deep down, I was wishing for someone like her, just that magic of instant fireworks but sustainable like Sam and Susan have.

I'm probably just seeing what I want to see, but it feels like it may have worked. The next morning was the start of a hot streak that's led me back here for a shot at redemption. I'm ecstatic to be driving into town again, feeling like this is gonna be the move that really changes everything for me.

I haven't heard from her, and for all I know, tracking her down might make me seem like the biggest loser ever, but I'm adventurous enough to give it a try. After all, the worst thing that could happen is that I get laughed at a little in a town that I may never visit again.

From my last trip to town, I remember a diner that seemed to be a local landmark. I find a parking spot along Main Street and begin to make my way toward the diner, hopeful someone there can help me find Rose.

It seems like fate is on my side when I'm not even halfway to the diner. I see a familiar figure and hair that I've dreamed about for the past five months in front of me. She's not wearing a sexy clingy dress this time, just some denim with a cozy sweater, but I know her as soon as I see her. "Rose!"

She keeps walking, and I call out again, a bit louder this time. She stops, turning, and time seems to slow down as her eyes, those same gorgeous baby blue that I remember, meet mine. Her eyes widen slightly and lock onto mine, a shock like lightning jolting down my spine and making me grin like a damn fool. I guess playing it suave was over in about half a second flat. Fuck it, I have to tell her how these past five months have been for me.

She finishes turning around, and something for the first time catches my eyes. Her belly is decidedly fuller than the last time I saw her, her sweater not hiding her growing form at all.

I feel like someone's just punched me right in the stomach. I half stumble to a stop a few steps away, the smile sort of locked on my face but wavering, my brain spinning. Was I an idiot these past few months? Did I just attach all of my loneliness and dissatisfaction with my life onto her without knowing what the fuck is really going on?

"Uh . . . hi, Nic," Rose says, obviously as shocked as I am.

Smoothing out my face, I tilt my head. "I thought that was you. I was hoping to see you."

I can see the surprise on her face, but it quickly turns to puzzlement. "You were hoping to see me? What brings you back to Great Falls?"

I nod, feeling a dark spot of sadness at my core at her question. I think I was more dedicated to the idea that she'd be somehow waiting for me to return than I realized. Fuck, my being here is probably just going to complicate things for her. It kills me that I can't tell her that she's been on my mind since I left here, but I really hope she's happy with the obviously big changes in her life in the last few months.

"Well," I say, forcing a smile on my face and half pointing up the mountain toward the resort. "The resort wanted me to come back, sort of talk some things over more. I was feeling hungry, so I remembered the diner, but then I saw you. So . . . uh, how're you doing?"

There's a spark of irritation in her eyes that I don't understand, and she pulls her sweater closed, wrapping her arms across her body to keep it that way. "So you're back in town for work and thought 'Hey, I know a booty call in that town. Guess I'll track her down for another round.' Is that what you're telling me?"

I'm taken aback by her unexpected anger and struggle to regain my balance. "Huh?" I stammer, still unsure what the hell's going on. "No, not at all. I just—"

She interrupts me. "Look, Nic . . .Nicolas." I instantly cringe inwardly, hating her saying my full name, like there's more distance than just time between us. Rose notices but continues. "We had fun, obviously. But when I reached out to you and left a message three months ago and didn't hear anything back, I got your response loud and clear. I get it. It's fine. I'm a big girl and I think we both were surprised at that night. Or at least I was. But I can't do this. I have other responsibilities now, and you don't have to worry about that. I'm fine."

She starts walking away, the dismal bleakness of utter rejection settling over me like a shroud. I see her shoulders lift as she takes a big breath and exhales.

What the fuck was that? That's definitely not how I expected things to go down. I get that it's been months, but that stings. I should've fucking called, but shit, we didn't exchange numbers. How was I supposed to call her? And what's this about reaching out three months ago? That would've been about the time I was in Oregon with Sam, and when I came back, things were crazy around the office.

Still, I mean, I guess I deserve it. She did tell me she ran a boutique, and there can't be too many of those in this town. But I've just been so busy and time flies. It didn't seem like calling her after she snuck out that morning was the right thing to do. I thought that's what she wanted, but judging by her reaction, maybe I was wrong? Especially after she said she left a message.

I burst into action, chasing after her down the sidewalk, but I lose her somehow in a meandering group of tourists. By the time I get myself untangled from a man totally overdressed and wearing a University of Miami ball cap, I don't see her at all.

I look up and down the street, wondering where she went because I need to talk to her, straighten this out somehow. I can't go on and never see her again on that note. The least I can do is apologize and wish her well, even if I hate the thought of some other lucky fucker being the one who snagged her.

He'd better treat her right, that's all I can say. Not knowing where she is but knowing where she *will* be, I walk back up the street the direction Rose was coming from. It takes me about two minutes to see it, the sign hitting me between the eyes as I make the connection again. Quickly, I cross the parking lot to the Mountain Rose and step inside.

A younger woman with brown curls cascading down her back and a bright smile cheerily greets me. "Hello. Welcome to the Mountain Rose. Can I help you find something today?"

"Yes, I've been in town before and met the owner. Will she be in today?"

The girl nods, eager to please. "Absolutely. Rose just stepped out for a moment to get our lunch."

I nod, directing my gaze to a rack of clothes, although I don't think I'll find anything for me here. Other than a few items in the corner that are more . . . effeminate men's fashion than my style, everything here is obviously meant for women. "Great, I think I'll just browse a bit till she gets back. Thanks so much."

The girl hangs nearby, giving me a curious look as I flip through a few hangers. "So, how do you know Rose? I just met her a few weeks ago. Today's my first day, actually."

I grin, realizing that's why she's so enthusiastic to be of service. Newbies . . . and probably looking to make a good impression. "Just old friends. We met a few months ago and I'm in town for work, so I thought I'd look her up."

"A few months?" the girl remarks. "That's not exactly 'old friends', now is it?"

She laughs at her own joke and I smile. "Well, it's not exactly like we went to kindergarten together, but you know how it is. What's your name? I'm Nic."

The quickly introduced Devon and I make some small talk about the town, just buying time. The store's quiet, not much of a lunch rush for places like this, and about twenty minutes later, the boutique door opens. Rose walks in, almost pushed by the light wind that's kicked up to make her hair blow back like gossamer strands of gold around her face, her arms laden with two bags of what smell like the diner's famous, or infamous, depending on whom you ask, gut bomb cheeseburgers.

Her smile is bright and her voice is light as she moves toward the desk and calls out, "Lunch is here, Devon. If you don't mind, can I eat first? Gotta feed this hungry monster and then you can take your lunch."

Devon grins as she finishes, pointing toward me. "Sure, you've got a visitor anyway."

"Huh?" Rose asks, turning. She sees me and I watch as she ignites, angry all over. "What are you doing here? Get out."

Devon flinches, worried that she fucked up on her first day at work. "Oh, no, I'm so sorry, Rose. He said he was an old friend."

Rose's flashing eyes don't leave mine, but she answers Devon, giving her a little wave of assurance. "It's fine, Devon. You couldn't have known."

"Rose, I just want to talk," I say placatingly, softly. I don't want to beg, but right now, I'm just being moved by the same feeling I felt five months ago. I have to know what's going on. "Can we sit down while you eat lunch? Or I can come back tonight when you close, if that's better?"

Rose firmly shakes her head while out of the corner of my eye, I see Devon grab her bag and disappear to the back, probably wishing she were anywhere else right about now. "No, I don't want to talk. Just go. I'm fine."

Being a salesman, my bullshit detector is sharper than most people's, and while Rose is putting up a decent front, my alarm bells are ringing loud and proud. "You're obviously not fine. You're mad at me and I don't know why. What's gotten you so upset?"

Something flashes across her face—hurt, maybe, or regret—and she sighs, shaking her head as she admits defeat. "I can't do this. Not now and not here."

"Where?" I ask, stepping closer.

"I don't—" Rose says, freezing when I reach out and take her hand gently. Another tingle jumps between our fingers, and I feel like something inside me moves. To hell with the meeting at the resort. This woman's my future.

She glances at Devon, who's about half a step from the back room door, and steps back, breaking our contact almost reluctantly. "Fine, come at six tonight and we can talk, but not now."

I see the stubbornness on her face, and even though I want to hash this all out right here and now, I sense that will be counter-productive, so I give in. For now. But this deal's far from done. "Thank you. I'll be here at six."

I turn to walk out, but I can't resist and turn back at the door to look at her. Her cheeks are flushed and her chest lifts with every breath, reminding me of . . . before. "Rose, I missed you."

Before she can reply with more than her eyes, I walk out into the chilly air, knowing I've got to get up to the Mountain Spirit Resort anyway. Hopefully, she's ready to talk tonight.

CHAPTER 11

ROSE

*a*s soon as Nic walks out the door, I collapse against the counter, my head and my heart pounding like I just got done slamming down a few bourbons. "Oh. My. God."

Devon gives me a worried look and comes back over from the door. "Is there anything I can do?"

I shake my head, standing up. "I'm okay. I just need . . . to call someone. Eat your burger up here."

I set my lunch on the counter, forgetting entirely about my earlier hunger pangs, and grab the phone. I punch a couple of buttons and begin to dance around impatiently as it rings.

Brad answers quickly. I guess there's a lull at the salon too. "Hey, bitch-a-roo, what's new?"

All of my breath leaves in an audible huff, and I collapse into a chair near the door. "Brad, I need you. Something happened. He's here."

Brad is instantly all business, dropping his lisp, all of his humor evaporating, and I hear the man who, despite all of his protestations to the contrary, could be a great father someday if he wants. "What happened? Are you okay? Is the baby okay?"

I'm stumbling over my words, trying to make the swirls in my head into sentences. "I'm okay," I reply, and I hear him let out a breath in a long whoosh that makes me tear up. He cares about me so much and I'm lucky to have him as a friend. "Jelly Bean's ok. But Nic . . . he's here. I don't know what to do."

I trail off, and Brad jumps in. "I'm already on my way down the street, honey. Be there in a couple. Sit down, put your feet up, and breathe. We'll figure this out."

I hear the click as he ends the call and sink into the chair behind the front desk. It's only a second later that Brad swoops through the front door, looking like I've never seen him before. Instead of his usual fabulousness, he's wearing a . . . I swear it looks like a camo military jacket, lending an even more surreal air to the day.

Brad surveys me quickly, taking in my pale face and Devon's questioning look. I'm sure she's wondering what the else could happen on her first day at work here.

Brad approaches her, his hand outstretched. "I'm Brad. You the new girl?"

Devon looks to be in shock, but she nods. "I'm Devon."

"Nice to meet you, although I wish it was under better circumstances." He turns to face me, even as he talks to Devon in a brusque tone. "Look, Rose and I need to talk. Can . . ."

She straightens her back, stepping behind the desk and giving us both a reassuring look. "I've got this. Don't worry."

I smile at her, giving her a pat on the arm. "Helluva first day, huh? I swear it's not usually like this."

Devon shrugs and smiles. "If this is unusual, I'm just glad I'm here to help."

She really is the best helper I think I could find. Keep this up, and she's going to find herself with a pay raise before the week's out.

Brad shuffles me into my office and plops me into my chair, dragging another chair to sit in front of me. "Okay, start at the beginning. What happened?"

I give him the rundown, seeing the look of pride he has when I say that I told Nic I wasn't a booty call and could take care of myself. "You can, you know? You're doing great with it all."

"Thanks. You know it's because of you guys though. Takes a village and all that shit."

"For sure, but why did Nic find you now? Is he just in town and wanting a repeat of some grade-A nookie?"

"I think so. He seemed happy to see me until . . ." I gesture at my belly. "He definitely wasn't expecting this."

Brad sits back at the news and pops a hand under his chin. "All right. So now what? What do you want to do? He needs to know this is his baby, Rose. He may run right back out of town and basically be the sperm donor you thought you were getting in the first place, but at least you'll have given him that respect."

"I know," I admit. "He knocked me for a loop, but he said some things . . . anyway, he's coming back tonight at six so we can talk. I'll tell him, but then what? What if he wants to be involved? What if he doesn't? And custody, child support, and I don't even know what else because I didn't think he was ever gonna show back up!"

I'm getting hysterical, my hands covering my belly protectively. Brad leans forward and puts his hands over mine, soothing my nerves and making me look up at him with trust and hope. "Chill. He's not taking Jelly Bean here. Just hear the man out and go from there."

I take a big breath, letting it out slowly. "You're right. I can't do anything about it until tonight. No use getting myself worked up. Then I'll tell him everything, see what he says, and go from there, I guess. Thanks, Brad."

There's a still a touch of worry in his eyes, but his demeanor lightens back up, his voice pitching a bit higher. "There's my girl. Cool, calm, and collected. You've got this, Rose."

*R*ight at six, I flip the sign on the front door to *Closed*. Devon has already gone home with an epic first day at work story that I just hope she doesn't spread all over town. Still, I wanted to make sure, so I let her go at five, along with my thanks and a smile.

I've still got my hand on the sign when the door opens. It's Nic. He's so intense and so handsome, my heart starts speeding up despite myself. "Hi, Rose. Can we talk now?"

An ugly fear in my gut makes me want him to go away, get out of my shop. Run away, you perfect memory who hurt me. I can't and won't be hurt by you again. I feel like pouting, sticking my fingers in my ears, and immaturely chanting out, "Go away . . . I don't wanna talk to you . . . la la la la . . ."

Instead, I rally, digging deep for some maturity to act like an adult. "Sure. Come to the office. We can sit and talk there."

I lock the door and he follows me back to my office, settling into one chair while I sit down in the chair across from him. I have a flicker of humor at how my position with Brad earlier has been reversed and now I have to be the adult one who handles shit.

"Okay, so . . ." I begin, my voice trailing off as my ability to put together a coherent sentence thoroughly fails me. So much for handling things. Part of it is the subject at hand, but another part is how my brain's whispering to me just how handsome Nic looks. He's dressed nicely, in an open-throated dress shirt underneath his jacket and dress slacks that tell me he came directly from a business meeting. That same little voice in me wonders if he cut his meeting short in order to come see me, and if so, it's impressed.

Nic smiles, and I shiver inside, desperately trying to hang onto my anger. I'm not going to let him off that easily. "Yeah, so . . ." he says, trying to sound relaxed but still with a slight undercurrent of nervousness that helps me all the more. "Maybe we start at the beginning? You left the morning after." He clears his throat awkwardly, not sure how to discuss that night. "And then what? How did you end up . . .?" He seems to stumble over his words a bit.

I hear the pause in his voice, the unwillingness to come out with the elephant in the room, my obviously fuller belly. I look down at my hands, nervously playing with my fingers. "I guess I should tell you that before our night, I'd been looking at starting a donor cycle. I've been wanting a baby for a while. After we had our night, I went to the doctor for a checkup, just to make sure everything was healthy down-stairs and my body was ready. Everything was fine, but the blood test showed I was already pregnant."

Nic flinches, and I realize I'm walking a minefield here. "Donor cycle? You were *trying* to get pregnant?"

I realize how that sounds and quickly try to reassure him. "Yes, but not with you. That night, I'd made the decision to do a donor cycle, ready to be a mother even if I wasn't a wife. That's what I was celebrating the night we met."

Nic looks at me sternly, his eyes flaring. "Just to be clear, you were trying to get pregnant and then somehow did get preg-nant the one time we had sex. Is that what you're saying?"

I nod, quietly agreeing. "Nic, I wasn't trying to use you or trick you. I mean, we did use a condom. But they're not 100%, and while it might not have been intentional, I'm happy this happened."

"Did you . . ." He seems hesitant, but he continues with a deep breath of courage. "Did you tamper with the condom?"

The accusation stings. How dare he make it sound like I did this on purpose! I vault to my feet, my voice rising. "No, I did nothing of the sort. The condom might've been a little old, but not like it was expired or something. I just don't fuck random guys that often . . . or ever, as a matter of fact."

I see the betrayal in his eyes, feel the anger radiating off him in waves, but I'm still unprepared when he pops the question that's been hanging between us like an elephant in the room. "Are you sure it's mine?"

Like a knife right to my heart, he goes for the kill. Like it fucking matters if it's his or not after basically accusing me of seducing him for his sperm? I grit my teeth together, my eyes narrowing as I get to my feet, pointing toward the door. "Get the fuck out! Get out!"

I dissolve into hysterics, yelling and pushing at him, my arms flailing wildly as I maneuver him toward the front door. "Go! Just get out!"

Nic lifts his hands defensively before turning to walk out the door. There's a pause as he has to twist the lock, not quite the dramatic 'rip open the door and walk into the evening darkness' maneuver you see on TV. He turns back just before opening it, his anger still flaring in his eyes but his voice calm and determined. "This isn't over. We're not done talking about this."

He gets the door open and disappears into the night. I hold it together for one more breath, just long enough for him to get out of sight, and then collapse to the floor, my body wracked with sobs as I wail.

God, I fucked this up so badly.

CHAPTER 12

NICOLAS

I can't help leaving Rose's boutique in a near-rage, stomping across the parking lot before hopping in my car and driving back to the Mountain Spirit Resort. Before I know it, I find myself in the hotel bar, ironically the same hotel bar I first met Rose in.

"What's your whimsy?" the bartender asks. "You look familiar."

"Been here once before . . . and a double scotch, Glenlivet if you've got it. Neat," I reply in a tone that says very clearly, 'don't ask.' Besides, I seriously doubt he remembers me, probably something to spark up conversation.

The bartender gets my drink and I take a sip, the aged oak burn sliding down my throat and evaporating in my stomach while my brain swirls, lost in thoughts of what just happened.

Rose is pregnant.

Yep. That's pretty much a given.

Pregnant with my baby.

Well, we could still call Maury Povich, but yeah, there's a good chance that you ARE the father.

How did this happen?

You know, when a man and woman love each other very much, they wiggle their bodies together and that sends a signal to the land of the storks . . .

I never expected anything like this. I was coming back to town for a work trip, again, as always, and thought maybe I could see Rose one more time. Not for a booty call, though I admit I wouldn't have complained about a happy ending.

We'd had such a hot night, and I've never felt chemistry like that with anyone before. Beyond that, I hadn't really given it much thought until I saw her, her blonde hair floating out behind her like there were wind currents flowing by just for the chance to caress her hair.

I knew it was her instantly, but all of my joy faltered when I saw her rounded belly. Granted, it didn't cross my mind that the baby she was carrying was . . . mine.

The word smacks me right in the brain. And again, I'm lost. Pregnant. My baby.

"I'm going to be a father," I say to myself out loud. The words seem alien to me. Not that I never wanted to be, but I never expected it to be like this. I press back from the bar, tossing the rest of my scotch to burn down my throat, needing some privacy for the panic attack I'm afraid is coming.

Now? Of all the fucking times? I mean, I went through an

acre of shit after meeting her the first time, and I've just started to pull myself out of that rut.

I virtually stomp to my room, leaning back against the door as it closes. I lift my chin, closing my eyes and talking out loud to the empty room. "I don't know *how* to be a father. I barely feel like I can take care of myself half the fucking time. What am I going to do?"

I need to talk to someone, someone who'll help me get my shit straight, because I'm veering a hard left into uncharted territory. I honestly feel like I just stepped off a bridge, intent on BASE jumping . . . and I now realize that's not a parachute I'm holding but an umbrella from the dollar store.

Grabbing my phone, I dial Wes. He's one of my only friends and I'm glad when he answers on the second ring. "Hey, buddy, you already get the contract approved and signed? Damn, I figured it'd take you until at least tomorrow. You're a beast, man!"

It takes him a moment to realize that I'm silent, just breaths coming through the line. Contract? Shit, of all the things to think about. I've got more obligations now, and I don't know how the fuck to balance it all. I take a deep breath, calming myself.

Wes speaks up again, his voice more subdued and concerned. "Hey, Nicolas? You there, man? Everything okay?"

I let out a shaky breath, running a hand through my hair as I feel my throat constrict while I try to fight back the tsunami of feelings inside. "Wes . . . she's pregnant."

There's a stunned silence on the other end, and when Wes answers, I can hear the confusion in his voice. "Huh? Who's pregnant?"

Pulling myself together with sheer will, I try to get it all out. I'm not sure if I'm going to be able to get through this again for a while. "Rose. She's the woman here that I met last time. Remember when I told you about her? I saw her today and . . . she's pregnant."

Wes hums soothingly, supportively as he lets the news hit him. "Okay, she's pregnant. First things first, I guess. Is uh . . . well, is it yours?"

I clear my throat, trying to get the words out. "It's mine. Yeah, it's mine." Saying it out loud to another person makes it feel a little more real somehow. There's no running, no hiding, although I'm not sure that's even what I want to do. I'm just shaken, surprised at the turn of events I never saw coming.

Wes has always been the rational, proactive side of our Yin-Yang. That's what makes our business so successful, and I'm reminded why I appreciate him when he automatically goes into planning mode. Instead of offering congratulations or condolences, his mind just shifts into 'well, now what?' mode. "Okay, so it's your baby. What do you want? What does she want? And are they the same thing?"

All very good questions. I can almost imagine him scribbling them down on the legal pad he keeps next to his laptop for brainstorming ideas, but I have no idea of the answers. "I don't know. She got mad and kicked me out."

Wes's voice raises a notch, in surprise or anger, I'm not sure. "Why would she do that?"

"I kinda fucked up. Long story short, I asked if she sabotaged the condom. And I asked the same thing you did, if the baby is mine."

Wes sighs loudly, and I can picture him pinching his nose between his fingers like he always does when he's exasperated. "Fair questions given the circumstances, if you ask me, but maybe not the best phrasing. I mean, this isn't like asking if a customer intentionally fucked up something on a shipment."

"I know," I reply, starting to feel slightly calmer. "I was just surprised and confused and wasn't thinking before I spoke. Holy shit, man, I'm going to be a father."

Wes's voice calms me as he continues. "Okay, back to the original questions. What do you want and does she want the same thing? Do you want to be involved? You've always been a man on the move, nomadic and chasing after the next new thing. This could change your life. Or not."

I try to imagine myself traveling for work every week, going from place to place, all while Rose would be here creating a home for our baby. Our baby who wouldn't even know me. Imagining myself as the guy who comes through every once in awhile with presents from afar, t-shirts from Tacoma and bumper stickers from Brooklyn or something, begging for awkward hugs, only to run off again.

The image makes me sick. I try to imagine an alternative, one where I'm holding a little blonde baby girl, sitting in the grassy yard with her as we wait for Rose to come home from work.

While that sounds idyllic, I'm not sure I'm set up to stay here all the time. What would it mean for me and my career? Besides, am I ready for that sort of life, the same day on repeat like it's that *Groundhog Day* movie I've watched on reruns late at night?

Reruns about a day on repeat . . . the irony there makes me huff a bit, considering my life.

"Wes, I'll do the contract while I'm here," I finally say, "but I'm going to need some time. Check in with my assistant about my upcoming visits for the next few weeks and see who you can get to cover them. Also, Rose insisted that she tried to get in contact with me about three months ago, but I never got anything. I know that was right about the time we were busy as hell and having a few IT issues, but still, that was an important fucking message. If you need me, give me a call, but I need to stay in town here. I hope you can understand."

"Sure thing, Nicholas. Let me know if you need anything and I'll take care of things here. And man, good luck. It sounds like you're gonna need it."

"I appreciate that, and thanks for not saying it . . . contract first, then Rose. Don't worry, I'll get that handled quickly and then see what's here and how this is gonna work."

Wes makes a sound that I swear sounds like a cheer. "All right, Nic. Get your personal stuff settled and then we'll talk."

"Talk?" I ask. "About what?"

Wes sighs, I know he doesn't want to bring this up right now. "Nic, you're my boy and I understand that family comes first. But we need you. Hell, I need you to keep us growing and selling. I'll do what I can to rearrange everything for the short term, but long term, we might need to revamp your role if you want the chance to be a father. If that's your plan. Some food for thought. Good luck, man. It sounds like you're gonna need it."

I hang up the phone, a new fear settling in my heart after the feeling wears off.

How in the fuck is this gonna work?

I can't go and leave my baby. I don't even know if she wants me to stay. But I know that's my baby in her belly, and I can't imagine being an asshole who never knew his child.

CHAPTER 13

ROSE

*A*fter my wild and crazy fit last night, Nic is the last person I expect to see in the shop today. What I really want is to finish up the day's work, flip the sign on the door, and hide in a nest of comfy blankets and eat ice cream with pretzels. At least my weird cravings have settled a bit, the desire for salty pickles at least giving way to pretzels, which seems a bit more normal with the sweet, creamy ice cream.

But right at six as I go to turn the sign over, here he is again. Nic walks in like he's stepping on eggshells, visibly making himself smaller and less threatening somehow, and I can't decide if I like that he's deferring to me somewhat or if I hate it because that's not who he really is.

Crossing my arms over my chest, I stare him down. No way am I letting him off the hook after the bullshit he tried to pull last night.

"What?" Nic looks at me calmly, no sign of the fight we had, his voice even. "Can we talk, Rose? Not like yesterday. We need to have a real conversation."

I know he's right. If nothing else, we need to do this so that we can move forward and he can move on, if he's doing what I expect.

"Fine, come on."

Just like last night, we walk to the back room. I settle into my chair and Nic grabs the same chair he used last night and flips it around, straddling it as he faces me. Probably a bad omen, but we need to just get this done.

He looks at me for a moment, like he's gathering his thoughts. "First, I want to apologize. I didn't intend to sound so . . . mean last night. I was just in shock, I guess."

I nod, wanting to get this over with. If he's here to say he doesn't want any part of things, then I can deal with it. But I don't want to drag the whole fucking thing out. "Fine. Just so we're clear, I didn't do anything to the condom, and I'm sure it's yours because you're the only guy I've slept with in . . ." I pause, chastising myself for not just stopping at 'it's yours.' Jeez, what a way to sound like a desperate baby-making wench. "Let's just say it had been a while."

Nic nods, giving me a hint of that same amused smirk that made me want to fuck him three times in one night. "I know. I mean, I figured. It had been a while for me too. Work. I love it but I hate it."

There's a tender note in the room as we both let that sink in. Somehow, in this weird roll of the dice that is the universe, two people who were running long dry streaks met, clicked, and in a single torrid night of passion that obviously made a memory for both of us, we kindled the life that's now growing inside my belly.

I continue, setting aside the philosophy lesson for later. "And contrary to what you seem to think, I'm not some conniving shrew who wanted to lock you down. That's why I left you alone. You didn't ask for this then, and I don't need you now."

Nic's voice is gravel, his eyes going flinty as he figures out his reply. "Why didn't you at least tell me? I would have liked to be given the choice."

I shrug, not knowing exactly how to explain it all. "I did call. In fact, it took a little work to track you down. I found your number, called your office to speak with you, and left a very precise message with your conscientious-sounding assistant. She said you were out of state, but she'd give you the message. I didn't hear from you, so I figured you didn't want anything to do with me."

Nic shakes his head, looking up at the ceiling. "I swear I never got a message. I did go out of town . . . well, I'm always out of town, actually, but I went off-grid for a few weeks. I got back and had tons of messages but nothing from you. There were some IT problems at the time. Things might have gotten lost."

I fall off my high horse a bit, the honesty in his voice telling me he's not just giving me a line of shit to try and assuage my feelings. "You didn't get my message? You didn't just ditch me as a random one-night stand in a place you never planned to visit again?"

Nic leans forward, taking my hands in his and looking into my eyes. "Rose, that night we shared was amazing. When you were gone the next morning with barely a *Thank You* note, I just figured it was a one-night stand that would never be topped. And when I never heard anything, it just confirmed it. I've spent the past five months trying to get you out of my mind, and I haven't been able to. I did come here for work, but I was hoping to see you again."

I smile, a little bit of ice around my heart melting. "It was hard making that call. Really, you didn't want this so I'm not going to be angry. I didn't ask you to get me pregnant. If you're out, it's okay, no hard feelings."

Nic smiles back at me, a dimple popping deep into his cheek. "You're pregnant with *our* baby."

"Yep, that's how it works. Unless it's an immaculate conception."

He squats down so fast I think he's going to fall to his knees, and I worry for a second before he smiles more, bringing his face close to my tiny baby bump. "*My* baby." Sitting back on his haunches, a huge smile breaks across his face as he shakes his head, looking up at me with an innocent wonder that makes him look not only handsome and sexy, but young too, like some impossible figure who's wise and youthful at the same time. "I have no idea what to do, what to say, what to think . . . but I want to figure it out. Together."

I smile back, wanting to reach out and take his hand, but I stop myself. We're not there yet. "That sounds great, Nic. Because we don't even really know each other. We're about to be parents and I don't know you."

Nic hums and nods. "All right, so we may be doing this backward, but I *want* to know you. You're going to be the mother of my child, after all. So, Rose, how about some dinner?"

I laugh a little. This is just so damn ridiculous that it's the only reaction I can have. "You mean like a *date*?"

He nods, reaching forward and taking my hand, another little spark jumping between us as he does. "No, not *like* a date. A date. That's what people usually do, right? So let's date, get to know one another."

It's a little crazy, and he's right, we are doing this backward. But it sounds like the best idea I've ever heard in this moment.

"Ok, Nic, let's go. But it's gonna have to be a pretty awesome one. My last date ended up pretty incredible."

CHAPTER 14

NICOLAS

*W*hen Rose says yes to the date, my heart soars at the same time my stomach plunges. I literally have no idea what I'm doing. I don't know where to take a date in this town besides a hotel bar that we've already been to. This is probably going to end in disaster, but I have to at least try to get to know her as best I can and figure out how this might work.

She looks beautiful in her dressy but casual clothes as I pick her up in my SUV at her shop. I get out, coming around to escort her to the passenger side, ignoring the man in a pink tie giving me the stink eye as he watches from down the street. He's tall and lean but apparently being held back by an even taller, broad-muscled guy who is physically blocking him from moving, although the block seems rather intimate even from here. It's a funny sight, but I don't dare laugh, bringing my attention back to Rose. "You look beautiful."

"Thanks," Rose says, blushing lightly in the evening chill. "Nice car."

"It's a rental. Who's the welcoming committee?" I ask as I come around and get in. "The guy in the tie looks like he wants to slice and dice me a bit."

"Nah," Rose says with an amused smile. "That's Brad. He's basically my best friend and has spent quite a bit of the last few months looking out for me. The other guy is his boyfriend, Trey. They're good people."

I can dig that, although my flash of jealousy when she said Brad was her best friend and had been taking care of her is a bit of a surprise. I'm not usually jealous to begin with, but the momentary twinge was mitigated by the follow-up that Brad has a boyfriend. At least there hasn't been another guy coming in to take care of my girl romantically. *My girl? Shit.*

We settle into my SUV and I follow her directions to a small Italian restaurant just off the main drag toward downtown. Walking in, the smell of garlic and tomatoes is overwhelming, but in a homey mom-cooked dinner sort of way.

"One of the little secrets around town," she says, seeing my eyes light up.

I nod, taking off my jacket and handing it to the staff member, who hangs it up. "Smells good. Must be a good choice."

Rose grins, nodding as the hostess leads us into the dining room. "You have no idea. Their pasta primavera is my favorite food, and for months, I couldn't even think about it without getting sick, much less eat even a bite of it. I'm so glad I can indulge again."

It's an off-hand comment, but I realize that she's had this whole experience so far without me, alone with our baby . . . the good and the bad. It makes me feel like a total asshole for blowing up at her that first night or worrying about my damn job. I tell myself that regardless of what happens between me and Rose, I'm not going to leave her hanging again.

"Well, let's make sure we make up for it tonight?" I ask, and Rose gives me a smile that makes my cock twitch in my pants. *Down, boy.* Fuck.

We sit, ordering drinks immediately, and a silence descends over the table as we both nervously sip our sparkling waters. We're not right back where we were that first night, but I think we can both sense we could be . . . and that's scary as fuck with the amount of water that's gone under the bridge the past five months.

Clearing my throat, I decide to take the plunge. "So . . . tell me about the pregnancy, about the baby? I have no idea where to start."

Rose smiles, relaxing. "I'm about twenty weeks along, about halfway there. Everything is going well, my morning sickness is gone, and I'm feeling good. Jelly Bean, as we call the baby right now, is totally on track. The heartbeat always sounds good. I haven't felt movement yet, but hopefully soon, and my next appointment is a sonogram."

It's a mouthful, and I try to take it all in, let the reality sink in, but there's still a sense of shock. I mean, it's probably a shock to most men, but to get that shock plus twenty weeks . . . maybe I should have a designated driver so I could indulge in something harder than the water I guzzle as I try to process. "Wow . . . that all sounds great. Um, Jelly Bean?"

I watch as her cheeks flush, an adorable shyness coming over her. God, she's fucking sexy, and in my mind, I can't keep thoughts of that night from coming back.

Thankfully, Rose doesn't notice. This isn't the time. "Yeah, that's just what I call the baby because I don't know if it's a boy or a girl yet. "

My eyes widen. That's a milestone I haven't missed. "When do you find out?"

Her eyes drift off into space for a second, and I can see her mentally counting. "Probably in four days, at my next appointment on Friday. Do you . . . want to go with me?"

There's a hopefulness in her eyes that pierces my soul, and while the fear inside me makes me want to run and pretend none of this is happening, I know that I need to grow the fuck up. Besides, there's another part of me that is ready to say *Yes* just to see her beautiful smile again.

"Of course I want to go," I say, reaching across the small table and taking her hand. "I'd love to see Jelly Bean."

I can see the relief cross her face. "Great. I'll send you the address and we can meet there."

"One thing."

"What's that?" Rose asks warily.

"I'd like it if the baby's name doesn't end up being Jelly Bean after birth," I say, smiling.

Rose laughs, nodding. Feeling like we've reached a tipping point on pregnancy talk for the moment, I try to direct the conversation to something more neutral, ironically something more along the lines of first date talk since really, that's what this is.

"How's business going? I guess the store is doing well if you've hired help. I remember before you were saying you worked the boutique by yourself."

Rose lights up, grinning. "Yes, business is booming, and this year's ski season is looking to be the biggest yet. Devon was a good choice, and I think by the time I really need to take things easy, she'll be ready to run things on her own with just a few check-ins each day. Speaking of work, isn't that what brought you back here?"

I nod, wishing I could say I'd come back for her, but I know if there's any chance of healing the inadvertent wounds of the past five months, honesty is the best policy. "It is, but I'd like to say fate played a part in it too. The deal with the Mountain Spirit fell through when I was here last, but a week ago, they called us back and wanted to give us another shot. So I'm here to make the arrangements. The ideas we discussed that night were a great help in making our offer more appealing. Not sure I ever really thanked you for that, so . . . thank you."

Rose dips her head in acknowledgement and says lightly, "So glad I could be helpful. Guess that business degree paid off."

I hum, sipping my water. The waiter comes by, and we place appetizer orders, garlic toast and calamari. After he leaves, we continue. "Where did you go to school?" I ask. "How'd you end up here?"

Rose smiles, something that I'm finding I like more and more with every passing second. "I grew up in a small town up north, the quintessential tomboy with scraped knees who spent most my time in the woods, hanging out in the trees I climbed, reading comic books, and skipping rocks."

I'm struck at how much a parallel our childhoods were, and my eyes widen slightly. "Sounds idyllic. What pulled you into running a boutique?"

"When my teen years hit, they were kind to me, and I discovered the fun of clothes, dressing up and all that. My town mostly had folks who dressed for function, and fancy clothes weren't really understood. Standard first-date clothes for most people when I was in high school were just your cleanest pair of jeans. My love of dressing up made me an oddball, so I escaped with magazines, envisioning a different life than my small town could provide."

I try to imagine the beauty across from me as a little girl, dirt smudged across her face from climbing trees, and it's surprisingly easy to do. The image morphs into a teen girl-next-door-type in fancy finery with a town full of jeans and workboot types, and I can see how that would feel isolating. I remember how it felt being the guy who wasn't into the typical high school sports, who'd rather go rock climbing than carry the 'rock' downfield for the football team.

"So, what did you do? How'd you go from home to here?" I ask as again, that sense of fate seems to whisper in my ear.

Rose shrugs her shoulders and points toward the window. "School, more or less. I worked my ass off and was valedictorian of my class. Universities give scholarships to valedictorians, even if the high school is tiny, so I was able to go to my choice, and the state school just to the south of here has a good business program. I double-majored in business and fashion merchandising, figuring out that I liked the business and marketing side better than the designing. I'll let you in on a secret. While I can sew, I can't draw to save my life. All of my attempts at designing look like stick figures scrawled in Crayola."

I grin. "Most models look like stick figures anyway, but go on."

"As part of my degree, we had to write a business plan and

mine was the Mountain Rose Boutique. I'd researched towns all over the state, and at the time, Great Falls wasn't so great, but I knew it would be because there were proposals for the resort to come in as a boom for the economy and tourism. That business plan was good enough to get me an A, but more importantly, good enough to get me a small business loan when I graduated. As soon as I graduated, I moved and opened Mountain Rose, and it's been hard but rewarding ever since. The boutique has been my everything for a lot of years now. But I'm ready for something more."

She smiles at me, absently rubbing her tiny bump, and in my mind, I wonder how much of that *more* I can be involved in. Before I can interrupt, she asks, "So that's basically my life story. How about you?"

I laugh a little, suddenly feeling self-conscious. "This feels like Life Stories 101."

She laughs back, pausing while our appetizers come. "Well, first date basics, at least. Whatcha got, Nic?"

I pause, trying to figure out where to start. "Well, my mom and dad were great, always traveling or planning our next trip. If there was a three-day weekend, we were loading up in the RV to go somewhere. We had our favorite spot, a national park a few hours from home where we'd hike, swim, and just *commune with the trees*, as my mom always said. I always thought she was perhaps born a little too late. She'd have made a great back-to-nature hippie."

"Sounds very Left Coast," Rose says, and I nod.

"That's Mom. In the summer, we'd load up and be gone for all twelve weeks. By the time I graduated high school, I'd been to every state in the US, even Hawaii, although we had to fly there, obviously. Too bad, Dad really wanted to make a go of sailing it until Mom pointed out that a storm on Lake Sherman is nothing like a storm on the Pacific Ocean. But they brought me up loving everything to do with the outdoors, and I always pictured myself doing something like that. But when I was eighteen, they were adamant that I go to college, finish my education. I ended up doing an internship and met Wes, my boss at ADRENALIN Sports. He was still a bit of an upstart then, but even during the internship, we clicked, so he offered me a full-time job as soon as I graduated. It seemed like the best of both worlds. I could be outdoors, travel and see the states, meet people, and get paid to do it. Surprisingly, I was even good at it. Now, Wes is like an older brother-slash-best friend to me, and I've been the VP of Sales for several years now."

Rose grins, and I'm momentarily distracted as she dips a bit of calamari in marinara sauce and wraps her lush, sensual lips around it before speaking. When she does speak, I have to listen carefully, because a lot of blood's left my brain to run down to my cock again, and I can barely pay attention. "What about your parents? Do they still travel?"

I grin, nodding. "You won't believe this, but they travel all the time. After I was done with college and they knew I wasn't coming home, they sold the house and upgraded the RV, and they live on the road full-time now. Dad's invested well, and he and Mom have jobs that allow them to work online most of the year. We talk every week, and they're in a new place every time, having a blast. They even have this little sticker map of the US on the back of the RV that they fill in with tick marks every time they go through that state . . . again."

Rose laughs, her beautiful blue eyes sparking in the candlelight from the table. "That's amazing! That seems like such an adventure."

We talk some more, and before I know it, we've worked our way through pasta, bread, and a delicious tiramisu, the whole time laughing and talking, our connection from before just as freaky, deep, and profound. I pay the bill and help Rose on with her coat, feeling warm enough inside that I pull mine on with great reluctance.

Walking outside, Rose jokingly complains as she rests her hands on her belly. "Oh, my gosh, why'd you let me have so much food? You're going to have to roll me out of here. Or get a forklift!"

I smile back, looking over her curvy frame, not seeing a single flaw. "You look fine to me . . . in fact, you're beautiful, but if you need a hand, I could carry you to the car?"

Rose groans but blushes at my compliment. "Definitely not, you'd probably break your back!"

She's such a tiny thing that even with a few pounds of baby weight, I easily swoop her up, one arm below her knees and the other wrapped around her upper back. "Upsy-daisy!"

Rose squeals in terror and delight, grabbing my neck tightly. "Whoa . . . what're you doing?"

Without a single complaint, I start off across the parking lot toward my SUV, looking half ahead and half in her eyes. "You're busy growing our baby. The least I can do is feed you, tell you you're pretty, and carry you home. Well, or to the car."

She laughs, settling in my arms as she relaxes her grip around my neck enough that I'm not being half choked the whole time. I place her gently in the front seat, reaching the seatbelt across her. I can feel her breath on my cheek, and when I turn to her, I can only think of kissing her . . . but I want this night to be storybook, and in storybooks, the kiss happens at the end of the night.

The drive to her house is full of easy banter, both of us comfortable after an evening of sharing, and she tells me the address quickly, again giving me directions. Pulling up to her house, I open the passenger door and walk her onto the dark porch. It's a trim little house, what my mother would call a gingerbread house, and with the light frame of frost on the windows, it certainly lives up to that name. "Well . . . here we are."

Rose looks up at me from under thick lashes, and I can see the conflict inside her before she can even say anything. "Nic, thank you for a lovely date. I, uh . . . contrary to before, I don't usually move too fast."

I interrupt her, knowing she's trying to tell me not to expect anything, and place a hand on her shoulder, stroking down to take her hand, where I can feel her pulse racing like a baby bird's. "Rose, it's fine. It is a first date, after all." I wink at her, and she relaxes but doesn't let go of my hand at all. "But maybe just a good night kiss?"

I see her bite her bottom lip and it makes me want to be the one to nibble the pink fullness, and when she nods slightly, I go for it, leaning in as I pull her close. I cover her mouth with my own, gently taking her. Her lush body presses against mine, and again, that feeling of fate throbs in the air.

I bring my hands up to her cheeks, holding her to me as our kiss deepens, and I probe her lips with the tip of my tongue. Her lips part slightly on a breathy sigh, and I slip my tongue to caress hers. She tastes me back, and soon, my body is crushed against hers, my cock throbbing in my pants and my heart hammering in my chest.

"Mmm, Rose . . ." I murmur as I feel her arms wrap around my waist, pulling me flush with her body, her bump pressing against me.

Unexpectedly, the thought of her round with my child makes me even hotter, a streak of masculine alpha pride racing through me. The kiss explodes, and I reach up, cupping a breast through her jacket, stroking gently. Our hands begin rubbing and squeezing along our bodies, our moans of passion getting louder, tongues licking and mouths sucking along warm, delicate flesh. I reach down, squeezing her ass and grinding against her, a low groan sounding deep in my throat.

The deep vibration seems to wake Rose up from the spell we're both under, and she pulls back. "Nic . . . wait, wait. We can't."

She's right, and I let go, releasing her enough to take a half-step back. I take a big breath, exhaling slowly, and bend down to rest my forehead against hers. "You're right. I should go. Rose, I want this to be more than one night. Can I see you again? Tomorrow?"

Rose shakes her head, and it feels like a punch in my belly as she replies, "I can't. I have a new shipment coming in tomorrow. Devon and I will be busy for a couple of days getting it all processed and displayed. But Friday, we can go to the doctor?"

I meet her eyes, the desire as naked in mine as it is in hers, and I smile. Friday? That gives me a few days to get things settled with the resort, and I think this time, the manager I'm meeting with up there, Gavin Adams, will be an easy meeting.

"Oh, I want, Rose. I definitely want. I'll see you Friday."

CHAPTER 15

ROSE

*M*y fingers are aching and my lower back isn't far behind as the clock creeps past three thirty Friday afternoon. It feels like it's been the longest few days of my life. I'm sure I pulled some longer days in college. I was an expert at all-nighters, but I know I'm more exhausted now than I was when I was cramming marketing theory at two in the morning.

Part of it has been a mini-business boom. In addition to the new product and restocking, the shop has been crazy busy with customers, and Devon and I have stayed after hours every night to get the new items out on the floor.

I don't know what caused the boom, but it's been great for the bottom line. One of the spring dresses I'd bought an entire rack of completely sold out already, and I even had to rush-order a few more to keep up with demand. The Etsy dealer must be doing backflips themselves . . . or shitting themselves trying to keep up with my demand.

But for now, we're finally done. I glance over at Devon, who's looking just as exhausted as me. "Devon, thank you so much! I don't know how I would've done this without you. You're a life-saver."

She smiles back, her chin lifting proudly as she surveys the shop and all our hard work. "No problem, Rose. I'm happy to help. And I appreciate your teaching me so much. I know unpacking and hanging clothes isn't exactly fun and games, but your telling me about how you choose what to order and the quantities helps me understand the whole process better."

I snicker, smirking back at her. "I love how you make my rambling about business stuff that only interests me sound like something you actually enjoy. Thanks for indulging an old lady."

Devon bursts out in giggles, shaking her long, dark locks. "Old lady? You make it sound like you're ancient. You're a few of years older than me, and I'm twenty-two."

I half-close my eyes, nodding sagely while putting on a false philosophical accent. "Ahh, but it is the wisdom and life in those few years' difference that change everything."

She rolls her eyes, heading for the back room where I know we've both got water bottles stashed. "All right, Dr. Phil-etta, you'd better get out of here before you're late for your prenatal appointment, or did you forget about it?"

I can't help but bounce up and down a little bit, despite my aching lower back. "Of course I didn't forget! It's sonogram day and I get to find out if Jelly Bean is a boy or a girl. I really hope it's a girl or Brad is gonna be so pissed. He already bought pink booties with humongous bows on them and a onesie with a tutu attached. Can you believe that? A tutu. I guess I'm just thankful he hasn't bought a tiara yet. Well, at least not one for the baby, but between you and me, I'm certain he has one for his own use."

Devon snickers. "He definitely has at least one, and don't tell him that I snitched, but he already bought a headband with a big tiara printed on it, complete with blingy rhinestones."

I laugh, waving it off. "I can definitely believe that." Giving her a quick hug, I grab my purse and head out to my appointment. I'm supposed to meet Nic there, even though he offered to pick me up. With the way I've started feeling every time I see he's sent me a text, I wasn't sure I wouldn't detour the car straight back to my house for a quickie before the appointment. As much as I want him, I don't want to jump the gun.

Speaking of texts, I check my phone to make sure he hasn't sent anything while I was working today. It's another habit I've gotten into, just sneaking my phone out for a moment to see if he's sent me anything. In some ways, I feel like a teenager again.

Nope, nothing new since his simple confirmation of the appointment he sent me this morning, but I see the few texts we sent last night, full of double-entendres and dirty talk. I swear that man can get me off when he's not even in the same room. Actually, that was literally the case last night because after we signed off for the night, I had to finish what we started, rubbing myself until I yelled out his name.

Shutting off the phone for the drive, I soon pull into the doctor's office lot and see Nic waiting outside. He looks handsome as always, dressed in a business suit with a long overcoat to keep out the chill.

He waves, immediately rushing over and opening the car door for me, taking my hand to help me stand, and then wrapping his arms around me in a big hug. "No carrying me through the lot, you big ape," I tease, relaxing into his arms. "How was your day?'

His lips press to my cheek, and my heart speeds up as he whispers in my ear, "I've missed you."

Smiling, I reply back, "I've missed you too, but we've been so busy I've been working like mad the last few days. I don't think I've sat down once before ten in the evening."

Nic raises an eyebrow as he looks down at me, and I can tell he knows I'm exaggerating just a little. Actually, last night, I was lying in bed with my legs spread, my fingers busy, and my mind on nothing but him at ten . . . but he gets the idea. "Well, maybe we can go to dinner after we see the doctor and then I can give you a reason to sit down."

I lean back, patting his chest playfully. "Any particular reason in mind?"

I'm flirting, half-hoping he says something sexy back but cautiously reminding myself to go slow. It's just so damn hard with Nic. Everything with him seems natural, easy, and about a hundred miles an hour.

He nods somberly, playing Mr. Serious. "Definitely something in mind." He leans back down to whisper in my ear, his breath tickling me and making my stomach flutter. "Maybe I could interest you in a foot rub since you've been working so hard?"

I moan, my mind already filling with ideas of candles, oil, lingerie, and Nic on his knees easing the exhaustion out of my feet before moving up my legs. "That's not at all what I thought you were going to say, but that sounds amazing. Just don't judge my pedicure. I slapped a fresh coat of polish on for the appointment, but my toes are getting further away every day so I'm sure it's sloppy."

Nic laughs, letting go enough to let me catch my balance. "Trust me, I'm not judging your polish." He takes my hand, and we go inside, quickly getting escorted to the sonogram room.

Within moments, Dr. Stevens enters and I introduce Nic to him. "Nice to meet you, Nicolas. We would like to do some bloodwork on you too, and there's a questionnaire if you're up for some paperwork? I just want to make sure we screen for any possible complications, not that I think we'll find any."

I look to Nic, uncertain about his response, but his voice is unwavering as he answers Dr. Stevens. "Sure, we can take care of whatever you need today. I'm here for Rose and for Jelly Bean."

His steadiness puts me at ease, a coil of tightness loosening in my heart to let Nic sneak in just a little more. I lie back on the table, Nic moving politely up to stand by my head and hold my hand.

I jump a bit as Dr. Stevens squirts cold jelly onto my belly and begins moving the handheld wand around. I watch as he points out various body parts and takes measurements, my eyes flicking back and forth between the screen to see for myself and then back to Nic to see his reaction.

Nic looks a little terrified, but mostly excited, probably exactly how I looked at first, and I remind myself that to him, this is all brand-new. Dr. Stevens presses a little bit, getting a view of the heart flickering on the screen. With a press of a button, the musical rhythm of Jelly Bean's heartbeat fills the room. My eyes lock with Nic's and his jaw drops open in wonder. "Is that it—the baby's heart?"

Dr. Stevens nods. "Yep, sounds good. Everything's looking good, for that matter. Measurements are right on track for your due date. Are we finding out the gender today?"

I nod, grinning foolishly as I think about the idea. "Yes, please! I can't wait any longer. And Auntie Brad will probably kill me if I don't call him within minutes of leaving here."

Nic squeezes my hand, and I look up to see him gather his courage and strength. In his steady gaze, I know that somehow, everything's going to be all right. "We're ready."

Dr. Stevens draws a circle on the screen before declaring triumphantly, "Looks like you're having a . . ." He pauses dramatically, and we nod like bobble heads until he explodes into a huge grin. "Girl!"

The news is stunning somehow, as if knowing that I have a baby girl inside me makes this all real, and I burst into tears. Joy fills and explodes inside me like someone's just set off a whole value-pack of fireworks, and I've got sparklers, Roman candles, pinwheels, and more running all around inside me, and the only way to let off the pressure is through tears.

Nic looks back at me, suddenly confused as he wipes the tears away, wrapping his arms around me and whispering in my ear. "It's okay, Rose. We're having a girl, and she's going to be beautiful and perfect, just like you."

Vaguely, I realize he's trying to comfort me, like I'm disappointed, and I laugh. The combination of tears and laughter do him in, and he looks to Dr. Stevens for help. "Uh . . . Doc?"

This isn't Dr. Stevens's first rodeo, though, and he smiles, patting my shoulder with a neutral gesture that can be both reassuring and celebratory. "Congratulations, Rose!"

He exits the room, and I wipe the last of my tears away, getting control of myself. "I'm not sad, Nic. I'm excited and happy. It's a girl! I'm having a girl!"

He wipes my tears once more, lowering to press a light kiss to my lips. "*We're* having a baby girl."

CHAPTER 16

NICOLAS

*A*fter the doctor's appointment, I hug Rose a few more times, pulling her close. I'm still in disbelief at the surprising change in my life in such a short period of time.

A baby girl . . . *my* baby girl.

I carefully help her into her car before following her home in my rental SUV. I normally try and drive something that's less than a rolling penis compensation, but around here, the big tires and four-wheel drive are actually helpful. Twice, as we leave stop signs, I feel the tires have to bite a little extra before accelerating, and part of me wonders if Rose's very practical and very small car is the right vehicle for the winters here.

"Stop freaking out," I laughingly chide myself as we pull up in front of Rose's house. "I'm sure she can drive just fine around here. She's been living here a lot longer than you have, mother hen."

I feel warm and very self-aware as Rose invites me inside her place, and from the moment I cross the threshold, I can see Rose's personality all over the place. Her style is warm and cozy, neat and tidy. Along the short hallway to her living room, I see four pictures, and I smile when I see an obviously younger Rose holding a diploma while wearing an emerald green gown and cap. "Graduation?"

Rose stops, then smiles as she shrugs off her coat. "Yep. That was me, eight years ago. Can I take your coat?"

I hand her my coat and my suit jacket, leaving me in just the dress shirt and slacks that I wore for my meeting with Mr. Adams, the resort's owner/manager, earlier today. I can feel her eyes on me as she slips both onto hangers, making them disappear into the closet before leading me into a comfy-looking living room with a long overstuffed couch along one wall. "I might be all about fashion at work, but at home, it's all about poufy pillows and being able to let my body relax."

"You'll get no arguments from me," I tell her as we sit down on the couch. "My living room still has the same secondhand sofa that I picked up and have kept because I swear there's no place better for catching some sleep after a long flight. Now . . . about that foot rub."

I reach down, pulling Rose's feet into my lap, encouraging her to lie back along the length of the couch. The corners of her mouth tilt up, her smile growing as I slip off her shoes and take her feet in my hands, rubbing and kneading lightly.

She groans, her eyelids fluttering as I start to work the knots in the sole of her foot loose. "Nic . . . what are you doing?"

"What do you mean? Exactly what I told you I was going to do," I reply as I run my thumb down the arch of her right foot. I can't help it, the intimacy is turning me on even though I'm not trying to seduce her. My cock is stirring in my pants. "You've been working hard and you deserve a reward for doing so much. Tell me what you're thinking about our baby girl."

I get a little catch in my throat as I say 'our baby girl', but I don't think Rose notices, thank goodness. Instead, she's almost purring. "Well, I'm thinking I want to name her Amelia and paint her room pink. Well, Brad wants to paint her room pink, but that's fine because that's what I want too."

I chuckle, lifting an eyebrow while wondering. I don't mean to pry, but I do need to find out more about Rose's life. Besides, she's in a good mood right now, about two glasses of wine from being jelly if that was still allowed. "Brad seems like a good friend. You said he's been taking care of you?"

Rose smiles, biting her lip as I work on her big toe. "Oh, yeah, he's gonna spoil this girl rotten if I'm not careful. Between him and Trey, her feet may never touch the floor."

I smile back, my cock growing as Rose shifts, and I can feel the warmth of her left calf coming to rest on my growing bulge. "I'm glad you've had friends and support during all of this. I'm sorry I wasn't here before, but I'm glad I'm here now."

"Me too," Rose admits. "Don't tell Brad, but he sucks at foot massages. Although come to think of it, that might be on purpose because pedicures aren't really his favorite job."

I chuckle and keep massaging, my hands moving up Rose's lean legs, creating tension in the quiet house as I get higher and higher. As I trace lightly across her inner thighs, the back of my hand grazes up to her pussy as she starts to squirm. She opens her eyes and looks at me with a small smile, inviting me in. I cup her mound, my thumb sweeping across her clit, and even through her clothes, I can feel her heat.

Rose bites her lip again, her breath catching when I stroke her clit again. "Nic . . . oh, God . . . what are you doing to me?"

I reach up, hooking the waistband of her leggings, shifting her a little to the side and easing them down along with her panties in one long, exhilarating pull. My mouth is already watering to taste her as I remember our last encounter. "Driving you as crazy as you drive me."

I spread her legs, sitting back on the couch facing her so that one leg is half slung over the back and the other half on the floor, open on either side of me. Rose looks at me with desire coursing through her beautiful blue eyes and reaches back, grabbing the cushion behind her head. I slide my hands up her legs to her pussy, bared to me now. "You're so damn perfect, Rose," I murmur as I massage her lips, spreading her wetness along my thumbs and using it to slip along the pearl of her clit and back down to her tight asshole. "Five months, and every night I've thought of you . . . and you're more beautiful now than ever."

She writhes, her hips chasing my fingers to get more, and her fingers clench around the cushion, her breath coming in short gasps. "Please, Nic," she moans sexily as I keep rubbing her clit in feathery little circles with one thumb and sink my other thumb slowly into her wet folds, spreading her open a little and watching the dark pink of her inner lips be massaged by my digit. "Oh, fuck, yes."

I feel her squeezing me, and it's enough to make me groan out loud, my cock pressing painfully against the fabric of my suit pants. I switch, replacing my thumb with first one finger and then two, moving them in and out slowly in time with the teasing to her clit. "My sweet Rose," I murmur, watching her. "Let me help you feel good."

Speeding up to match the rhythm she sets with her hips, I can feel the flutters starting deep in her core as her honey drips down toward her ass, and I pull back. "Not so fast, Rose," I tease. "We have all the time we need."

She whimpers, whining desperately. "More . . . I need it so much. I need you."

I pull my fingers out, dipping my pinky finger in once and then moving it to press against her tight asshole as I slide my other fingers back inside. She squirms, a sound of uncertainty squeaking out, but I reassure her, kissing her upraised knee. "Just relax, baby. I'm gonna give you more than you ever imagined possible."

Rose nods, her eyes full of concern and trust, but with just a few deep breaths and a few circles on her clit by my thumb, she relaxes enough, letting my finger slip inside her tight ass. I hold still, relishing the interplay of feelings across her beautiful face, and I realize . . . I'm her first back there.

"Good girl," I rasp, nearly overwhelmed with the gift she's giving me. I let the two fingers in her pussy sink in further while I keep my pinky still. When she adjusts, I start sweeping back and forth across her clit faster, filling her with slow strokes from all of my fingers. She squirms, loving the new sensation of being totally filled and taken by my hands as I stroke her clit with feather-light caresses that are meant to light her body on fire.

Rose's reaction is immediate and sexy, and she plunges herself deeper onto all of my fingers, looking down with her mouth dropping open in pleasure. "Oh, God, Nic . . . fuck."

Quickly thrusting my fingers in and out of her, I give her clit a small pinch, and she shatters under my touch, shudders wracking her body as she yells out my name. It's beautiful to behold, and I feel lucky to be the man sitting here with her in this moment. I ignore my own desire for this instant as I watch her, and I realize again that something powerful exists between us and I need more.

As she comes back down, her eyes focus on me and I'm shocked at the pure heat I see in their depths. She tries to sit up, and I help her, easing her legs down. Without saying anything, she reaches out, cupping my cock and massaging it, making me gasp.

"Strip," she says, more fiery than I've ever seen her before. "Now."

I stand, doing as she says while she pulls her shirt and bra off, exposing breasts that are bigger but even more perfect than five months ago.

I do my best to give her a little show, playfully opening my shirt and easing the zipper on my pants down, but after five months, I'm too eager, quickly kicking my shoes off and nearly tearing a seam on my shirt as I yank it off. I sit back down on the couch, pulling her to straddle me, and she rubs along my shaft, coating me in her honey as her hips move up and down.

I groan, not sure I can hold back much longer. I mean, other than my hand, it has been five months for me too. "Rose, is it okay . . . you know, with the baby?"

She smiles at me, wrapping her arms around my neck. "Yeah, Dr. Stevens says it's fine. A few positions I can't do, no pressure on my tummy, but other than that, we're good."

"Well, thank you, Dr. Stevens." I chuckle, leaning in and kissing the hollow of her throat. "And just think, don't have to worry about condoms."

"None at all." She lifts her hips, and I hold the base of my cock to angle inside her as she slowly lowers down, taking me into her heat inch by inch. We both moan, my hands going around to support her back as she settles balls-deep on me. There's a snapshot moment where we both look into each other's eyes before she grinds her hips against me, throwing her head back in pleasure.

I lean her back, kissing down her chest to her right breast, sucking on the stiff nipple until her pussy clenches around my shaft and I tear my mouth from her skin, hissing as I pull her back up until our chests are pressed together again. "God, Rose . . . you feel so good. Fuck me or I won't be able to hold back."

"Then hold on tight, cowboy," Rose says as she rolls her hips, lifting up and down on my cock. It's all I can do to not come right then as I squeeze her ass, encouraging her movements.

She feels so good and it's been so long, I feel like my eighteen-year-old self trying not to bust so quickly when losing my virginity. I try to focus, bringing her tit up to my mouth to lick and suck as she rides, letting her be in control as long as I can. She's breathless and collapses against me, resting her head on my shoulder as she nibbles and sucks at my neck.

"Fuck me, Nic . . ." she pants in between licks of my skin, "I can't anymore, but I need you."

Her words ignite the animal within me, and I growl, taking over with all the power inside my body. My hands grab low on her hips, holding her up so I can piston my cock in and out, forceful but not too hard, even if Dr. Stevens says it's okay. Sex is one thing, but I don't want to push it.

Rose's moans are right in my ear, egging me on, and I'm on the brink. "Touch your clit for me, baby," I pant in her ear, squeezing her ass again. "I want to feel you come all over my cock."

She moves a hand between us, and with a few flicks, she's twitching in my hands and I feel the pulses of her walls as she climaxes again, unable to make any noise it's so intense for her. That's all it takes as I come too, feeling like I'm in heaven as I fill her body with my seed.

"Rose . . ." I growl her name as it gushes out, filling her with pulse after pulse. As the last bit comes out, I pull her tightly against me, mashing our bodies together and claiming her mouth in a tender kiss. Finally pulling apart, we lie down on the couch face to face, legs and arms tangled together to have room. We're silent as I trace little circles on her belly, happily satisfied to stay just like this forever.

Suddenly, Rose twitches, her eyes widening in shock. "Did you feel that?"

"No, what?" I ask, a spear of fear piercing my heart and making me worry that maybe I'd just done something wrong.

"I think the baby just moved," Rose says, smiling. "Right here." She points to a spot low on her belly and lays her hand flat. "There it was again!"

Her voice is full of excitement, and she moves my hand to the same spot. I don't feel anything, but she does, and I'm just as excited as she is about this new step.

I talk toward her belly, caught up in the wonder. "Hey,

Amelia, sorry if you didn't like all that bouncing. I'd say we won't do it again, but . . ."

I lower my voice and whisper in Rose's ear. "I'm sure hoping your mom wants to do it again soon. And again and again and again."

Rose laughs, pushing on my shoulder, and I hug her back in tight. "Watch yourself and you may get that chance."

CHAPTER 17

ROSE

*S*ometime in the darkness of night, long after the moon has trekked across our piece of inky sky, we wake up still curled together on the couch. After a little wiggling and Nic falling to the carpet with a thump, he carries to me to my bed without a single complaint. Instead, he stretches out with me, where he makes me come again and again with imagination and a thorough devotion to my body's responses that has me wondering just how many different ways he has to make me scream out his name in ecstasy.

Our initial heat, the fire that led us both to give in to a one-night stand even though it was uncharacteristic for us, still burns just as brightly. For the next two days, at least when I'm not thinking about sex, I marvel at just how this has all come to pass.

For the entire weekend, we've barely found time to eat and shower, opting to snuggle up naked as we rest for our next round. Nic has at least pulled on enough clothes to pay the pizza guy who brought in a so-called 'family four-pack' so we don't pass out from lack of calories.

"You sure Devon hasn't robbed the store blind?" Nic asks as we munch through the last of the twisty breadsticks.

"I'm sure she did fine," I reply, shrugging. The real world is starting to loom over us again, both of us coming down from the lovers' high we've been on. "She's been fine on her own before. Still, I wish it wasn't almost time to go back to work."

Nic chuckles, the bounce of his chest vibrating me and making my breasts jiggle. "If I were an independently wealthy multi-millionaire, we could just stay holed up here forever."

"Naked and fucking and recovering to do it all again," I add, smiling some. My pussy aches . . . but still wants one last knockout before our mini-vacation ends.

Nic seems to read my mind, bringing his right hand up to cup my breast, rolling my nipple between his finger and thumb. "Mmm, that does sound like a good plan. Too bad folks would eventually come looking for us. And the fact that we do have jobs."

"I didn't hear from Devon all weekend except when I called her to check in. She's doing great, so maybe I could disappear from the shop for a few more days. You?"

Nic shakes his head, a regretful sigh escaping. "I have to check in with the deal here, and then first thing Tuesday, I have to fly out for a few days to go to Maine for another contract. My boss cleared my schedule on most of the stuff, but that one's a tough one we couldn't shift onto someone else. I'd say you could come with me, but snowmobiling in your condition probably isn't recommended."

He smiles, but I have a small stabbing pain in my heart. I sit up, looking into his eyes, the accusation clear but I can't help it. "You're leaving again?" It sounds bad but I just can't help myself, the emotions rolling inside me.

The smile falls from his face, a serious look taking over as he pushes my hair behind my ear and looks me in the eyes. "Just for a few days," he vows. "I'll be right back, I promise. Like I said, my boss is clearing my schedule as much as he can, and I'm taking some long-deserved vacation time too. I'll be back, Rose. I'll call you every night to check in on you and Amelia."

He moves forward, sealing the vow with a kiss. I feel a bit silly for my melodramatic reaction, but I can't help it. The last time he left, I didn't see or hear from him for months, and I don't want that to happen again, especially when it feels like we're doing something big here. "Okay," I tell him when our kiss breaks apart.

"So, where were we? Let's see what we can do before we actually have to sleep and behave like adults again."

---

*N*ic is as amazing as ever, but by Friday, I'm missing him physically and mentally. We've gotten pretty damn good at Skype sex, especially after I figured out how to hook my laptop up to my TV. *Watching Nic's cock in even larger than life-size is very . . . motivating*, I think with a blush as I get the morning stocking done at the shop.

Before this week, I'd never done anything like that, just some dirty talk over the phone and maybe a little sexting. But every night this week, Nic has called me, and after a quick check-in and chat, we've resorted to telling each other all the wicked things we want to do to each other when we're together again. I'd never known that masturbating while Nic's deep voice, gravelly with lust, tells me what to do would be so amazing, or that I'd find it so erotic to watch him jack off as he watches me.

Twice, we've even come together. It's not as good as having him here, but not a bad backup for a few days.

At that, my brain screeches to a halt . . . a few days? Yeah, that's what he said, but it's quickly turned into a week, and last night, Nic said not to expect him back until Wednesday at the earliest.

"I'm sorry, babe, but these guys in Maine are being . . . well, let's just say *Flinty-Eyed Yankee Traders* isn't all just hyperbole," he'd said. "I'll make it up to you, I promise."

It was okay last night, but now I'm trying not to be upset. After all, he has a job to do and I can't expect him to change everything in an instant. His boss is supposedly trying to be cool, but in the end, he has to do what's best for the company. I'm still busy working the boutique, so I have to give him some leeway to do what he needs to as well. It's not like I could just close up shop and traipse around the country with him right now either.

I'm just in a vulnerable moment and I miss him. That's why I'm going out to dinner tonight after work. I called Brad, and the Four Musketeers are going on the town tonight. Yeah, there's supposed to be three, but none of us do what we're supposed to anyway, so for tonight, four it is.

As usual, I'm the last to slide into the booth next to Ana as Brad and Trey sit across from us. Brad looks tired but happy, while Trey's buffer than ever and Ana looks . . . well, to be honest, she looks like she's seen better days. I hope the ER shifts aren't wearing her out too much.

"Well, hello to you, Bitch Mama!" Brad says, raising his mixed drink high. Only Brad—what the hell could he be drinking that is violently neon blue with a pineapple chunk on the rim?

I look down my nose, the sass that Brad has taught me dripping from every word. "I think you'd better correct yourself. I'm Mama Bitch, not Bitch Mama, unless you're calling my baby a bitch. And if that's the case, we're gonna have more than words."

"Is that so?" Brad asks, raising a finely sculpted eyebrow. "What's *more than words* supposed to mean?"

"It means for the first time in your life, a woman's gonna have her hands on your balls as she lifts them high in the air as a trophy before she makes them into some Rocky Mountain Oysters."

There's a pause of silence before we all burst out laughing.

Through snorting laughs, Brad toasts me. "That was so classic! Mama Bitch, Bitch Mama . . . Rocky Mountain Oysters." He rolls his head around on the last bit as he mimics me, thrusting his hand into the air like Wonder Woman holding her sword high.

Beginning to sober, he continues. "I've taught you well, Rose. Maybe a little too well. Although I do like the way you defend Jelly Bean, because if anyone says one word to that little baby, I will have their hide. Trust me, I know people. Scissors and lug wrenches are just the beginning."

We laugh a little more until I'm holding my belly because my abs hurt from the shakes of the giggles. "Enough, enough . . . before I spill Jelly Bean all over this floor."

Trey snorts before leaning forward, his eyes wide with curiosity. "Okay, now that that's over, spill it, girl. Brad hasn't told me what the doc said and I'm dying here."

I look to Brad, who calmly takes another sip of his blue concoction. "You didn't tell him?"

Brad smirks back, shaking his head. "Not my story to tell, and I don't gossip, you know?"

I'm incredulous, glancing at Ana, who snorts herself. "You liar, you're the biggest gossip queen I know! Half the things that go on in this town I know because you told me!"

"Only the interesting things," Brad says, defending himself. "And only people I don't count as family. Jelly Bean's gender isn't anyone's business but ours. But your weekend boinkfest, on the other hand . . ."

"You didn't!" I squeal, but one look tells me the truth. Looking back to Trey, who's blushing lightly, I shake my head. "Holy shit, Trey. I'm sorry. I figured you already knew from Mr. Knows-All-Tells-All here. Jelly Bean is . . . drumroll, please." I bang on the table lightly for myself. "A baby girl!"

Trey and Ana squeal, excited for me, and their excitement is so infectious that all four of us are shaking as we holler in delight. Ana wraps an arm around me, hugging me.

"I'm so happy for you, Rose!" she says with a sweet intensity. "A baby girl! You're gonna have to be careful that Brad doesn't snatch her away and put her in baby pageants."

Brad's eyes light up like that's actually a good idea, and I know I need to squash it before the idea takes root. "Absolutely not. No tiaras and poufy dresses unless you're playing dress-up at home. And by the way, Devon sold you out on the rhinestone tiara headband. Really? That's probably a choking hazard or something anyway!"

Brad deflates, his lower lip jutting out in a pout. "Fine, bitch, but pageants are awesome. She could win some scholarship money or something, you know?"

I smile back, trying not to roll my eyes. "You don't give a rat's ass about college money. You just care about the glitter and stomping down a runway. Hell, if there were a way to do it, you'd be out there yourself." I pull my lips into a duck-lip, squinty-eye model look and we all bust out in laughter again.

"All right, you've got me there. Just don't ever do that face again. Definitely not model material there." He continues, not even letting me poke him back. "So, I know I said I'm not a gossip, but I totally already told Trey about Nic showing back up, and presumably, he told Ana. So what's the deal on the daddy front?"

I smile, the thought of Nic warming me up from the inside. "Things are going good. We had a bit of a miscommunication and a blow-up initially, and some shock on his part, for damn sure. But he's great."

"Bit of a blow-up, she says," Brad grumbles. "You had me ready to call in the cavalry!"

I smirk, knowing Brad's right, and continue. "We've gone on a date or two, he went to the last check-up with me, we spent last weekend together, and he seems really onboard now. We're doing great."

Brad eyeballs me, his chin tilted down a bit. "Like I said,

Boinkfest. Boinkfest Two, actually. Isn't that how you got into this pickle in the first place?"

Trey rolls his eyes. "Ignore him. It's like he's thirteen sometimes. But he does have a point . . . a weekend together?"

I'm sure my eyes go slightly glassy as I think back, and I can't keep a hint of wistfulness out of my voice. "Yep, a whole weekend of naked, sweaty awesomeness. And I'm ready for an encore."

Ana whistles lowly, and probably a bit jealously. "So, where's he at now?"

My drink comes, a virgin margarita, but that's okay. No booze for the next few months. "Maine. He had to go for work for a few days, but unfortunately, it's turned into longer."

Trey looks thoughtful, forming his next words carefully. "He's traveling? He does that a lot, right?" He continues as soon as I nod. "So you said 'he's great' and 'we're great' and those are two very different things. Which is it . . . or both?"

That's Trey, a ton of muscle, but he's also smart as hell too and has good insight. "Hopefully both. He seems okay with the pregnancy stuff now, and we had a really great weekend. I think we're on to something. We just haven't figured it all out yet. I mean, the timeline's still really sudden."

Brad and Trey look at each other, a silent conversation flashing through their eyes before Brad turns to me, concerned. "Rose, babe, you're a Disney Princess kinda girl. You believe in romantic fairy tales where princes ride in on white horses to save the day and whisk you away to a castle for a happily ever after."

I shake my head, grumbling. "I'm not some sappy naive girl."

Brad raises a hand, shaking his head. "I know you're not. That's not what I'm saying. I'm saying that you're a dreamer, and in your heart, you've always wanted the husband, kids, dog, and picket fence picture. And sometimes that happens, but I'm just not sure that's happening right now. I mean, he's here for what, a week or so? And then he's gone again."

I know Brad's trying to help me out, but I still feel a little pissed and I'm ready to argue back. "Yeah, he's gone, but he's called every night. And it's not like he can just give up his work. He has responsibilities."

Trey reaches across the table, taking my hand. "I get that, Rose. He does have responsibilities . . . you and the baby. Just don't get so caught up in a fantasy that you don't see reality. We're just worried and looking out for you."

CHAPTER 18

NICOLAS

*I*t's been the most pleasant version of hell the last few days. On one hand, I've gotten to do a lot of things that I love—snowshoeing, cross-country skiing, and snowmobiling as I work with these tightfisted potential customers who all want demonstrations that ADRENALIN's gear is up to the challenge. But I miss Rose, and every morning, I wake up feeling worse about that. I'm just thankful that it's over and the contracts are signed. Hopefully, that'll keep Wes off my back for a little bit longer too.

I slipped off to Maine for what was supposed to be a few days, promising to call Rose every night and be back as soon as possible. But a trip that was supposed to be three or four days has turned into over a week now, and I'm hating that.

Our nightly phone calls were the only thing keeping me sane, even as I enjoy my work of talking to folks about our products and getting to do some real demos out on the machines in the woods. Each conversation started with her telling me about her customers at the shop, but she's also told me how she discovered that our little Amelia apparently loves hip hop music because she squirms around to the beat, and how she was doing some online window shopping with Brad on furniture for the nursery.

That last one hurt a little, the stab at not being involved in choosing a crib a surprise to me, but mostly, I've been glad she's happy. I've told her about the deals I was working, the adventures I had out in the woods, even the bears we'd accidentally come upon in a cave when we we're getting out of the cold on a hike. In every word, though, it's been great, because Rose has been positive that she and I would see each other soon and that I'm going to be a part of Amelia's life.

It touches me, it really does. And I want to be a good father, but that's more than money. Honestly, the Skype sex is the only thing saving me from quitting on the spot and running back to Rose, knowing she wants me just as much and that soon enough, we'll figure out our future.

I've been thinking more about that as my few days in Maine turned into a week, and I'm excited to see her in person again after the up and down of missing her, having fun with work, missing her again, and then getting to talk to her. It's going to help me figure out that next step.

Rapping on the door, I'm prepped for a hot reunion, and when the door opens, I can't help but look Rose up and down, taking her in. She's dressed in a sweet little dress, hugging her curves and totally inappropriate for the weather . . . but I don't think we're going to be leaving the house for a while anyway.

"Damn, Rose, looking good," I say, pulling her in tight and sweeping her into my arms, hugging her as I kiss her deeply with all the passion we've been keeping on simmer while I've been gone. Pulling back, I drop to my knees in front of her. "I've missed you so much."

Rose looks shocked, blinking at me as she reaches for my hands. "Nic, we're right in the doorway. The neighbors can see!"

I hear the embarrassment in her voice, but I hug her belly, kissing just to the side of her belly button. "Just wanted to say Daddy's home to my baby too, that's all. Let 'em watch."

Rose blushes, rubbing my hair as she struggles to find her words again. "Oh, that's not what I thought you were doing."

I look up at her, offering a wink as I get up. Of course I knew what she thought I was doing, and I'll admit that I've mused about it. But this isn't the time, I know that. "Oh, I want to, but not where the neighborhood can watch."

Getting to my feet, I put an arm around her shoulders as we go inside and settle onto the couch, Rose curled up in my side as I keep her snuggled against me. For the moment, I'm happy just to hold her and trace little circles around her growing bump. Has it really been that long? Or is she just growing that quickly?

Rose lets me keep stroking her belly through her dress but turns to look me in the eyes. "Hey, Nic, can we talk?"

The tone in her voice worries me, but I nod, looking at her with a slightly distressed smile. "That sounds ominous, but of course."

Rose shifts, turning a little to look more directly at me, and while my arm's still around her, it's not as close as it was before. "What are we doing here? I get that you have a job, and I don't really expect you to just stay here. But . . . what are you thinking is going to be the reality of things after Amelia is born?"

I've known the question was coming. I've been thinking about it in the back of my mind myself. But somehow, it doesn't make it any easier to answer. Mainly because while I've spent a lot of hours thinking about it. I still don't quite know what the hell's going on. Everything's moving so fast.

The hardest part was waiting at the airport to come back. I'd talked with Wes, who I was glad was mostly supportive. *"Glad to know that, man. Listen, can you set aside some time next week for a serious Skype conversation?"*

I held in a chuckle, thinking about the sort of 'serious Skyping' I've been doing for the past week and some change, but kept my voice level. "Sure, man. What about?"

"About the next few months for you," Wes said. "I don't want to be a dick, but you know that the next three months are a big time for us. The summer season's kicking in and all the new lines are coming out. That means a big deal to ADRENALIN's bottom line."

"I know, but she's just past the halfway mark. I mean, I just learned I've got a daughter on the way, and her name's gonna be Amelia. How can I be running around the ass-end of Vermont or rolling down some whitewater course in Kentucky when Rose might be in labor?"

There's a silence on the other end, then Wes sighs. "You're right. I didn't want to bring it up right now. Listen, we'll still talk, but I want you to give me a plan on how the rest of the sales staff can handle the territories on a more permanent basis, not just an 'oh, shit, cover for me' way. Maybe some of them need to step the fuck up and start earning their keep. Time to stop earning base and earn some commission."

Now, with her question about what's next, the conversation comes back to me full blast, and I swallow. Wes wasn't trying be a dick. He's legitimately concerned, and that's the tough part about it. He's trying to be cool, and I can see he wants to keep me and my skills in the company. But in a single mention, he sent chills down my spine. My salary is base plus a commission on sales over my target.

Granted, my base salary is more than my team since I manage them all, and the VP title comes with some sweet stock options, but I've got a daughter on the way . . . one who'll need diapers, baby food, and braces, and violin lessons. I have to keep the money flowing in somehow, and that worries me.

"Nic?"

A momentary flash goes through my mind to lie to Rose, that my space out was just jetlag, and not to worry. To tell some placating story, because I want to keep her happy . . . and also, right now, my cock wants a little attention too. But instead, the stronger part of me speaks up to tell the truth. "Rose, I'd like to have an easy answer for you. But really, I don't. But I'm working on it and I'm doing my best here. I've always traveled for work, and I can't change that at the drop of a hat."

Rose's eyes fall, but she nods in understanding. "Be honest with me. Do you even *want* to? I get it, Nic. You've always been a nomad, chasing the next adventure. Mixed in with work stuff, of course, and that's what makes you good at your job. Your passion. Hell, it's part of what makes you sexy as hell. You're the sexy wanderer who lives life by his own rules. But this isn't about hookups anymore. It's about Amelia and me, and you, if you want it to be. I need to know if you're going to be in and out forever. Or are you ever going to settle down? Because I'll admit that I'm getting caught up here in what could be. We could be a family, a real one, but I don't want to get my hopes up if that's not what you want."

I stand up, pacing the floor for a little as I try to form the words that have been burning in my heart for the past week. "I want to. I don't know just how the hell it's all going to work out yet, but I *want* to. Boss is trying to help me, but he's got expectations and is worried. I'm worried too. God, if I don't get out there, how is Amelia ever going to afford Harvard, or to learn to play piano or—"

Rose laughs, making me stop. "Slow down, Nic. She's not even born yet. Let's get her to walking before we book her future, let alone Harvard. I mean, it's cute as hell and answers some of my questions, but chill."

I swallow, shaking my head as I realize what she's saying. "Rose, I'm gonna sound stupid, but from the moment I first saw you almost six months ago, I felt deep inside that my life was going to somehow change at the fundamental level. I think you feel the same way, or else you would've told me to get the fuck out that second night I came back to the boutique."

"Maybe," Rose admits. "But what if I just wanted another dose of Grade-A dick?"

I snort, laughing lightly. "Something tells me that's not your style. But what if I just wanted some of your Grade-A pussy?"

Rose laughs, and I continue. "Rose, you're right. I'm an adrenaline junkie and I love my job. Hell, the name of it fits me perfectly. But the way I see it . . . this is my next adventure, here with you and Amelia." I gesture to the house around us with its simple, practical things, and I smile. "You planned to do this alone, but you don't have to. I want to be here."

Rose blinks, and I can see the tears shining in the corners of her eyes, and as they begin to roll down her face, I'm lost.

"Isn't that what you want too?" I ask, coming back over and kneeling in front of her. "I mean, you've had months to adjust to this, and I've only had a couple of weeks, but I'm doing the best I can. I'm trying to get to know you. Hell, I'm falling for you and having all these thoughts, picturing us showing Amelia the woods, teaching her how to swim and ride and explore, and being a family. My search for another place to stay here in town hasn't gone so well because . . . well, I keep wanting to share your bed. Isn't that what you want too?"

Rose nods her head, sniffling loudly. "It is. I just didn't know if you did. I'm falling for you too." She tries to wipe her cheeks, and I reach up to help her, sweeping the droplets away with my thumbs. She laughs at my attempt, finally using the neckline of her shirt to wipe the rushing tears as her smile gets larger. "God, I'm sure I look horrible." She swipes under her eyes, smearing her makeup more than wiping it off.

"Well," I admit, trying not to laugh out loud, "you do kinda look like a raccoon right now, but not a rabid mean one, just like one of those cute big-eyed stuffed animal ones you want to snuggle. Hold on, let me get you something better."

She laughs at my attempt at humor, finally using a tissue I quickly grab to wipe the rushing tears, and her smile gets larger. "Sorry, these hormones are like whiplash. The other day, I cried at a dog food commercial."

Smiling, I run my hands over her arms, marveling at the texture of her skin. Hormones might make Rose cry at dog food, but it also leaves her with skin that's smoother than silk. "It's all right, baby. I'll just call it practice for when Amelia cries and I have no idea why. Just rock and shush and hope for the best . . . it seems to work on you, and hopefully, it'll work on her too."

To show her that it works, that's exactly what I do, pulling her to stand with me and swaying her body with mine as we dance to imaginary music. She wraps her arms around my waist, and I gently run my hand through her hair, inhaling the heavenly scent that is undeniably Rose. "It's gonna be okay. We can do this. You and I are gonna figure this out, and we're gonna be a family."

She relaxes in my arms, the tears replaced with soft scratches as she runs her nails up and down my back. Our bodies press closer together, and my cock, which has behaved itself long enough, says it's ready to take over.

Rose feels it too and hums in appreciation. "God, I missed you."

She tilts her head up to look at me, and I see her eyes zero in on my lips. Taking her cue, I move to kiss her, soft butterfly kisses at first but quickly, the fire we've been stoking with our Skype chats for the last week flares. I sweep her into my arms, moving toward her bedroom and setting her down gently on the edge of the bed.

"I see you missed me too." Rose laughs softly as I reach for the tie at the back of her neck. Her dress is sexy but simple and is thankfully easy to remove. Sliding it down her legs, I take a moment to watch as she lies back on the bed, her 'angel's wings' hair spreading behind her and down over the swells of her breasts. It's breathtaking, and I admire her changing body until Rose squirms a little. "What is it?"

"You look gorgeous, glowing and round as you grow our little girl," I reply, my throat thick with desire and emotion. I take off my shirt, letting her get an eyeful before I move down to kiss her belly. After a soft kiss on her tight little bump, I slide to my knees in front of her, running my hands over her knees and easing them apart. "Seems like I promised a little something more than belly kisses earlier."

Rose smirks down at me, getting to her elbows to watch me. "It does seem like you did, but—"

Before she can finish her sentence, I pull her panties down and off, diving in to lick and suck her. I'm voracious. After watching her play with herself in HD for the past week, I've thirsted deep in my soul for her, and as my tongue laps her juices into my mouth, Rose moans my name deeply, running a hand through my hair. "Fuck, yes . . . I've so dreamed of your tongue."

"Hopefully, not just that," I tease before I start sucking on her clit. Rose makes a squeak that's half gasp, half scream of pleasure as I nibble and let my tongue flutter over the tip of her clit, cupping her ass and not letting her squirm away at all.

It doesn't take long. Rose has been on edge as much as I have despite our nightly masturbation marathons, and soon, she's trembling, grinding her pussy into my mouth as she starts to come, bathing my lips in her honey.

The drink of her precious sweetness only ignites another

hunger deep inside me, and I get to my feet, undoing my belt and stripping off my pants and boxers. "How do you want it?"

Rose bites her lip, licking once as she thinks, then gets onto her hands and knees. "We can do it this way almost until the delivery, I found out," she teases me. "And if you're good . . . well, you used fingers there once. Maybe you can do more."

"And if I'm bad?" I tease, running my hand over the curve of her ass. Her offer is amazing, but right now, I need a little distraction or else I'm going to be a two-pump chump as turned on as I am.

"If you're bad . . . then you can definitely do more," Rose purrs, looking back over her shoulder.

So not fucking helping. I don't care, though, and I take my cock in hand, lining up and filling Rose in one long stroke. It's like completion, coming home, whatever you want to call it, and we both moan deeply. "Fuck, you're perfect for me."

"Keep telling me that," Rose moans, pushing back until my cock is all the way inside her. We pause, both of us breathing deeply as the moment stretches out. Finally, Rose wiggles her ass, telling me without words what to do next.

Every movement is natural as I start stroking in and out, swirling my hips and pumping deep into her. There are no words needed, nothing beyond the gasps and moans that come from deep within our bodies, so deep I swear they're coming from our very souls.

This isn't fucking . . . this is something more. My cock is squeezed and massaged inside her with each inch I thrust, and I can feel her body electrified as I return the pleasure. It's amazing. I've never felt this close to someone before, even Rose herself during our hot encounters.

We speed up, my cock pumping fast and deep inside her before switching to shorter strokes that draw out our pleasure, making sure we don't rush. Reaching underneath her, I cup her breasts, pulling her up to nibble at her neck while my cock stays buried inside her, stroking her body and memorizing every curve with my fingertips.

"Nic . . ." Rose finally moans as I pinch her nipple lightly while sliding my other hand down to stroke her clit. I can feel her heart thundering under my fingertips, and I let go, lowering her carefully to the bed before taking her waist in my hands. My fingers sink into the soft curve there, and I take hold, stroking fast and deep inside her. Faster and faster I go, not hammering her but driving deep with every pump, giving her what we both need and making my eyes roll back in my skull it feels so fucking good.

Our orgasms hit us like a lightning bolt, simultaneous and massive. Her pussy flutters and squeezes me tightly, and I explode, filling her with everything I have. Sure, I know I can't get her pregnant again right now . . . but there's nothing like filling her and claiming her as mine just as she claims me as hers.

We collapse into the bed, and I gather Rose in my arms, holding her close as she's not the only one on the verge of tears after how intense that just was. "You okay?" I whisper, and she hugs me tightly. "Rose . . . thank you. For everything."

"Tell you what. You're paying for half of the electricity, at least," she says, turning to look me in the eye. "And the food. Do that and you can stay as long as you want."

I smile and kiss her little button nose. "I plan on doing a lot more than that. But let's start there and with breakfast in the morning. I want to take my girl out for pancakes."

Rose shakes her head, sighing. "No good pancake restaurants in the area. How about waffles?"

"Deal."

CHAPTER 19

ROSE

*O*pening the front door after a long day at the boutique, I'm greeted by the tangy smell of tomatoes and garlic with an undercurrent of porky deliciousness that tells me it's the good stuff. It smells divine and my now almost eight-months-pregnant stomach immediately rumbles to be fed.

Amazingly, only a few months ago, this smell would've sent me running for the hills to toss my cookies since I couldn't enjoy my favorite pasta, even if I could cook it, which I can't. I'm a lot of things, but a gourmet cook isn't one of them, and the smell of cooking in my kitchen was a warning for the neighbors to call the fire department. But now . . . it smells like heaven.

And it's all due to one man. "Nic? Whatever you made for dinner smells amazing. It's my new favorite."

There's a laugh from around the corner and Nic steps out of the kitchen with a smile, waving to me. "Yeah guys, that's Rose. No, I haven't been hiding her from you Mom. Here."

Nic turns his phone around, and I see two people on his screen. One of them is definitely Nic's father, so I can only assume that the smiling woman with him is Nic's mother. "Hi. . . uh, I'm Rose."

"Yes, Nicolas has been telling us about you for the past half hour," his mom says, smiling. "We're so excited to meet you and our granddaughter!" Her voice goes high and a little wild as she says 'granddaughter' and I'm glad she seems excited, not upset at the situation. "Welcome to the family, honey. I'm glad to see I raised my son right."

"You've done more than that," I assure her. We start talking about Nic as a boy, their myriad of adventures, and how she worried he'd never settle down. All in all, it's a wonderful first meeting with Nic's parents, if all too short.

"Okay, well one of the drawbacks of our lifestyle is limited internet, but unlimited minutes," Nic's dad says. "And we've got a date with a meteor shower tonight at dusk, so we need to run. You look famished, so we'll cut this short for now so that boy of mine can feed you dinner. Rose, it was such a pleasure to meet you."

"You guys too," I say, grinning as Nic starts plating dinner in the background. "By the way, whoever taught him to cook, thank you."

The call ends with them promising to see us soon. I set the phone down with a smile, glad that went so well, and turn to admire my man. He's still in his gym clothes, probably relishing the slightly unseasonal warmth, but to me I just like seeing his arms and chest rippling with muscle in his tank top.

And he can cook, how perfect is that? "So, you've got two plates of heaven for me?"

Nic laughs. "You haven't even tasted it yet, how could you know it's heaven?"

"If it tastes half as good as it smells, it's got to be close," I tell him, finally undoing my jacket to hang it up on the coat rack. "How was your day, besides the talk with your folks?"

Walking over, he plants a big kiss on me, tongue and all, definitely not bad for a pre-dinner appetizer. "Much better now. Not that it was bad before, but... well, seeing you makes the day near perfect. So, you up for some linguini with my secret tomato sauce?"

"Can't wait," I reply, feeling Amelia turn in my tummy. She's so big we've actually been able to watch her squirm now, it's sort of weird and wonderful at the same time. "Just give me time to get to the table."

Nic shakes his head and guides me towards the living room. "Have a seat on the couch, I'll bring yours to you. There's dessert too, chocolate pudding."

Not needing to be told twice, I plop down and perch my feet on the edge of the coffee table. "You're a figment of my imagination, aren't you?" I call out, earning another laugh. "Nope, no way are you this good. I've got to be imagining that you worked all day and made dinner and are serving me. I've officially gone off the deep end."

Nic calls out from the kitchen, a playful note in his voice. "Nope, not imagining things. I'm just buttering you up."

Oh, shit, what's he got up his sleeve now? I was teasing about his working all day and still handling dinner, since really, in the last few months, that's become our standard operating procedure.

It's been two months of bliss in a lot of ways. After he got back from Maine and we had our 'Come to Jesus' talk, along with mind-blowing sex afterward, Nic has been with me every step of the way. He's cut way back on his travel and has spent the majority of the last few weeks permanently delegating his accounts over to his sales guys and taking on a more managerial role versus his usual more hands-on approach.

I know it's been tough on him, mostly because he's put himself under a lot of pressure. I don't know what the deal is with his boss, but Nic hasn't complained. Still, he's trying to please everyone when all I want him to be is . . . him.

There have been two overnight trips where he went almost as much to teach as to be the salesman, from what he told me. He's shown the ropes to his newer associates, introducing the new agents around and making sure the right people are getting to know each other. Mostly, though, he's spent the past two months working out of the house, remote officing everything possible while I run the Mountain Rose.

At the end of the day, we meet for dinner. Sometimes, he brings takeout, but most nights are like tonight where he cooks. I guess I shouldn't be surprised he's an amazing cook and an even better griller. Nic's joked that his skills come from all the campfire cooking he's done. "When the only thing you've got is a survival knife, two sheets of tinfoil, and some stuff you dug up in the woods . . . you get creative."

Creative, indeed, and so far, no 'mystery mushrooms' from the nearby woods. Bringing in the plates, he sets them on the coffee table and sits down beside me, handing me a wineglass of sparkling water. "My lady."

"Ooh, fancy," I reply, sipping my Perrier. "You're pulling out all the stops here, mister. What's up?"

There's a tiny piece of me that's worried because as awesome as Nic has been lately, I know that he's still a bit of a wanderer and I sometimes feel like I'm waiting for the other shoe to drop, especially after hearing his parents talk about going here and there and the magic of meteor showers. And here in Great Falls, it's just... me. The stress of his job and, from what I understand, the loss of his sales commissions, have to be weighing on him. But I'm putting my faith in him, and so far, we've done awesomely. If anything, I've told him numerous times that we're a team. The Mountain Rose is continuing to do well, and we'll be fine. I think my reassurances have helped. At least, they seem to.

"I checked a few more boxes off the to-do list today," Nic says as he tells me about his day. "Well, I got a good workout this morning, and yeah, I know I'm still dressed, but you see . . . the nursery is done."

"That's great news!" I cheer, knowing Nic's been working hard to try and get everything squared away there. "Even the crib?"

"Double-checked and verified by Brad himself. He said that he's got your baby shower under control and not to worry about a thing. I signed over two more contracts to my team for monitoring and support, just one big one left. And—"

I interrupt with a smile, knowing where this is leading. "And that one deal is why you're buttering me up?"

He nods, and I lean back against the couch, looking at him expectantly. "That obvious?"

"A little. All right, well hand me a piece of garlic bread. Nothing can be that bad with garlic bread in my mouth."

He smiles and hands me a slice, waiting till I take a big bite and wave my hand for him to continue.

"This last contract is the one I want to keep as my own. It's not about the sale itself. Their monetary value really is small potatoes compared to some of the other contracts I've handed off. I want to keep this because I like the couple that runs the company a lot. They're the ones out in Oregon I told you about. And well, they're sort of a sentimental place for me because of some of the stuff they told me."

I search my mind for a second then make the connection, as Nic mentioned it one night when we went for a moonlit walk. "Sam and Susan, right? The off-grid adventure tours?"

Nic nods, smiling a little. "That's them. Look, for me to be able to stay home for a while with you and Amelia after the birth, I need to make a trip out there to do a meet-and-greet and make sure everything's running smoothly. And with your being thirty-two weeks now, I need to do it sooner rather than later and as fast as possible to get back."

"That's it? You need to run to Oregon for a quick trip?" I ask, surprised. I thought this was a big deal or something, what with the spread he's got in front of me. "What's the catch?"

Nic tilts his head, and I can see that he's got more to tell. "Well, 'quick trip' is relative here. These guys are totally off-grid. Last time, I spent a few weeks there all told with getting there, the sales and stuff, and then ferrying back and forth to a damn internet connection to get it done and then back. Don't worry, though. This isn't anything like that. But I'll need at least a week . . . and I'll miss the baby shower."

I smile, relieved. "It's okay, honey."

"Are you sure?"

I nod, taking his hand. "I'm sure. I'm sad you'll miss the shower, but I'd rather have you here after Amelia is born to change poopy diapers and to deal with my hormones going apeshit again. I'll be using this as a bargaining chip for a long time, Daddy. Brad and Trey can help me get to and from the shower and take care of me for a week if I need anything. Devon is doing great at the shop, and Dr. Stevens says everything looks great so I'm still fine to work for a few weeks. It'll be fine."

Nic lets out a big puff of breath, the tension leaving his shoulders. "God, I'm so glad you're okay with it. I really don't want to leave you, and I knew that'd be a hard thing for you to handle, but I need to do this so that we can hibernate after Amelia is here, just turn off the phones and disconnect from the world to be our own little family. I just want you to know that I don't want to go, but I need to so that I don't have to leave for a long time after this."

"I get it, and I do appreciate how much work you've done to stay here with me and to plan ahead to be here for Amelia," I reply. "I can handle a week apart when I've got at least six weeks to go."

He leans in to give me a kiss, smacks and sweetness, and whispers in my ear, "I love you."

The words still thrill me, and I kiss him back, loving the tenderness in his every move. "I love you too."

He lowers down to my belly, pushing my oversized maternity top up to kiss my belly too. It makes me giggle. I'm unfortunately very ticklish recently, but he knows just how to do it so that I'm not laughing out of control and peeing myself.

Talking to my belly, he croons to Amelia. "Daddy will be

back before you know it. Be nice to Momma while I'm gone, okay?"

Unable to resist, I lift my belly up a little toward him and mimic a little kid voice. "Only if you feed me some of that damn spaghetti right now. Bitches gotta eat."

Nic shakes his head, leaning back and putting his hand to his forehead like some sort of wannabe Southern belle. "Oh, my poor ears! The mouth on this kid already. She's gonna be a spoiled brat if Brad has anything to do with it. Look what he's done to you."

He smirks like he got me good, but he still goes to my plate and twirls up a forkful of pasta that looks so delicious I'm thinking I'm the winner here either way.

CHAPTER 20

NICOLAS

*A*ll of my bags are packed and it's nearly time to go. Just one last call, and it's gonna be a bitch, but I need to do it. I've taken care of as many other things as I can, even speeding up the process by taking this ungodly early flight today so I can land tonight and jump right in the rental to get out to Sam's camp early tomorrow. After a couple of rings, Brad answers, the sound of a high-pitched motor going in the background. "Bitch, there'd better be a damn fine reason you're calling so early in the morning."

I cringe, knowing he's not too happy with me, but there's nobody else I can really trust with this. "I know, I know. Sorry, but I needed to check in one last time before I get on my flight. You've got my back here while I'm gone, right?"

Brad *tsks* through the phone, and I can practically imagine him rolling his eyes at me. "No, I don't have your back, but I have Rose's. Anything she needs, I'll take care of. Just go do what you gotta do and get back here."

I can live with that. "Thanks. I hate that I'm leaving," I say before adding, hoping this'll get me a few brownie points, "and that I'm going to miss the fabulous shower you're throwing for my girls. Jesus, man, what the hell is that sound in the background?"

"Gasoline-powered giant vibrator," Brad replies. "Why, wanna ride?" he pauses a beat like I'm actually gonna answer that before continuing, "It's the blender for Trey's smoothie."

"Very funny," I shoot back. "But seriously, man, thanks. I'll be back as soon as I can, but I have to do this so I can be here."

My plea seems to have worked as Brad's voice sounds a little less grumpy when he answers. "I know. I'll handle anything that comes up. It's fine. I'm just grumpy at this time before the rooster even crows, and it's my turn to make the damn breakfast smoothies. But now that I'm up, I guess I could go for a little cock-a-doodle-doo, if you know what I mean."

I laugh but attempt to cut off details before he thinks he can give them to me. "Well, thanks again. See you guys when I'm back."

I'm not sure if he realizes he hasn't hung up yet, but before the line goes dead, I hear him in the background. "Tre-e-ey, I have a nice breakfast sausage for you!"

Thankfully, that's all I hear. I take one last look at my sleeping Rose, memorizing the spray of hair across the pillow, her mouth soft in sleep and her hand resting protectively on her full belly. Not wanting to disturb her nest of pillows, I land a light kiss to her forehead and whisper in the bedroom air, "I love you, baby."

---

*I*t's a long day of travel, commuting first to the airport and then flying into Oregon. My secretary arranged all the travel and assured me that the best option was to stay at a hotel my first night in Oregon so that I could safely ride an ATV out to Sam's place in daylight hours. Admittedly, my first reaction was 'fuck that', and I'd planned to travel straight through, but now I'm glad I listened to reason because the long flight has me exhausted, and a ride as the sun sets and the woods become darker and more dangerous is definitely not the best option.

Settling into the hotel, I look around and realize how alone I feel. "Homesick already," I muse out loud as I fire up my computer, glad the motel's got Wi-Fi. Dialing up Rose, I hope she's still awake. Time zones can be a bitch at this distance. After a couple of rings, her face fills the screen and I feel my heart jump in my chest.

"Well, hello there, stranger. I missed you this morning," she greets me. "Didn't even leave a note."

I chuckle, knowing that her soft chide is just a joke. "I couldn't bear to wake you up. You were sleeping so well, and I know that's harder these days, so I wanted you to get your rest."

Rose smiles, leaning back on the bed. "I did sleep well for a bit and then went into the shop for a few hours. Two hours after I got there, Devon sat me in a tall chair behind the register and told me not to move. She helped all the customers and just sent them to me to ring out."

I laugh, knowing that Devon's totally one of those people that I'm so glad is in Rose's life. "Sounds like she's got it under control . . . the shop and you."

Rose fakes indignation, pointing a finger at me. "Hey, I don't need anyone to control me. I'm doing just fine."

I tilt an eyebrow, thinking that a little bit of control is exactly what we both need right now. I drop my voice down, letting the gravel rumble the way I know she likes. "Rose . . ."

I see the smirk cross her face as her eyes light up, realizing that I'm shifting the mood. She almost wiggles, and I wonder idly just how far we could take this if we ever wanted to. "Yes?"

I lean forward, undoing the top button on my shirt and showing her a little bit of my chest. "I was thinking back to when I traveled before and missed you so much. Do you remember what we did?"

I watch as her eyes go to my exposed skin while she bites her lip and nods. "How could I forget? And I am rather . . . needy tonight. These damn hormones make me horny all the time."

I smirk, knowing that it's not just the hormones that are making her feel so needy for sex. Because I feel the same way every time I look at her. "I know, and I fucking love it," I half growl, undoing my cuffs and rolling them up my forearms. "You just do what I say, and I'll take care of you, okay?"

Rose purrs, looking into my eyes. "Okay, and just what do you want me to do?"

"Thought you didn't want anyone to control you?"

Rose smiles, trailing a finger down her neck to her chest, where I can see her nipples already poking through the thin cotton of her t-shirt. "At work, I'm the boss there. Like this, with you, it's different. Now, are we gonna have a therapy session or are you gonna make me come long-distance?"

I laugh a little. No matter what, the woman's got sass. "Oh, I'm definitely gonna make you come, but not till I say you can. Deal?"

Rose grins, and I realize again that somehow, I've found the perfect woman for me. "Deal."

"Take off your clothes and lie back on the bed, spread your legs wide, and set the laptop down between them so I can see your whole body."

Rose does as I ask, and I say a little prayer of thanks for HDMI cables, because after plugging my laptop into the TV in the motel room, I can see every inch of her body in sexy thirty-six-inch detail. My cock's already throbbing, and we've barely begun.

"Lift your shirt and tease your nipples nice and slow," I command, my voice raspy. "Just like that. Now, lick your fingers and circle them around your nipples. Slow circles, baby . . . tease yourself for me."

I watch as she does as I ask, circling closer and closer to her peaked nubs with each hand. Through the video feed, I can see her eyes almost glowing, staring as she watches me.

Rose's fingernails catch the sensitive tips of her breasts and she takes a huge inhale, trying not to give herself away.

"Nuh-uh," I playfully admonish her. "I didn't say you could touch your nipples, naughty girl. You do exactly what I say and only what I say. Understood?"

Rose whimpers but nods. It's not quite domination. We both know that as much as I'm commanding her, she's just as much in control . . . but whatever it is, it's sexy as fuck. "Yes, baby."

I nod, making my voice stern even as my hand reaches down to massage my cock through my pants. "For that, you'll have to be punished a little bit. Pinch your nipples, both at the same time."

Rose does as I say, throwing her head back to gasp, and I reward her by stripping off my shirt, letting her see all of my upper body.

"Now," I continue, standing up to let her see me better, "push your tits together. Lift them up and let me see how big and full they've gotten. And slide your thumbs across your nipples. Soothe that bite away from the pinch."

She does as instructed but suddenly jolts as her nipples start dribbling a little milk. She stops, blushing nearly bright pink as I watch the whiteness dribble down her skin. "Oh, shit, sorry."

As far as I'm concerned, it's sexy as fuck. I don't want her to be embarrassed. "Move your hands. Let me see those milky tits. You're gonna feed our baby with those, and I'm gonna get plenty of it too. You're the mother of my child. Everything about you is sexy. I'm just wishing I were there to suck and lick you right now."

She calms at my words, getting back into the mood and beginning to rub her nipples again. "Nic . . . you make me feel so good."

I groan lightly and undo my belt, showing her just a little bit of the happy trail of hair that goes from my belly button down to the base of my cock. "When I get back, you're getting a nice big surprise. Cup yourself for me. Grind your pussy into the heel of your hand."

She does as I say but stops just before her hand makes

contact with her pussy. "You, too. Take off those pants and put the laptop where I can see you stroke yourself. Show me how turned on you are to watch me because God knows, I want to watch you."

I whip my pants off easily, adjusting the laptop on the table so that she can see everything from my knees to my hair, sitting upright on the edge of the bed so she can see me grab my cock in my fist, giving it a few strokes. "Is this what you want? You want me to jack off for you?"

Rose moans, her hand moving to massage her pussy and her palm grinding down on her clit. "Fuck yes, Nic. Tell me . . . tell me what to do."

I keep stroking, slow and easy to stay in control. I don't want this to end quickly. Not until we're both totally satisfied. "Slide a finger into your pussy. Slip it in nice and slow." She groans a bit, and I see her pussy clenching around her finger, searching for more. "What do you feel?"

She looks me in the eye, slowly moving her finger in and out in time to my strokes. "Hot, so hot and slick like silk. I'm dripping wet for you."

I hiss, my mind filling with the memory of what it feels like to slide my own fingers inside her, the way she clings to me. "Fuck, I want to feel your heat, wrapping around my fingers as I open you up, making you squirm while I stroke your G-spot just how you like."

She whimpers, spreading her lips for me, and I pump a little faster, grinning. "It's not as good as my cock when I pound into you, is it? Keep yourself open with your other hand. I want to see your hard little clit pulsing, greedy for attention."

She moves her hand up, pressing her pussy lips wide, and I

see her clit peeking out from its hood and throbbing with her heartbeat. "Like this?"

I nod, a clear drop of precum already oozing from the tip of my cock and making my shaft glisten as I smear it up and down my throbbing shaft. "Yes. Take your fingers out and rub your clit . . . slow and easy. Keep yourself spread so I can see."

As she does, I can't help but jack myself a little faster, already close to coming. God, it's hot to watch Rose, my perfect mix of innocence and naughtiness. And all mine. She smiles, her breath coming in short gasps. "Slow down or you're gonna come before I do. Or can I speed up to match you."

Her fingers blur as she matches my tempo, and I growl, shaking my head but letting up a little on my strokes. "No, I told you slow and easy. I think you need a smack for that. Now."

She meets my eyes, a hint of defiance, but I know she likes it and won't hurt herself. Her eyes don't leave mine as she gives her open pussy a little spank, her fingers centered right over her pussy as she makes contact with her clit, her hips jerking at the sensation. I watch in lustful awe as her pussy contracts and more of her honey leaks out. "I think you liked that. Scoop that gush of nectar out and smear it all over your clit, get it nice and wet, then smack it again."

She groans as she spreads her juices before crying out as she smacks herself lightly again. My cock jerks in my hands and I grin, knowing just how to torture her. "You're my dirty little slut, aren't you?"

"Just. Yours." She moans, shaking her head. "Fuck, Nic . . . I'm on the edge, Nic. Please . . . please, let me . . . I need to come."

Unable to wait much longer myself, I give her what she wants. "Rub your clit, Rose. Fast and hard, and watch me come for you. We're gonna come together, no matter how many miles are between us. Got it?"

She moans her agreement as she starts to strum across her clit in a blur and I move my hips to fuck my fist. It's hard, watching her and trying to keep in time, but with Rose, I find the ability to keep going to give her everything and deliver on my promise.

Rose sees my torture and smiles, helping out like only she can. "Grab your balls, squeeze them just like I do, and come for me."

I use my other hand, never stopping the rhythm of my hips to do as she asks, and giving my own instructions in between whimpering grunts. "Slide two fingers in, Rose. Fuck your fingers and come for your man."

There's a moment of silence, just panted breaths as we stare at the screens, eyes locked on each other, and then we both erupt, shudders and shakes overtaking us as our moans echo both in our empty rooms and through the screens. I spurt all over the floor in front of me, but I don't give a shit.

Riding the high as long as possible, I open my eyes again to see Rose catching her breath too. She smiles, and it's like sunshine on my heart. "Eight months, and you still want me like it was the first time."

"Damn, Momma." I pant, wiping the sweat from my forehead. "You're sexier now than ever. As fast as you make me come, maybe this traveling thing isn't so bad after all."

Rose chuckles. "Mmmhmm, that was just what I needed, but I still wish you were here in person."

"Me too, baby. This is it, though. Last trip for a long while, and then it'll just be you, me, and our little girl."

"I like that . . . kinda hard to do Skype sex with a baby around. We'll just have to be boring."

"Oh, I can help you be quiet," I tease. Rose laughs, nodding. We talk for a bit longer, and while my cock says it still wants a little attention, I know I have to get up before sunrise to head out so I start to wrap things up. "I think I've gotta get some sleep. I'll be off-grid for five days to ride out, do the checks with Sam, and ride back. I won't have phone service till I'm back in town, out of the forest. Brad promised to take care of you, and if there's an emergency—"

Rose interrupts, shaking her head. "There won't be an emergency. I've got this handled, and you're right. I've got great friends if, by chance, there is. So no stress, Nic."

"I know you do, but if there's an emergency, have someone call Wes. I left his number there, and he can get in contact with me if he really has to. If you need me, that's how to reach me."

Rose nods. "Got it. It's fine. Go get your work done, play in the outdoors, and feed your spirit, then haul ass home as soon as possible."

"Will do. I'll be back before you know it."

CHAPTER 21

ROSE

olling out of bed, I scowl at the alarm clock, its *beep-beep-beep* an annoying reminder of all the things I need to do today. I'm opening the boutique, and Devon comes in to cover the afternoon shift so I can hole up in my office to place an order for our next shipment before she closes down.

The spring lines are in full swing, and I'm already looking for this summer's lines, knowing that's another of the big tourist seasons. May through August pays for September through November, when the ski season starts around here. Just not enough fall foliage, I guess. Too many pine trees, even if they smell great.

Mentally running through the list of clothes I've already selected, I try to decide what bonus pieces I want to order as well.

One of the major ways I can add to my bottom line and provide exceptional customer service is in not only providing the one piece a customer is looking for, but in providing an entire ensemble, from dress to jewelry to shoes to jacket. The difference between 'oh, that's nice' and 'holy shit, I gotta get me one of those!' often comes down to these little accessories. Those detail pieces are what I need to determine this afternoon to finalize the order.

Finishing up my mental prep as I brush my teeth, I slip on a slim-fit cotton dress that hugs my curves and highlights my baby belly. Amelia's really far too big to call her a 'bump' any longer. While the mornings and evenings are still cold around here, days are nice and the shop can get really warm. Devon has insisted on keeping the shop at exactly the temperature that Ana's told her is perfect for me. Ah, well, better to be over-loved than under, I guess.

Turning sideways to check myself in the mirror, I really am stunned by how huge I've gotten. I always thought the expression 'she swallowed a basketball' was funny, but when it's your own body stretched, it's shockingly odd to see yourself that way. I'm thankful that most of my pregnancy weight seems to be contained to my belly, breasts, and if I'm honest, my butt, and if the mirror isn't lying, I look good—glowing, healthy and happy. Especially my ass. I'm gonna have to figure out how to keep that cushion for the pushing after Amelia is born. Eat your heart out, Kardashian family!

Slipping on low-heel booties that will be comfortable all day, I decide to just grab dry toast and decaf coffee on my way out the door. My stomach is a little upset and I don't know if it's from Amelia dancing inside me all night or because I miss Nic so much. Probably both. Amelia seems to get antsy when Nic's not around. She's gonna be a total Daddy's girl for sure.

Unlocking the boutique, I get to work straightening racks, putting away the few things left in the dressing room area before deciding that the mannequins up front need new outfits. With the change in weather, it's time for a new series up front.

This is one of my favorite parts of my job, creating a look that is eye-catching and interesting to get folks to stop in and buy the outfit I'd put together. Every time that happens, it feels like a pat on the back for creating a look that someone wants to actually wear on their body for their daily life.

By the time noon rolls around, I've helped several customers and selected the mannequin outfits, trying to discreetly wrestle the clothes onto the unhelpful forms while there's no one in the shop but me. If anyone can ever make a mannequin that doesn't make you half rip a seam getting a blouse on, I'll kiss them.

"Come on, you son of a bitch—" I grunt as I wrestle with a light pink blouse that's going to be part of a set inspired by Amelia, who seems intent on pink becoming my favorite color even before she gets here. The bells jingle merrily as the front door opens, and I call out, "Welcome to the Mountain Rose . . ." as I look up, but it's not a customer.

Devon comes in with takeout boxes from the diner, and as her eyes find me, her face screws up in exasperation. "Rose, what the hell are you doing? Why are you kneeling on the floor? You're about to pop, for gosh sakes!"

She sets the boxes down on the desk and offers me a hand, helping me up. I accept the helping hand, grunting as I get up. "I'm fine. Just decided the mannequins needed to have some fun so I picked them out new outfits. And I'm kneeling because if I sit all the way down, I'd never get back up. I'm pregnant, not broken."

Laughing, Devon brushes off my butt, which I guess has gotten a little bit of carpet fuzz on it. "All right, pick them out some goodies and then leave the clothes for me to do it. That's what you pay me for, Boss."

I smile, glad that she is such a good worker but more importantly, that she's become a good friend in the months that she's worked here. I don't know what I'd do without her and I'm glad to have her so that I can go on maternity leave in a few weeks, secure that she's got the boutique well in hand. The Mountain Rose isn't going to miss out on the kick-off to the summer sale season, and I'm not going to have to rush back either.

"Thanks, truly. You're a lifesaver."

Devon shakes her head and heads back behind the register to drop off her things. "That's what I'm here for. So, besides doing too much," she says, giving me a knowing, reproachful glare, "what's up?"

I smile, quietly loving her mama bear instinct because I already have quite a serious streak of protectiveness over Miss Amelia. "Nothing much. Saw some customers, sold several items, including one of the long layered maxi-skirts and one of those chunky turquoise necklaces to the same lady."

Devon does a little fist pull as she makes a *cha-ching* sound. "Money, money, money, baby."

"Yep," I agree, not mentioning that I'm going to be giving Devon a bump in her paycheck this month because that necklace was her idea. "Good sale and a nice lady. She had me cut the tag off the necklace and wore it out—said it was her new favorite." I smile at the memory of how excited the woman was with her new treasure.

"I'm glad," Devon says. "All right, let me finish this up and you can get to whatever else needs done. Don't forget your lunch. I got us soup and sandwich specials today."

I grab the takeout box, inhaling the delicious aroma and realizing that the dry toast didn't exactly last me long enough and I'm suddenly starving. "Thanks again. Holler if you need anything, otherwise I'm hibernating until I'm done."

I get to the office and sit—well, more of a controlled fall— down on the couch, resting my food box on my belly and laughing that it's become a convenient place to perch things. I sip at the soup. It's good, light but filling, and helps me feel reenergized. For a diner that has a reputation for being a bit of a great side-of-the-highway comfort food place, they really know how to make a damn good high-quality soup . . . and today's ginger and chicken with vegetables really kicks ass.

Deciding to save the sandwich as a pick-me-up treat for later, I set the box on the little table and stand to switch over to my desk. As I stand, my belly tightens, a strong squeezing sensation moving from under my ribs to down deep in my pelvis. It takes my breath away for a moment before I remember to breathe slowly, in and out.

"Whoa, baby," I mutter, grabbing the edge of my desk. "What the—" My mind whirls, and I realize I just had a contraction.

As it passes and I feel fine again, I'll admit that I'm a little excited. Dr. Stevens and the nurses who'd done my birthing classes had talked about how most women have practice contractions for weeks before they actually go into labor— Braxton-Hicks contractions, they call them—to help their bodies prepare.

"It's like a marathon runner doing training runs beforehand," Dr. Stevens told me when he explained them. "You've got to get your muscles ready and learn how to stay calm and breathe through the contraction. There's another benefit too . . . for Amelia. The practice contractions will help her get in position and be ready for her birthday."

All right, first practice contraction . . . handled like a boss, and that means I'm getting one step closer to meeting my little girl. I wish I could call Nic to tell him, but he's still incommunicado out in the forests of Oregon, and I don't want to scare the shit out of him by using Wes to get in touch with him. But he'll be back in three days and I know he'll be just as excited as I am.

I picture him holding my hands, telling me to breathe as he puffs his chest out, breathing with me, rubbing my belly lightly to feel the contraction himself and help me get through them as they become stronger.

We're gonna do this. We're gonna be parents. I can't believe it. Trying to focus my buzzing brain, I sit at the desk, focusing on clicking all the right buttons as I go through item after item for the order. I don't have any more contractions, just a general sense of tightness as I work, but I'm comfortable enough considering there's a human being doing somersaults inside me. "Hope you're having fun down there, babe," I tell Amelia after clicking the *Pay* button on the last order. "Just think, soon enough, you'll be outside and then the real fun starts."

By late afternoon, I'm exhausted and hungry so I grab my earlier sandwich, thankful I saved it. After munching it down, I decide a little walking would do my back some good. The hours spent hunching in my office chair have not been doing my back any favors.

I step out into the boutique to see Devon making final

adjustments to the mannequins, which are now placed in the display windows. Devon hears me and calls over, doing a final flourish with her feather duster. "Whatcha think, Rose?"

"Looks great. Thanks for finishing those." Her eyes stay locked on her work as she brushes a little lint off the top and tweaks the necklace.

"No problem, Boss. You did good with the picks. Miss Madison-the-Mannequin looks ready for a night on the town. Heard she's been talking to that mannequin they're using for the Nike compression gear at the sporting goods store. Wonder if he's enhancing any bulges in all that spandex."

"Well, if anyone can find out, it's Maddie," I say as I laugh a little, the jiggle causing me to inhale sharply as another contraction shoots across my belly. "Oof!"

Devon is instantly sober and rushes over to me. "Rose, what's wrong? Are you okay?"

I breathe, nodding my head, waiting until it passes before I reply. "I'm fine, just having some Braxton-Hicks contractions today."

"You sure?" Devon asks, her eyes searching my face, looking for a sign of . . . something. "You do look a little pale."

I roll my eyes. Devon's more freaked out by all of this than I am. "Gee, thanks, honey, but I'm okay. I do think I'll head out for the day, though, if you have things handled."

Devon smiles and gives me a hug back. "Everything is under control. Go home and get some rest. Call me if you need anything."

I nod absently, wishing I was already curled up at home on the couch to get some sleep. I bend down to grab my purse from behind the counter, slipping it over my shoulder, when I feel a tiny little cramp deep inside and my panties feel suddenly wet. In my mind, I'm thinking that maybe I just peed myself, when I hear Devon gasp, her eyes locked on my leg. I look down and see a tiny line of blood trickling down the inside of my right leg, curling around to drip over my kneecap.

"Oh, my God," I whisper in a voice that doesn't sound like me. "That's not supposed to happen."

Devon's voice is panicked, her eyes nearly big enough to fall right out of her head. "Do you want me to call Nic?"

I shake my head, realizing he's in the wilderness with no phone. "Not yet. Call Brad and tell him I need him to take me to the hospital. And call Dr. Stevens so he can meet us there."

CHAPTER 22

*A*fter our night of Skype sex, I headed out dark and early to meet Sam and Susan. Sam was nice enough to meet me in town, his son coordinating for us to meet during Sam's supply run. He greeted me next to the biggest of his snowmobiles, a huge cargo job with attached trailer, with a hug that had damned-near taken my breath away, but it was good to see him again. Funny how a few days with just the two of you, working in the woods, could create an instant deep friendship.

"I gotta tell you, Nic, you were a lifesaver this winter," Sam says as we go up and down the aisles of the market, checking items off Sam's list. "Twice, we got huge snowstorms that woulda knocked out our old gear. But the stuff you got us, me and the family were nice and cozy. Haven't had a single snowmobile go down all winter, no matter how hard we've run them."

"Considering the amount of stuff you're putting in this cart, I guess you've been able to run them pretty hard too," I joke as Sam puts in a case of Dinty Moore beef stew to join the roughly hundred pounds of other stuff in the cart. I swear, anywhere you go in North America, you go into the woods . . . and someone's going to have a can of Dinty Moore nearby. It's damn near a law.

"You would've laughed your ass off at this city boy who came out, bag packed full of beef jerky and socks," Sam says, pausing his story dramatically to grab two twenty-five-pound bags of rice. "Damn fool had nothing else. Not a knife, map, flashlight, or even matches in there at all."

"What the hell was his idea? Was he going to build a tent out of socks? Keep the bears away with athlete's foot funk?"

Sam laughs. "I don't know. Susan geared him up properly with your stuff and we headed out, supposed to be a five-day trip. But wouldn't you know, by nightfall day three, we hadn't even made it halfway to the turnaround point, so the next morning, we took a shortcut out and I radioed Susan to pick us up on the main trail in the SAG wagon. That big boy ATV you left sure came in handy. Got us out and home for Susan's apple pie before dark, and city boy said he felt like he'd had 'a life experience he'll never forget'. Can you believe that?" He laughs good-naturedly. "Damn fool never even got to the peak I wanted to show him."

"At least he didn't die," I point out. "A credit to you."

"Your gear too," Sam says honestly. "He put a beatdown on your stuff with his bumbling ways, but it took it all. Even when he thought that you were supposed to hammer tent stakes into a tree."

After finishing his list, Sam and I load up the cargo trailer on his snowmobile and jump into the passenger cabin to drive deep into the woods. "I know it seems a waste down here, where the snow ain't deep," Sam says as he adjusts his throttle, "but once we go about two or three miles, you'll see why. While you're out here, I'll give the ATVs a test run. Some of the trails are clear enough."

"They'll handle anything you put in front of them without a problem," I assure him.

As soon as we're surrounded by trees, I feel a tightness in my chest loosen. The fresh air, bright in my lungs, rejuvenates me, and the pine boughs waving in the breeze as we slowly roll by seem to welcome me home.

Susan's greeting is much the same as Sam's, although her hug isn't nearly as backbreaking since she's less than half his size. "Good to see you, Nic. How's civilized life?"

"Lots of good, but I'll tell you about it inside. I see you've built a fire and I don't wanna waste the good oak," I reply, looking at the idyllic looking cabin. "And I heard something about pie?"

"Of course," Susan says with a knowing glance at her husband. "Come on in."

To say the dinner is delicious is a ridiculous understatement. The stew is venison, shot by Sam himself, while the pie is mountain berry, picked and canned by Susan back in October and aged just right. As we eat, we catch up more, and I tell them about what's been going on over the months since we last saw each other.

"So after our last visit, I flew around a bit, same as always, visiting with customers and negotiating with potential customers. A resort that had gone another way called us back, and I flew out to Great Falls, a town back east that I'd been to right before seeing you guys. Ran into a woman there I knew from my last trip."

Sam looks over at Susan, mouthing 'a woman he *knew*' as he waggles his eyebrows. She giggles, slapping his arm lightly. "Be good and let the man finish his story. Tell us about this young woman."

They turn back to me, and I smile at their easy camaraderie. "So, I see Rose—that's her name—and she's pregnant. She uh, well . . . she didn't know how to get ahold of me, and there was a bit of a mix-up with a phone call message when she finally did find me, but long story short, we're having a baby."

Susan claps, tears springing to her eyes as she rushes over to hug me. "Congratulations, Nicolas! That's fabulous, honey!"

Sam offers a hand-crushing shake and pats my shoulder. "Well done, Son. I had a feeling, the way you were talking out in the big woods." Before I can reply, he squeezes down a little more warningly while giving me a mean hard-eyed look. "You're doing right by this lady, aren't you?"

I smile through the pain, glad I've been drinking my milk or else I might have a broken hand right now. "Well, I'm damn sure trying. It was a little rough at first, as you can guess. The first meeting again when I walked in to find her five months pregnant . . . yeah, that was a little dramatic. She thought I wouldn't want to be part of the baby's life, but we got it all straightened out. Now, I'm looking forward to it being the three of us. I'm moving to Great Falls permanently to be with Rose, and ADRENALIN is working with me to help make that happen. I'm just riding out my lease on my old apartment and already arranged for a company to send me what I want from there and donate the rest to the Salvation Army."

Sam nods and gets up to pour the after-dinner coffee. "Well, if you got a guy that'll come all the way out here, I'll work with whoever you recommend. Don't you worry about a thing."

I shake my head, getting up to help clear the dishes. "Nah, if you don't mind, I'd like to stay the primary contact on your account. I won't be able to travel much, especially at first, but a trip out here every once in awhile sounds like the reprieve I need from city life. Also, no buttering you guys up, but this place is just about next door to paradise in a lot of ways."

Sam nods knowingly, handing me a steaming mug. "Sounds good to me, but if it's too much, you just let me know. I sure like the gear you left and appreciate the deal we've got, so if you need to stay closer to home, we understand. We had babies once too."

Susan clears her throat, tossing a dish towel over her shoulder as she prepares to wash up. "All right, boys, if you're done with the business chatter, I have a question . . . when are you getting married and do I get to meet the baby?"

I laugh, feeling heat rush to my face. "Well, I've been living in her house for a couple of months now, working remotely to be there as we get ready for the baby, but we need to make it a little more official, if you know what I mean."

Susan's eyes are shining like diamonds as she nods. "I know, and I can understand that. But I want to know all your plans, about the baby, how you want to do the proposal, wedding . . . all the good stuff."

Sam chuffs, rolling his eyes as he takes the dish towel from his wife and starts running water. "You two go on. This could take you all night. About the only things that can make my tough as nails spitfire wife go all gooey are weddings and babies. Back when we lived in town, she'd watch these Hallmark movies every day, same damn story with different characters every time. Now she just reads them." He leans in to whisper, even though Susan can hear every word, "At least I don't have to listen to them anymore, and the books seem to get her going, so that works out just fine for me."

I laugh along with them, happy to bear witness to their love. When their eyes come back to me, I continue. "I am planning to propose, but figured I'd wait. We're moving about as fast as you can, and I don't want to overwhelm her. I do plan on visiting a jeweler in Portland before I fly back to Great Falls though. Just gotta plan when I'm going to pop the question, so not a word to anyone."

Susan mimics locking her lips and throwing away the key. "My lips are sealed."

I laugh and sit down on the couch. "We're naming the baby Amelia, and her room is already painted pink, like a Pepto-Bismol bottle got tossed all over the walls. I know that sounds cliché, but Rose loves it, so I do too. Best of all, she's got a good group of friends that rally around her, and a helper in her shop so that she can take off for several weeks after Amelia is born. It's not where I ever saw my life going, but now that it's here and it's happening, I can't believe how amazing it is."

Sam and Susan smile back at me, delving into a long story about how their son, Mason, had met the woman of his dreams. She'd hated him for being backwoods, but he'd eventually won her over, and now they live in the small town we'd shopped at today with their five kids. Sam laughs. "Trust me, keeping up with those five as they go running through the woods . . . the first time I let them, their mother was worried they'd get eaten by a bear or something, but I told them with all the noise they were making, the bears were heading over the mountains as fast as their legs could take them."

His story gives me pause. I might be excited about Amelia, but the thought of five kids gives me a good dose of fear, and somewhere deep inside, I hope that Rose doesn't want quite that many. Maybe one or two more, but definitely not five. I don't want to raise a basketball team. I mean . . . we'd have to have a chain of Mountain Roses and I'd end up having to take Wes's job to afford *that*.

---

*S*am and I spend the next few days running maintenance checks on every piece of gear he's got, checking his soon-to-be broken out ATVs from bumper to bumper, restringing fishing reels, and replacing a ski on one of the snowmobiles.

It's dirty, hard work but I enjoy it. Being outdoors, making sure that Sam has what he needs to be successful and safe, and generally being useful in a way that pushing papers around doesn't make me feel. This is a sort of life I could certainly get used to.

We chat as we work, and Sam's full of little nuggets of wisdom. "You know what will keep you in your lady's good graces?"

"Tell me," I reply as I oil a drive chain. "Figure you, of all people, might know, from what I've seen."

Sam chuckles as he checks a length of rope for wear and tear. "When your baby's born, you're gonna be tempted to swap turns getting up when she cries. You're gonna have days at work that'll make getting up at two in the morning seem like the toughest thing ever. But don't you do it. You drag your carcass out of bed when you're home . . . it'll pay off."

"Pay off, huh?" I ask, and Sam chuckles.

"Chances are she'll need to be fed or need to be changed. You can't feed her, but you can sure take her to her momma since she'll be the one staying up to do the feeding. And you can dang sure change a diaper. Lord knows I did my fair share of diaper duty once upon a time."

I store the advice away for later, sure that he knows what he's talking about if his marriage has lasted this long and is as good as it appears.

Sam finishes the last few inches of rope inspection and makes a quick coil of it, looking over to see if I'm done with my assignment too. "You ready? Let's run these babies."

It's great to take the ATVs out, heading out along the paths Sam's created as he shows me some hidden treasures along the property. The caves, huge trees, and a surprising hidden pond are amazing to see, and the machines run smoothly, not a single hiccup after our maintenance and care.

"They're purring," I comment as we come to a stop over-looking the pond. "Let me guess, your old ones were cranky as hell the first days of spring?"

"You could say that—" Sam says, but before he can finish, his radio squawks.

"Sam? Come in, Sam." It's Susan, and Sam cuts off his engine. I follow suit, the silence somehow sounding ominous after the pleasant drone of the engines earlier. I shiver, suddenly feeling the chill wind on my throat.

"Susan?" Sam asks, picking up the radio. "What's up, honey?"

The radio static quiets before Susan continues. "Mason just came out from town, said he got a call from a fella named Wes who's looking for Nicolas. You boys need to come on in."

She doesn't say as much, but I feel a knot in the pit of my stomach and my hand trembles on the controls of the ATV. There's only one reason Wes would go through the trouble of calling Sam's son to come find me out in the sticks. "Rose . . . something's wrong."

Sam meets my eyes, nodding once as I see he's come to the same conclusion. "All right, Son, keep your head. We're gonna get you back as quick as possible, but these woods and these machines ain't made for racing, so hold it together."

CHAPTER 23

ROSE

The hospital room is bland, but I don't care. I'm focused on Dr. Stevens. "Everything looks stable . . . for now. Your bleeding has stopped and the baby's heart rate is perfect, no signs of distress. Sonogram shows that there's a tiny separation of the placenta, but we're doing what we can for now to keep that baby inside you for a little longer."

I swallow my fear, knowing that Dr. Stevens is good at what he does "Okay, but what does that mean? What do I need to do?"

He gives me a reassuring smile. "The prescription is very simple, but also very difficult for someone like you. Bed rest, and plenty of it. In fact, I'm admitting you to the hospital for monitoring, and you'll be here until you deliver."

I gasp, unconsciously struggling to sit up. "Umm, until I deliver? Couldn't that be weeks from now? I mean, I've got so many things that need to get done, and I'm hardly—"

Doc puts a calming hand on my shoulder, shaking his head

gently. "And you have one of the best support systems in place that I've ever seen. This does increase your chances of delivering a little earlier, but mostly, we're just going to keep the contractions at bay as long as we can."

"What dangers are there for her?" I ask, reminded that this is about Amelia, not the boutique or anything else.

"Even in the worst-case scenario, if you gave birth today, odds are really good that she'd be fine and just have a little growing to do before she went home. The best thing you can do to keep her inside, though, is to be calm, stay in bed, and let us help you."

I nod, glad for his fatherly bedside manner as he walks out. I grab Brad's hand. He's been with me the whole time. "Thank you."

He turns to me, his voice a little deeper than his usual airi-ness, and I know I'm talking to 'Real Brad', not 'Fabulous Brad'. "You're fine. Jelly Bean's fine. I'm here and Nic's on his way. Just breathe."

I try to believe him and trust that everything is going to be fine, but inside, I'm freaking out. I curl up into a ball, protec-tive around my hospital-gown-covered belly. "Brad . . . I can't lose her."

He leans down, wrapping his long arms around my shoul-ders and rubbing my belly. "Listen up, Miss Amelia," he says in a lighter voice, closer to his normal voice, "you are not done cooking yet, little princess. And as excited as I am to meet you and spoil you rotten, you're not ready. Get a little bigger and then you'll be able to handle all the love your momma, daddy, and Auntie Brad can surround you with. Mmmkay?" He keeps talking, the words becoming a soft murmur as I feel myself doze off.

When I wake up, it's nine hours later. Brad's gone but left a note that he'll be back, and I realize that I've been here since last night. It's been sixteen mind-numbing hours of constant, droning beeps, half-understood voices over intercom systems just outside the door to my room, and far-off alarms that both bore the shit out of me and fill me with a dreadful terror. "How can I deal with this shit?" I ask the room. "I've potentially got weeks of this to look forward to."

I steel myself. I can handle some boredom to make sure Amelia stays safe. Of course I can. I'd do anything for her. I guess I'm glad that Brad finally had to go home. He probably really needs a shower and some rest. So for the first time, I'm alone with all of this.

Questions swirl in my head. Could I have done something wrong? Could I have prevented this somehow? I know that Dr. Stevens said that my working had nothing to do with what happened, but there's a little part of me that still feels guilty. Worried about getting a damn mannequin dressed when my baby was inside me? Fucking stupid idiot.

My brain races on to negotiating, begging my little Jelly Bean to stay inside and promising that I'll meet her soon, but not too soon. I promise her that I'll be the best Mommy in the whole world. I rub my belly, feeling the little flutters as she seemingly answers me, and I smile.

Suddenly, the door flies open and Nic races in, dropping to his knees at my bedside. He's a mess, hair disheveled like he's been running his fingers through it, a few days' scruff on his face, and rocking dirty flannel that honestly kinda smells. "Oh, my God, baby. Are you okay? I'm so sorry I wasn't here. Amelia, how is she?"

He's rambling, stuttering as the words rush out. It reassures me, and I realize that part of what I smell is sweat and pine tar. I wonder if he's even taken a chance to change his boots since getting the news. A man who'll race across the country to get to me . . . he's the man for me. I take his hands, looking him in the eye to get him to calm down and focus. "I'm fine. Doc says Amelia is fine and that I just need rest."

I can see the relief rush across his face, and then he presses his cheek to my belly, looking up at me. "I was so scared, Rose. I thought I was going to lose you both. Are you sure you're really okay?"

I nod, tears in the corners of my eyes to see him so upset, but also my heart swelling knowing that he's so concerned about us. "Really. We're okay, and you're here now. Speaking of, how'd you get here so fast?"

He smiles, but it's wavering. "I was out with Sam, miles out in the forest when his wife called on the radio. Sam's son arranged for me to grab a chopper to Portland, where I grabbed the first flight back here, landed, and got here as fast as I could."

I smile, cupping his scratchy cheek. Not his normal look, but there's a part of me that likes it. "Sounds like you've had a busy day. I've just been lying here, taking naps."

I'm trying to lighten the mood, but Nic isn't having it. "I'm truly so sorry I wasn't here, and I promise I won't ever leave you again."

"Nic," I reassure him, stroking his messy hair and pulling out a pine needle, of all things, "you're not gonna be by my side every second of every day. These things happen, but we're going to get through this together."

Somewhere deep inside me, the damn that's been holding it

all back bursts and I cry. Nic climbs up in the bed with me, probably against the hospital rules but who gives a fuck, and we lie face to face, the roundness of my belly surrounded by our protectiveness and love.

Nic wipes my tears, kissing my forehead and reassuring me. Eventually, the fear subsides and I feel the calm resolve that we're going to be okay.

Our first unexpected hiccup as parents, and our people came to our aid, supporting us, and Nic and I are stronger than ever, knowing we're in this together.

CHAPTER 24

NICOLAS

*T*hree weeks. Three weeks of daily hospital visits that Trey coordinated to make sure Rose was never alone for more than an hour at a time.

Three weeks of entertaining Rose with cards, puzzles, books, and talking about everything under the sun and then some. Three weeks of Rose and I spending time side by side in her hospital bed, or me sitting in the chair next to it, each with a laptop as we work. I've spent time checking in with my team as they continue business as usual. Doing a business Skype meeting in a hospital room is only unusual the first time. After that, everyone's been cool. I finally had that talk with Wes and we've worked out a way for me to manage our sales force from Great Falls on a permanent basis so I can be here as much as possible. I'll still have to take some quick trips, but he understands and agreed that as long as ADRENA-LIN's goals are met, he doesn't care if I'm working from headquarters or in my PJs at home. That was a huge weight off our shoulders as I feel confident I can be successful here, and Rose knows I'm staying by her side. I got word out to

Sam and Susan that we're okay. The next time he goes into town, he's supposed to give me a call.

For her part, Rose has been doing the accounting duties and window shopping for future orders for the shop. She calls Devon every afternoon for an update and Devon seems to be handling the whole thing like a pro. She's done so well that Rose has already given her a promotion to assistant manager, although technically, she has no employees to manage, but she got a well-deserved raise with the title.

Surprisingly, the whole thing has gone exceptionally well, considering how scared we all were at first. Rose hasn't had any more contractions or bleeding, and it's just become our new normal, a type of waiting game where we try to function while never leaving bed.

That sounds like some kinky version of heaven, but it's definitely not. Rose's body aches half the time, my back feels like shit until I'm halfway through my workouts, and quite frankly, trying to get things done with the background noise of a hospital blows.

Thankfully, our little crew is helping out too. Today, Ana is going to sit with Rose after she finishes her shift while I go handle some top-secret business outside the hospital.

Ana comes in, looking tired but still with a smile on her face. "Hey, guys, guess what I just saw?"

"Treat a man who somehow *accidentally* ended up getting a full can of beer shoved up his ass?" I joke, knowing that after being on her feet for twelve hours, she's gotta be exhausted. "Or was it a remote control?"

"Very funny," Ana says, sticking out her tongue as she lays out food, breakfast for Rose, dinner for herself. "Actually, it was a Bluetooth earbud up the nose. Guess there are draw-backs to those wireless systems."

I laugh, giving Rose a kiss and Ana a hug before leaving. While Ana is on Rose duty, Brad and I have plans to sneak out for a little surprise. I'd begged his help in choosing a ring for Rose, considering my first choice of the jeweler in Port-land is a no-go.

I feel confident that I know what she'll like, but when her best friend is a fashionista with an eye for detail and the finer things, I'm not going to discount his expertise.

I pull up to Brad's place, giving a honk to let him know I've arrived. His door sweeps open and I see him give Trey a blazing kiss and cock grab as he steps out. Not a bad way to say goodbye, I guess. Maybe I should have him tell Rose that for after Amelia is born.

Trey smacks Brad's ass, a sassy grin on his face, and then he waves at me as Brad climbs in.

"So . . . new truck?"

"Well, new to me," I admit. "I had a long-term rental for a while and then was just using Rose's when I drove her back and forth to work. Seemed like I needed something a little more mine, if you know what I mean. Seemed like a good buy."

Brad runs his hands along the console. "Well, it's cute. Big, black, rugged truck seems to fit you, not one of those fancy jacked-up ones that never goes off the asphalt, but a real work truck that'll git 'er dun." He laughs uproariously at his attempt at impersonating a country boy, and I grin back, hitting the gas as we roar into town.

"I appreciate your help with this, man. And more importantly, your keeping this a secret. I know that's not really in your nature."

Brad smirks at me, leaning back in his seat. "Definitely not, so you owe me big time. What are you thinking on the ring?"

I think back to my original plan, discarding it almost immediately as I think of Rose. "I want something different. I mean, like Rose different, unique without being way the fuck out there. Definitely not just a chunk of shiny rock on a band. Delicate, maybe, like lace made out of metal. Definitely a diamond, but maybe more than one or rows of them? I'm just saying . . . shit, I've got no idea, but I'll know it when I see it."

Brad nods, his finger tapping his lips while he thinks. "Well, I do think I have it on good authority exactly what she wants, if you're interested."

I look at him skeptically, glad we're at a red light so I don't have to worry about traffic. "How do you know '*exactly*' what she wants?"

Brad leans over, whispering. "I happen to know her Pinterest password is *FuckMeNic* so I can show you her entire wedding board."

He sits back, obviously pleased with himself. I'm left in shock, and when the light turns green it's only the guy behind me blasting his horn that tells me I need to go. "So many things wrong here . . . you hacked her Pinterest, her password is . . . I don't even wanna go there with you, and she has a wedding board? I don't even know what that is."

Brad waves a hand, like everything I said is totally obvious and totally unimportant. "And that is why I am here."

We pull into the parking lot of the best jewelry store in town and Brad clicks on his phone for a moment, quickly pulling up what is, in fact, Rose's Pinterest board titled *'One and Done'*. He scrolls through the pictures, and I can't help but picture our wedding like this . . . the dresses, the flowers, the gazebos covered in flowers and greenery, a tiered white cake, and then I see it.

The ring in my head is on Rose's board. "Stop, that's it! That's the ring."

Brad stops scrolling and looks where I'm pointing. "Well done. That's definitely her style, and she obviously loves it. There's hope for you yet, my Padawan. Let's go in the store and see what they have that's similar."

We walk inside and the salesman is instantly on alert, knowing a ring-buying man when he sees one. Probably an aura I'm giving off, or maybe just the purposeful way I stride in. Men don't go jewelry shopping like this except for one reason. "How can I help you today, sir?"

"I need an engagement ring," I reply, earning a hiss from Brad. He gives me a look, and I shrug. Fuck it, it's just money, and an engagement ring is not the time to be looking for a bargain.

"Of course," the salesman says, probably trying not to rub his hands together in glee. "Do you know what style, size, and price point you'd like to shop today?"

I gesture to Brad, who pulls out his phone, showing the ring picture to the salesman. "I want something like this. Or this ring, if you have it."

He tips his glasses down his nose to get a clearer view and whistles lowly. "Ahh, a beautiful selection indeed. I saw that at a gem show, and I do wish there were a market for such a design in town. I have a few things that are similar . . . solitaires with halo settings and filigree, perhaps even a few with diamond bands as well. Let's see what we can do."

He brings us over to a case, sliding a tray out to show me a few options. But none of them are exactly what I'm looking for. I shake my head, not satisfied. "I'm sorry. I understand this might be a specialty piece, but this is a special woman."

The salesman nods, sliding the rings back into the display case. "Well, I do have one other, very similar to the picture, but it's rather pricey. I hesitate to show it because if you fall in love with it, it is difficult to be happy with lesser. 'Tis the first rule of weddings—don't look at things that are out of budget."

He tilts his head at me, silently asking if I want to see the ring. What a stupid question. I do. I definitely do. "Without a doubt. Let's see it."

The salesman dips his chin once, and I swear I see the dollar signs flash in his eyes for a second. Motherfucker is probably counting his monthly bonus as he waddles over to the safe. After all, I'm a pro at this. I know a sales tactic when I see it, and while it's not my favorite, he just played me like a fiddle. I don't care. If it's the ring for Rose, it's going to be her ring, no matter the price.

Brad raises one eyebrow at me, silently asking if I'm sure. I shrug back, leaning in to whisper to him. "VP of Sales with no real responsibilities has helped me become a little . . . flush, if you will. I know babies are expensive, but I've been smart with my money, and this is a one-time thing. I want it to be all Rose has dreamed of. I'll do anything for Rose and Amelia."

He smiles, rubbing his hands together like a little kid about to get a cupcake. "You know, you're supposed to get a gift for the maid of honor too."

"Yeah, well," I joke, "I'll find out what Ana, Devon, or McKayla likes, whomever Rose chooses."

As the salesman returns, Brad smirks and I know he's going to get me back for that one. "Bring on the ice, my good man. He's buying!"

The salesman is unflappable and sets the box down on the countertop, opening it with a good amount of theatrics to create a sense of mystery and value without taking too damn long. The black velvet parts and I see the ring. Rose's ring, without a doubt. I pick it up, turning it this way and that, watching the light reflect off the large center stone and the glittering surrounding ones. The shining platinum swirls along the band do look just like filigree lace, giving the ring a feminine vintage feel.

It's precious, perfect, just like she is.

"I'll take it."

Brad lets out a whoop of celebration, patting me on the back so hard I damn near drop the ring back to the velvet, but I hang on tight. Laughing, I turn and taunt him a little. "Watch it, man. You're getting a little stronger than you realize."

He blushes a little, flexing his bicep as he pats the impressive swell. "Yeah, Trey keeps me right, making me work out and eat well. I'd say he keeps me on the straight and narrow, but there ain't a thing straight or narrow about either of us."

I chuckle, then turn to the salesman. "Got anything to celebrate a little girl's birth? Like a necklace or something?"

"I believe I might have just what you're looking for."

CHAPTER 25

ROSE

*T*he night is just like all the rest over the last few weeks, tossing and turning. Well, more like squirming and wiggling with the weight of my belly in an attempt to find a comfortable position in a not-that-soft hospital bed surrounded by my nest of pillows.

I glance outside, but all I can tell is that the moon's down, the arc sodium lights from the parking lot eliminating any trace of the stars from my vantage point. Nic is sprawled out on the pull-out chair next to me, where he's been every night for weeks, unwilling to leave my side lest something happen overnight and I need him. It can't be comfortable, and I know that Ana's pleaded with him to at least let her 'reassign' a bed or gurney to my room, but he refuses. God knows how he's able to keep his body working at all, but Trey told me he sees Nic at the gym on a regular basis so he's keeping it up somehow.

My bladder's giving me fits, but I don't think I need to pee just yet. Instead, I pick up my phone off the nightstand, blinking at the bright light showing me that it's four in the morning, hours before the nurses change shifts and come in to wake me for a vitals check.

I know what my problem is, really. I'm restless, physically and mentally ready to get this show on the road since I'm technically full-term now. Dr. Stevens told us yesterday that while he'd like the baby to bake a little longer, I'm officially thirty-six weeks so if I go into labor, they'll run with it.

The latest sonogram shows that the small separation hasn't changed. Woohoo for bedrest. Still, I hate being able to do nothing but waddle up and down a hallway for no more than twenty minutes a day and go to the toilet. But as long as everything goes well during labor, I shouldn't need a C-section, although Dr. Stevens warned me to never rule it out.

Trying to be quiet so I don't wake Nic up, I rearrange myself, rolling to my back and propping the bed up higher to get some pressure off my achy lower back. Even in the bed, my belly weighs my body down, the days of a cute basketball effect long gone. As soon as I'm out of here and have Amelia safe in my arms, I'm getting to work with Trey. He can help me lose the bits of Jell-O I'm rocking now, because while a little extra badonkadonk is one thing, postpartum Jell-O isn't. I moan, the ache in my back intensifying. Maybe he knows a chiropractor who can help get my sore back in working condition too. This bed is so awful and not doing my poor body any favors.

Halfway through my roll, a contraction shoots like a bolt of lightning across my belly, taking my breath away and obliterating all thoughts of my jiggly ass. It's not a slow-rolling squeeze like the few I've had before, gradually tightening. This is instantly tight and painful.

As it subsides, I whisper to Nic, trying to wake him gently so he doesn't freak out. "Nic . . . Nic, wake up."

He jolts despite my gentleness, instantly on his feet and by my side. "What? What's wrong?"

God, I love this man. A whisper, and he's here for me. "I just had a contraction. A pretty good one. I'm gonna call the nurse, see if she thinks we should time them or something."

Nic smiles in the dim light, leaning down and kissing my forehead. "Relax. I'll get her."

In a flash, he's out the door, jogging, I bet, down the hallway to the duty nurse's station to get someone's attention. They're back quickly, the nurse full of smiles and energy considering the hour. "Having some good ones?"

She flits around a bit, checking my vitals, which are all fine, and as another contraction comes on, she lays a light hand on my belly, feeling the hard tightness. "We'll watch you for a little while, and if you get into a regular pattern, it might be baby day. But it's still too early to tell for sure. I'll call Dr. Stevens to let him know the update, and I'll make sure the on-call docs are ready if you do decide to pop quickly."

She gives Nic a piece of paper and a pen with instructions to write down the times when I have contractions and to call her immediately if we need anything. I sort of find it silly. I mean, who's going to go 'hey, I'm having a contraction! Is it eight fifty-seven or eight fifty-eight now?' but I guess I've got enough on my mind. The nurse hurries back out, and I look at Nic, whose hands are shaking.

"Oh, my God, it might be today!" I say excitedly, and deep in my heart, there's a well bubbling and I feel like it's going to burst with love and joy at any second. Nic smiles back at me, but there's a flash of uncertainty in his eyes. "Nic, you okay, honey?"

He nods, taking my hand and patting it absently, but still, I can see that his mind's running a thousand miles a minute, everywhere but here. "Yeah, yeah, I'm fine. I'm just . . ."

He takes a big breath, his eyes rolling up to the ceiling, and my heart stutters. Is he bailing on me? I'd been ready to be a single mother, but that was a long time ago, and we've been resolute in our relationship and our parenting for months. We're in love and supposed to be a happy family now, together. But he definitely looks like he's looking for a way out right now as his eyes keep darting to the door. My voice wavers, and I know this is the last thing I should be asking, but I can't help it. "Nic? Talk to me."

He drops his chin down to meet my eyes, a blankness on his face, and my worry becomes absolute terror. "Rose, I'm . . . terrified. I'm freaking out here. I don't . . . what are we gonna . . ." He's rambling, and he stands to run his fingers through his hair.

I'm breaking apart inside, and my worst fears are confirmed. He's leaving, and at the worst possible time. Considering how this all started, I guess I shouldn't be surprised. I knew who he was from the beginning. He's been in Great Falls, with me, longer than he's ever stayed in one place, and I guess I should be grateful for that, but right now, I just feel disappointed and hurt.

I should be pissed, ready to throw the TV remote next to me at him. But I have a higher priority right now, this little girl inside me who's almost ready to come out and tackle this big world. And I'm gonna show her that she can do anything she sets her mind to, all on her own, if need be. I'll role model that for her the best I can. I find strength from somewhere deep inside and give him a sad smile. "It's fine, Nic. I understand. And I can do this."

He stops his pacing, looking at me like I'm crazy, confusion written all over his face, that handsome face that I've loved for months now . . . and probably always will, even if he's traipsing all over the globe and leaving me here alone with our daughter.

"Of course you can. You're the strongest person I've ever met. But I'm fucking terrified. My mind keeps running a swirling list of *what ifs*. What if something goes wrong? What if we lose Amelia? What if I lose you? God, what if I lose both of you? I can't handle that, Rose. God, I was so scared when I was rushing back from Oregon, more scared than I'd ever been before. But this tops that by a landslide. You're about to do this amazing, wondrous thing, and I'm just standing here, unable to help or make it better, writing down numbers on a piece of paper. I just want to ease this for you somehow."

It takes me a moment to process the babbling rush of words, but as they soak through my ears and into my brain, I realize what he's trying to say. "You're not leaving? Not running?"

Nic blinks for a moment before rushing over and grabbing both of my hands, staring deep in my eyes. "Leaving? What the hell are you talking about?" he asks before his mind rewinds what he's been saying, and he smiles, leaning down and kissing the tip of my nose. "Babe, I'm not going anywhere unless you are. I love you, Rose. And I love our baby. Right now, I couldn't be happier. I just wish I could *do* something. Anything."

I feel tears trickling out the corners of my eyes, and I reach up, kissing him firmly on the lips. "Oh, my God, I love you too. And you are doing something. You're here with me, experiencing this together, the birth of our family."

He leans forward to kiss me again, his lips soft and sweet against mine. I feel the commitment, the promise of our lives together in the kiss, our breaths merging into one as he strokes my cheek with his fingertips, wiping away my tears. He presses his forehead to mine again, his eyes twinkling. "Guess what?"

"What?"

"We're having a baby."

We've known that for a while now, obviously, but as another contraction hits, the reality of the coming baby somehow seems quite a bit more real, and I smile through the pain. Breathing as Nic coaches me, gliding gentle hands across my belly to ease the discomfort, I want every moment to be like this, this mix of comfort, joy, and love, with just a hint of pain to make sure this is reality and not heaven . . . yet.

I squeeze Nic's hand hard as my contraction reaches its peak, and I feel a gush between my legs. My mouth rounds in surprise as I gasp. "Oh, boy."

Nic pulls back, still holding my hand but looking around again, confused. "What? What's wrong?"

I smile back, exhaling slowly as the contraction passes. "It's definitely baby day. My water just broke."

He pauses for a split second, what I said sinking in before he jumps up and runs for the door, calling for the nurse before he even gets it open.

The nurse hustles back in, looking half amused because she's probably seen this a thousand times before. No wonder they make fathers wait outside or go boil some water or something just to distract them in the movies. "I hear you think your water broke?"

I glare at her, a little annoyed. Honestly, I either had my water break or I pissed the bed, and I haven't pissed the bed in twenty-five years. "I *know* it did. I felt it, big gush. Huge. Definitely broke."

My words are stilted as I try to breathe. These contractions are totally not cool. It's like trying to run a wind sprint with your nose pinched shut. The nurse is a pro, ignoring my wisecrack as she moves to my bedside and lifts the sheet up after donning gloves.

As soon as she lifts my hospital-issue gown, her whole demeanor changes and she presses some light-up buttons on the wall behind me. Still, there's tension in her voice the next time she speaks, the tired humor gone to be replaced with a crisp professionalism that's almost terrifying.

"Okay, Rose. It is definitely baby day. I'm not sure about your water breaking yet, but you are having a bit of bleeding. Dr. Stevens is already in the hospital, actually, so you're in good hands. We're going to head into the OR and get you ready for a C-section."

Neither Nic nor I have time to react or to question because three other people run in, their pink and blue scrubs decorated in ducks and bunnies. Somehow, that's the most terrifying part. Ducks and bunnies? Do these people even know what they're doing? This is my baby we're talking about here!

I look at Nic, alarm and panic written across both our faces. He finds his words first, looking at one of the Bunny Patrol. "Can I come too? Please."

The nurse doesn't even look at him as she preps my arm for an IV, hitting the vein in the first shot before stringing two bags and hooking monitors to the bed. "Yes. Follow us."

Without another word, we haul ass out of the room, rushing down the hallway. Vaguely, I note that the fluorescent lights really do flash by above me like they do on TV shows when they're rushing someone to surgery. Looking around half blinded, I need the reassurance of my man. "Nic?"

He answers me, right behind my head, and I feel strength flow from his voice. "I'm here, baby. I'm right here."

We burst through a set of doors, and I blink again. Christ, the OR is even ugly as shit green, just like on TV. Do they just film the shows in this hospital or something, and am I going to run into Ellen Pompeo sometime soon? I blink and realize I must have been given something to help with pain or something to be thinking such weird shit. Whatever it is, they've got me on the good stuff.

Still, the OR is freezing cold, and I hear the nurses call out for a NICU team on stand-by as rushed activity swirls all around me. Someone pulls the blankets off me, and I jerk, the cold instant. I see Nic flinch as he looks between my legs, and I wish I could see what he sees. How much blood is there? Is Amelia okay?

They shift me over to the hard table and pull this sort of half-cover up, making sure I can't see anything. Dr. Stevens comes in, his face obscured by a big blue mask as he slips into a gown and gloves. "How're you doing today, Rose?"

"Uh . . . I think freaked out might be an understatement," I reply. I look around for Nic, but he's been led out by a nurse, and I panic for a moment before I see him through a window, getting a gown on himself. "What's going on?"

"Okay, here's the deal, Rose. Seems like this baby is ready to come out today. You're in good hands here. There's no time for an epidural, so we're going to have to put you under general anesthesia, but when you wake up, your little girl will be ready to meet you."

I can tell that he's smiling by the crinkles at the corners of his eyes, and his calmness helps me calm down too. It's going to be okay. I have to believe that. Once I'm arranged the way they want, Nic is given a stool to sit on near my head. He runs his fingers through my hair, tears gathering in the corners of his eyes. "It's okay, baby," he says, and I'm glad he doesn't have to wear a mask sitting up here. I want to see all of his face. "We've got this. I love you so much."

I smile back, nodding. "I love you, too. Make sure you tell Amelia I'll wake up and be there as soon as possible. I can't wait to hold her."

Nic leans down, planting a kiss to my forehead, and whispers in my ear. "You're an amazing woman and already a wonderful mother. One last thing before you go to sleep. Rose . . . will you marry me? Will you be my wife? You're giving me such a gift, our little girl. Please let me give you one too . . . our little family, just like you always dreamed."

I smile at him, and I think I say yes, but I'm not sure as the anesthesia takes over.

CHAPTER 26

NICOLAS

*W*alking back and forth in the hallway because they wouldn't let me stay for the actual surgery, I keep kicking myself. I should've waited until after. I planned a whole fancy setup, the proposal of her dreams according to her Pinterest board. I worked it out with Brad, who was supposed to make all the arrangements, to get the setting just right in the woods and to arrange for someone to watch Amelia, the whole shebang.

But in that moment, with so many unknowns and so many questions, that was the only thing that I could think of to show her just how much she means to me and how grateful I am for the gift she is giving me, both her heart and our child. Our family.

She smiled after I asked, but whatever she tried to say came out as mumbled gibberish that sounded kinda like she said she liked hot dogs. I'd just sat there, patting her head, knowing better than to look beyond the blue curtain they'd erected at her chest before one of the nurses led me out here.

On one hand, I would love to see our baby being born. On the other hand, I know my limits, and though I'm a strong man, seeing Rose cut open like that would kill me, no matter how routine it is to everyone else in the room.

In what feels like only minutes, the door to the OR opens and a nurse waves me back in. I enter to see Dr. Stevens grinning broadly underneath his mask as he gives me a thumbs up. "It's a girl!"

"Where?" I ask, and the nurse leads me to what looks like a plastic tub on a table against the wall. I look, and it's love at first sight. She's purpley-red, a little streak of blood still in her beautiful dark hair, which is plastered down. Her eyes are puffy and closed, but her mouth is working, looking for something, and I instantly know she's hungry. "She's the most beautiful thing I've ever seen, next to her momma."

The tears I've been fighting to hold back break through and I'm openly weeping. "She is," the nurse says, taking a warm washcloth and cleaning the rest of the blood out of Amelia's hair, "but we need to get her examined while Dr. Stevens takes care of Rose."

At the mention of Rose, I turn back, going over and kissing her forehead. As I do, I hear a loud cry coming from Amelia. It's the best sound I've ever heard. "Hear that?" I whisper in Rose's ear. "You did it, baby. Amelia is here and she's just as beautiful as we knew she'd be. Good job, Momma."

The nurse who's taking care of Amelia calls over to me. "Mr. Broadmoor? You coming with us?"

I glance to Dr. Stevens, unsure what I'm supposed to do here. He looks up from his work, pointing with his head. "Go ahead, Nicolas. Rose is fine and in good hands. Go with your baby and hold her, let her know who her daddy is. When

Rose is close to waking up, they'll bring you to her, and if everything looks good with Amelia, you can place your daughter on her mother's chest right away."

I nod, thankful for someone to tell me what to do. I might be a take-charge guy in most situations, but this is totally out of my league. I lean down for one more quick kiss to Rose's cheek and then scurry out behind Amelia.

As we walk, the nurse gives me a rolling commentary on things. "The baby looks good. Vitals are stable. We gave her a little oxygen right at first, but she's doing fine without it now. We'll watch her closely, do some bloodwork, but it's all just precautionary measures. Congrats, Daddy."

I'm beaming, realizing that the nurse is right. I really am a Daddy now, and I'm going to be the best damn father I can be to this little girl. In the nursery, they have me wash my hands again and change gowns before directing me to sit in a rocking chair. "Would you like to hold her?" a nurse offers me. "She's wrapped up and looking better than ever."

I nod, terror and excitement coursing through me in equal amounts as the little blanket-wrapped bundle is lowered into my hands. She blinks up at me, looking sleepy now more than anything else as she puts a tiny little fist against her now pink cheek and yawns. I cradle her to my chest, cooing. "Well, hello, Amelia. So good to finally meet you. I'm your daddy. I'll take you to meet your momma in a little bit, but having you kinda wore her out. You've gotta be nice to her, baby. She's a real special woman, your momma."

I don't even know what else I say. I just chatter in a soft voice, telling her all about everything—her mom and me, how she'll have to be careful or Auntie Brad will have her in a tiara 24/7, promising to explore the world with her, showing her all the wonders that can be found in the simplest of things.

We rock for what seems like hours, getting to know each other, and I memorize every little finger and toe, finding a tiny freckle on her earlobe and inhaling her sweet baby smell. In all honesty, it's not quite the baby powder smell I was expecting, but then again, I guess that's a product of Johnson & Johnson, not natural baby smell. Still, it's enchanting, and I find myself kissing her forehead repeatedly, just trying to memorize how my daughter smells and feels.

Eventually, a nurse comes in. "Mr. Broadmoor, the recovery room called. Your wife is starting to wake up. If you want to be there when she does, you'll want to head over. Would you like me to show you the way?"

I nod, realizing that she called Rose my wife, and while it might not be true yet, I'm definitely not going to correct her because as soon as I can, I'm going to make that a reality. "One thing," I say, handing Amelia back to the nurse. "When does Amelia get to meet Rose?"

"She'll be right behind you."

CHAPTER 27

ROSE

I blink, each movement of my eyelids feeling like it takes about an hour and a half to open, slowly getting adjusted to light again. It feels like days have passed, but I know that in fact, it's only been a couple of hours.

When I thought earlier they'd given me the good shit, I must've been right. The anesthesia really did a number on me, giving me nonsensical dreams about swimming though ice cream, talking cars, and even a flash of Nic proposing. While wearing a dress. Wild, crazy stuff, for sure.

I blink, trying to get my eyes to focus on the room around me, my throat painful and my voice scratchy. "Nic?"

He comes into view beside me, smiling as his eyes look down at me warmly. "Right here, baby. How are you feeling? Need anything?"

"Water," I whisper. "I could go for a wine too."

He nods, grabbing a huge cup from the table and helping me catch the straw in my mouth for a small sip. "Take it easy," he warns me. "Dr. Stevens said you could have water, but not too much right at first. And definitely no wine, you goof."

I sigh, the room temperature water soothing the roughness in my throat. "Amelia? Is she okay?"

"She's better than okay," he says, his voice breaking before he clears his throat, still smiling widely. "She's amazing, beautiful like her momma. So tiny I thought I'd break her, but I held her for a long time while you were resting. She's doing fine. They said she won't even have to stay. She'll be ready to go home when you do in a couple of days."

The knot around my heart unclenches as the news settles in. She's okay. I did it. "Can I see her?"

Nic nods, hitting a button on the side of my bed. "Of course. You have to stay in here a little longer, but as soon as you get transferred to a room, she can stay with us."

I smile, the tears of relief and happiness overtaking me and running down my face.

Nic leans over me, hugging my upper body awkwardly in the hospital bed. "Hey, nothing's wrong, right? Your belly hurting? They said that would happen, but that the nerve block should still be in full effect for another couple of hours. I can get a nurse."

I shake my head, reaching up to hug him back. "No, I'm just so . . . happy."

I feel his cheek move against my hair, and I know he's smiling. "I'm so happy too, Rose," he whispers, and I can feel the warmth of tears on his cheeks too. "Thank you so much."

I think I say something else, but I'm not sure because the next time I wake up, I'm in a different room. Looking around, I see Nic holding a little bundle as he sways back and forth, pointing out the window and whispering. "Those are birds. They fly around and live in trees. Oh, and they like to poop on cars, people too, if they get a chance. Trees are those big green blobs you probably can't even see over there. But they're fun to climb. Maybe we can plant one in the front yard for you."

He keeps talking, and his soft chatter sharing the world outside with our daughter makes me smile. She's a lucky girl, and so am I. "You know that babies are totally shortsighted for like, the first month or so, right?"

Nic glances back at me and smiles when he sees that I'm awake. "Never too early to start. Amelia, this is Mommy."

He holds up our daughter, and I swallow. She's so beautiful that I want to cry.

"Here you go. I've been telling her all about you. She's excited to meet you." He lays the bundle in my arms, and I get to see my daughter for the first time. It's overwhelming how much I love this little baby, my heart literally walking around outside my body.

"Hi, Amelia, it's Mommy. I love you so very much, baby, and I'm glad you're out here to see this big world and all that it has to offer you. I can't wait to show you all the awesome things you can do and be, experience the world through your eyes, and get to know you. I love you, my little Jelly Bean."

I rub her cheek, pulling her hat off to see her full head of hair, dark like her daddy's, but her skin seems fairer, like mine. With her little pursed red rosebud lips, it gives her a Snow White appearance, and I wonder if she'll be at home in the forest with critter friends like her dad is.

Nic sits down on the bed beside me, careful not to jostle me since my belly is pretty sore. Jeez, I'm supposed to walk out of here in a few days? Someone must have helped themselves to my pain killers to come up with that crazy ass idea. "This is my favorite memory ever, right here, right now," he says before he kisses my forehead, then Amelia's. He leans back, looking at me while I mess with my gown. Amelia wants some milk and I want to see how it feels. "Do you remember right before you went under in the OR?"

I shake my head, everything a little fuzzy from the medications. "Everything is sort of mixed up, unless I really did take a swim in some butter pecan ice cream."

"Butter pecan?" Nic asks, raising an eyebrow. "Nope, but I did ask you to marry me, to be my wife, and to make our little family a little more official."

I smile, recognizing that the intensity of that moment had gotten to him, leading him to jump in deeper than intended. "You didn't have to do that. I love you, Nic. And we are a family, no matter what. It was just the heat of the moment."

He shakes his head, reaching over and stroking Amelia's head before returning his attention to me. "I'll admit, the moment did get to me. I didn't plan to ask you like that, but I did plan to ask you. And I think you might have mumbled yes right as you went to sleep. You going back on that?"

He's playful, light, but I see the seriousness in his eyes. He reaches into his pocket and pulls out the most stunning ring I've ever seen, dropping to one knee beside the bed. "Oh, Nic."

"Rose, you have given me everything I didn't know I wanted . . . your heart, a daughter, a family. My home is wherever you are, whether that's one place for the rest of our years or a million places. It's you and Amelia. Us. Always. I love you. Will you marry me?"

The tears are gushing down my face as he speaks, and I nod wildly. "Yes, yes, I'll marry you. I'd given up on the fairytale-happy ever after dream, but somehow, you gave it to me anyway. I love you so much."

He stands, leaning over to lean his elbows on the bed, cradling me and Amelia carefully, kissing me fiercely and powerfully before sliding the ring onto my finger. "I love you."

We spend the rest of the afternoon mostly talking about our plans, distracting me from the ache in my belly until, just as the sun touches the horizon, there's a light knock on the door. Before we can call out, the door opens slowly and Brad and Trey stick their heads in.

"Hello, Mama Bitch. Or was it Bitch Mama? Are you taking visitors?" Brad asks, smiling. "We'd have come earlier, but Nic said you were too doped up for visitors." He gives Nic an evil look, but there's a hint of humor behind it.

I adjust a little, making sure I'm covered and trying to slick my mess of hair into something resembling anything other than a messy rat's nest while chuckling. "Of course, come in, guys."

They come in and beeline for the baby in Nic's arms, making cooing noises. Nic looks over at me almost help-lessly, making me laugh lightly. "I guess I can see the priority here."

Brad's eyes don't leave Amelia, but Trey looks at me sheep-ishly. "How're you doing, Rose?"

I smile through the pain as I adjust myself, using the motorized bed to sit up a little more. "I'm doing awesome. Look at that baby girl we made. She's worth all the rest!"

Trey gives me a nod and comes over. "When you need it, I'll get you feeling good at your own pace. Don't worry, you'll be looking great."

Brad looks up at Trey, grinning. "Speaking of looking great, hang tight, gotta fix her up." He reaches into the bag he's carrying, pulling out a little pink hat along with what looks like a special hairbrush. He gently pulls the hospital-issued cap off and with feather-light touches, strokes Amelia's hair into soft waves before putting the pink hat on. "I knew they'd have her in one of those blue- and pink-striped generic hats, so I brought one more befitting. And voila."

He moves back, and I can see that the beanie is pale pink, but there's a hot pink tiara printed on the front of it. "Of course. How would I ever doubt you'd be the first one to give the Princess her crown?"

He mock bows to Amelia, stepping back. "Your Highness, your world awaits." Straightening back up, he claps excitedly, looking at Nic. "Now, gimme that baby."

Nic hands Amelia to Brad, who turns to Trey, and I see the bond between them stronger than ever. Beyond all the differences in their styles, beyond their unique points of view, they really are adorable together and I'm happy they've found each other. Trey seems to balance out Brad's melodramatic ways, and Brad adds a little bit of crazy to Trey's rigidly structured life.

Mentally jumping around the thought of finding each other, I clear my throat pointedly. "Hey, Brad, did you see this?" I hold my hand out to him, flashing the ring his way. His jaw drops, delight obvious on his face as he passes Amelia to

Trey, who takes her comfortably, looking like he could someday want one himself.

Brad rushes over to me, snatching my hand and oohing and ahhing as he tilts my hand this way and that to see the diamonds at every angle. Then he turns to Nic, grabbing him and planting kisses on each cheek. "Congrats, of course, but what the hell, man? We talked about this . . . picnic, sunflowers, down on one knee at sunset. She laid it all out there for you like a damn recipe."

I'm totally confused, torn between trying to pay attention to Trey with Amelia, and Brad and Nic, who looks sheepish. "What are you talking about?"

"Well, I sort of had an idea of what I wanted to do," Nic says, looking at me, "but I asked Brad because he's your friend. And uh . . . well, I don't know but I guess he hacked into your Pinterest boards so that I could do it the way you wanted. But I couldn't wait after everything that happened."

His words hit me and I realize that he'd been planning this well before Amelia was even born. I'd thought that his having a ring was a good sign that he hadn't just proposed on the fly, but knowing that he'd been preparing, researching, and asking for help somehow makes it all the sweeter.

And to think I was worried he was feeling flighty when my contractions first started. "I wouldn't change a thing about the way you proposed. It was perfect."

Nic blushes, coming over and stroking my hair. "Are you sure? I mean, we can do a reset, then do the whole picnic thing if you want?"

I laugh lightly, my belly won't let me do more, and kiss his knuckles. "No, I don't need you to propose like that. It was just an idle fantasy, and the real thing turned out so much better." I smile, thinking of new plans, plans that I never would have imagined earlier but now sound like the best thing in the world. "But we could go on the picnic with Amelia. I'm sure she's dying to hear more of your nature lessons about birds and trees."

He smiles, looking sheepish as he glances over at Amelia, who's tugging on Trey's finger. "You heard all that?"

"Every adorable word."

CHAPTER 28

NICOLAS - FOUR MONTHS LATER . . .

*I*t's still dark and early, barely five in the morning when I hear the soft wail coming through the baby monitor. I don't even have to open my eyes as I make my way out of bed and to the nursery, the path embedded in my mind from making it multiple times every night for months.

For a child who started her first twenty-four hours on a very quiet, very angelic run, my daughter's picked up a lot of bad habits from her little 'village'. Or at least, that's what I tell myself. I haven't been around many babies, but I don't remember them being this noisy.

Reaching the nursery, I gather Amelia up, cuddling her to my bare chest as I move to change her wet diaper. The movements are practiced and easy in the dim nightlight-lit room, and once she's dry and warm again, I head back to bed with her. "Snack time, sweetie. I know Mommy will be ready for you."

Rose is, in fact, already propped up, her breasts exposed as she readies to feed Amelia.

I leer at her a bit, settling our daughter in her arms and watching jealously as Amelia finds a turgid nipple and starts sucking. "Fuck, you look so sexy right now. I wish you were all set up for me to feast on."

Rose smiles, sensing the heat in my words. "Well, let me feed Jelly Bean and then maybe we'll see what we can do about that."

I smile at Amelia's nickname, which has stuck since she curls up tightly when she sleeps, completely compact and sweet like a jelly bean. But mostly, Rose's words hit me somewhere else. My cock throbs in my pajama pants, already thickening at the thought of taking Rose the way we both want, and I reach down, adjusting myself. Rose's eyes follow my hand and she bites her lips, letting me know I just need to stay awake. Plenty of motivation there.

As she nurses Amelia, I lie beside them, content to just watch them and *be* a family in the quiet hour before dawn. As she finishes and burps Amelia, I stand to take the drowsy babe back to bed.

Rose hands her to me, smiling. "How'd I get so lucky? You get her, change her, and put her back every night when she wakes up."

I smile back, thanking Sam again silently. "Well, a very wise man once told me that it was the least I could do since you're the one feeding her. Seemed like good advice. Happy wife, happy life and all that."

Laying Amelia down in her crib, I kiss her forehead, inhaling her baby scent again. "Sleep well, Princess Jelly Bean."

Stepping softly and carefully, I quietly leave the nursery and close the door. Heading back to our room, I see Rose still sitting up in bed, her shirt off and her round tits softer. She smiles, tracing a finger down her lush cleavage and teasing me. "Thought we could see about that feast if you're still awake? Amelia will sleep for a couple of hours ... hopefully."

I grin hugely, knowing there's so many ways I'd love to feast on her sexy body and already untying my pajamas as I cross the room. "Sam was sure fucking right. Happy wife, happy life. You might not be my wife yet, but damn, do I want to make you happy."

I climb across the bed on all fours, caging her in with my arms as I lower to kiss her. Rose reaches up to cup my face, taking control of the kiss, showing me how much she wants this. We've engaged in plenty of foreplay, and more than once, she's watched me relieve my tension or lent me a helping hand, but our actual 'sex' has been slow and careful since she gave birth.

Part of that, Dr. Stevens told us when Rose brought it up one time, is totally natural. Her body's been through a traumatic experience, and her body and mind needed time to recover. Part of it has also been exhaustion. When you're going on weeks without enough sleep, beds have one purpose only.

But obviously, both of us are ready, and Rose is done with slow and careful as she attacks me, yanking my pants down and surrounding my rock-hard cock with her fist. I moan into her mouth, loving it. Sure, stroking my cock for her is fine ... but her hand's so much better.

After just a few strokes, she swipes her thumb around the head, slicking my precum on her thumb and then taking it to her mouth. Her tongue darts out to swipe across the pad, tasting me, and she moans as her eyes close in delight. "Mmm . . . I've missed that. Delicious."

She presses against my shoulders, urging me to lift up to my knees, and I kneel beside her, my cock jutting out as she gets up to her own knees. As she strips her nightgown off, I devour her body with my eyes. She's beautiful. Even the pink line of the scar on her belly reminds me of just how wonderful Rose is, and the so-called 'baby weight' she's always worried about makes her look sexier than ever to me. "My God, you're fucking hot."

"Why, thank you." Rose chuckles as her eyes move from mine to my cock, making it jerk in anticipation. She locks eyes with me as she lowers her head down again, her tongue long and almost lewd as she licks a long line up my shaft.

At the top, she takes the tip into her mouth, swirling her tongue around and making me see stars. "God, Rose, your mouth . . ."

Rose hums around my cock as I take control, grabbing her head, holding her firmly but not pressing, just letting her know how much I want her right there. She presses down, taking more of me into her hot mouth, and I watch as her lips stretch wide around my girth, her throat working as she swallows me down deeper.

It's all I can take. It's been too long and I'm already on the edge, and I come, pumping my hips as I fill her mouth with everything I have.

"Fuck, Rose," I cry out, and she squeezes on my thighs, reminding me to be quiet so I don't wake up Amelia. I choke back the roar, letting it come out as a long hiss while I finish my orgasm and soften slightly in her mouth before she pulls back, wiping the corners of her mouth with her index finger to catch what she lost and then sucking her finger into her mouth.

"Damn, baby," I say as I lean back down, pushing her onto her back and capturing her lips in a searing kiss. "I have missed your mouth. But know what I've missed even more?"

"What?" she asks, scratching at my chest with her fingernails. She knows the answer, but she wants to hear me say it, I can tell.

I lean in close. "The taste of your sweet little pussy."

Rose hums as my lips find the curve of her neck and start working my way down her body. Layering kisses and licks with sucks and nibbles, I follow the line of her neck across her collarbone and down into her lush cleavage. I lie down farther on the bed, snuggling up to her round tits to swirl my tongue around her nipples, which are always turgid now, deliciously looking like little pink gumdrops.

I suck and tease, knowing that if I'm lucky, I might get just a few tiny drops of her sweet milk. Amelia's always hungry, but now that the full pressure is off Rose's luscious tits, I can suck deeply and forcefully the way she likes. I'm rewarded when I take a draw on her left breast, and Rose gasps as I look up at her, pulling back to lick my lips.

"Make sure you leave some for later," Rose teases, her voice shaky and her breath coming a little faster. "But damn, that felt nice."

"This'll feel even nicer," I promise her as I pull her leg up and around my hip, opening her up wide as I settle down with her pink pussy, already soaked for me. I hold her puffy lips open, exposing her clit as I blow a hot breath across it, watching her pulse in need.

Rose lifts her hips, silently begging before groaning. "Please, Nic. I need you. Suck my pussy and make me come."

Not needing to be asked twice, I dive in, devouring her like the starving man that I am, licking long lines from her slit to her clit, where I swirl the flat of my tongue against the little nub. Rose gasps again, reaching down and running her fingers through my hair as she grinds her pussy against my eager lips and tongue, both exploring exactly where and how hard she wants it.

I cup her ass with both hands, lifting her to my face so I can press my tongue inside her, learning quickly. It's not quite the same as before. She likes more strokes of her clit than before, but I'm happy to comply. As I do, I knead her cheeks, pulling them apart to let my pinky fingers graze her asshole before pressing them back tight together. Rose moans, looking down at me. "You want it that way?"

I grin, looking up as I brush my fingers over her ass again, watching her eyelids flutter. "Yes . . . but first, I want your sweet pussy. Your moans, your body are driving me crazy and I'm already recovered. So I'll leave the choice in your hands. Where do you want me?"

"Let me think . . ." Rose teases, and I bury my mouth around her clit again, sucking and licking while my fingers continue to probe her puckered back entrance. Over and over, I press, relaxing her and exposing more for my exploration until I slip inside and she moans thickly. "Fuck!"

I pull out, pressing everything tight so she feels the difference before repeating the whole process again, the shock of me spreading her wide making her gasp every time. The whole time, my tongue flutters around her clit, feather-light strokes that send jolts through her body and make my cock throb, steely hard as I let her decide.

She's writhing in my hands, and I can't wait anymore. I need to be inside her, feeling her heat around me. I sit up, lining my cock up with her needy body, and look her in the eye. "You made your choice?"

Rose bites her lip, completely undone with desire, as she nods. "Surprise me."

I grin as I thrust deep into her pussy, amazed as I feel the waves of her orgasm all along my shaft. "Fuck, baby. You're already coming on my cock."

She whimpers, grabbing handfuls of the sheet as she tries to fuck me back. I keep pounding in and out, prolonging her orgasm, and she gasps, wrapping her legs around me and pulling me in tighter. "That's it, squeeze me tight, Rose. Milk my fucking cock, show me how much you want it."

Rose tries to look me in the eye, grabbing my shoulders to try and hang on, but she's in too deep, and her eyes roll back in her head. Halfway senseless, her pussy clenches tighter than ever around me as she breathes out my name. "Nic . . ."

It's all I need to explode, coming hard and filling her with rope after rope of hot come till it's too much for her pussy to hold and our combined juices run out around me, covering us both with stickiness. Collapsing over her, I kiss her neck. "Fuck, Rose," I whisper in her ear. "That was . . . wow. I love you so much."

She turns her head before a big, happy smile breaks across her face. "I love you too. Amelia will be asleep for another hour or so."

She looks at me playfully, and I know that once upon a time, she'd be angling for round two, but we're new parents, and with satisfaction already humming through our bodies, I tell her exactly what she wants to hear. "Sleep while the baby sleeps? I'm sure I've heard that advice before too."

"And round two?" she asks. "I know you want my ass."

"I want all of you, and this evening, maybe we can take a long, hot, nasty shower after you get back from the gym with Trey."

"But your parents will be here this afternoon," Rose murmurs. "Do you want them to hear us... you know?"

I chuckle, kissing her neck softly. "One, they'll be in the driveway, sleeping in their motorhome. If I make you cry out that much... well, I've got some legit skills. And two, I've heard them get frisky from time to time. If the Winnebago's rockin', don't go a knockin'."

She grins sleepily, hugging me tightly as we snuggle up, messy, exhausted, and so very happy.

EPILOGUE

ROSE

"Uncle Trey will be here any minute to hold his girl. Yes, he will," I coo to Amelia as I change her morning diaper. I try not to baby-talk to her too much, but sometimes, I just can't help it. "Now remember, we talked about this . . . no pooping on him if you can help it."

I keep up the chatter, walking into the living room to see that Nic has already let Brad and Trey in. Trey walks directly toward me, the least formal of everyone since he knows what his duty's gonna be. "Uncle Trey is already here, now gimme my girl."

He takes Amelia confidently, walking back toward her nursery to play and entertain her. He'll make an appearance later, but for now, a tuxedo is totally not necessary.

Watching them disappear down the hallway, I turn to Brad. "Uhm, he's gonna give her back, right? You two will have to get your own because that little one is mine."

Brad blushes, a rare occurrence, whispering back. "We've been talking about finding a surrogate mother, actually, or

241

maybe adopting. I swear, Amelia is like a fuse. I don't think either of us ever seriously thought about that before, but now I understand what you meant about there being a constant tick-tock in your head. At least neither of us will have to give up our girlish figures," he jokes as he looks me up and down. "Seems like you just got a bit more curvy in all the right places, though."

I laugh, smoothing my hands over my casual clothes I'm wearing before I put on my dress. "Really? Think I'll look okay today?"

Brad tsks, dropping his hand from his waist. "Okay? Do I think you'll look okay? Hell no, you will not look okay. You're gonna look bombtastic, and I'll make sure of it. Hell, you already dropped a bomb on Nic. Might as well do it again, wedding day style."

I don't know what I'd do without Brad. He's been the best pseudo-wedding planner a girl could have. He adjusts the bag under his shoulder and I wonder what he's got in there for me. A stroke of appreciation courses through me and I lean forward, giving him a big hug. "Thank you for this, for everything."

He winks at me, already leading me toward the dining room which I know he's co-opted as his makeup room. "Just a wedding, we can do this. Trey is on Amelia patrol, and he'll get her dressed later. I'm doing everything for you but your hair, and McKayla will be here later to do that. Devon and Ana are out in the woods setting up your wedding arch and the reception table. Those girls are on fleek with their organization and get-shit-done attitude, so it'll be perfect I'm sure. Check, check, check. Got it all covered, my dear. Now, are you ready to get ready for the most amazing day of your life?"

I nod, knowing that while today will be amazing, I've already had the most amazing day . . . when Amelia was born. "Let's get fabulous."

Brad goes to work, lightly brushing all sorts of things to my face and refusing to let me look in the mirror even once, promising me the end result is what matters most.

After a bit, McKayla swooshes in, her pink hair primped and a fluffy petticoat peeking out under her full skirt. "Okay, m'dear, time for some hair flair!" She goes to work, careful not to mess up my makeup but Brad keeps making little 'tsk noises until she can't take anymore.

McKayla eyeballs Brad, "That's it, you're out. Go fuss over something else Wedding Planner-zilla!" He huffs at her, their bitchy banter always making me giggle and it's just the stress relief I need today.

"Fine. I'll go pack the car, but you two better be ready in fifteen minutes. And not a second longer." With a sharp snap and a declared deadline to show he's still the boss, he swooshes out, leaving us with gaping mouths and wide eyes.

McKayla turns back, rolling her eyes at Brad's antics before meeting my eyes with a smile. "Hey, listen, I'm so happy for you, Rose. I know I haven't been around as much lately, but the extended honeymoon trip and uhm. . . newlywed activities have just eaten up my nights. Work all day, play all night. You'll see what I mean." She winks at me.

"I know, honey. And I completely understand. I was so happy for you and Evan to get married, and even though we haven't gotten to hang out as much, the whole town has seen how happy you two are together. And if you can turn that man's frown upside down, there's hope for all of us. You'll always be one of my best friends, the gang is just getting bigger and busier these days, which is why I appreciate everyone taking time to make today be the best it can be."

Brad's head pops around the corner, "Load up, bitches! Time to roll!" McKayla makes one last adjustment, and we're off.

It doesn't seem long before I'm standing ten yards away from Nic. Still, these last ten yards make it seem like he's so far away. There's a swath of rose petals spread out in front of me, at the end of which he stands under an arch made of intertwined young pine branches, draped lace, and wildflowers. The sun shines from behind me, lighting him in full relief and creating a halo effect around me. It's my 'magic wedding', totally natural and over-the-top and delivering on every single box in my mental list.

Most important, though, is the man standing under the arch. I see him swallow, his eyes looking up and down my simple spaghetti-strap white dress that swirls around my calves. My hair is pulled up, creating a wispy free style with little flowers woven in, and I do feel natural and beautiful right now, like a forest fairy, Nic's outdoorsy nature girl dream come to life.

He's brought that out in me, the carefree girl I once was, climbing trees and staying outside as much as possible, the one I was before I grew up and felt like I had such serious responsibilities. It's been great for my 'baby recovery' too. While I put in my time with Trey, more for friendship than anything else, I enjoy packing Amelia in her baby backpack and hiking the trails around the Mountain Spirit resort more.

It's been freeing to rediscover that girl with him leading the way, showing me and Amelia the beauty of the world and having some great adventures. His eyes shine with happy tears, and I know that I'm going to spend the rest of my life with this man, my happily ever after.

I walk slowly, carrying my bouquet of sunflowers to meet him as we're surrounded by Brad and Trey, who's holding Amelia, Ana, McKayla and her husband, Evan, Devon, and Wes with his wife, whom I just met recently. These are our people, all we need to witness this moment.

We'd decided to not have an officiant, instead doing our own vows. Brad did some online course that means he can file our certificate for us and make it official, but no matter how many times he begged, we just want to say our own thoughts and promises to one another. Still, we did agree to let him stamp and sign the form. I'm sure that's going to be fabulous, but I've been keeping my eyes out for a huge feather-plumed pen just in case.

After I walk the aisle, Nic takes my hands, going first. "Rose, when we first met, there was no denying our connection. It was like nothing I'd ever felt before, and leaving you then was hard. Later, when fate conspired to bring us back together, you challenged everything I'd ever thought about myself and my future. And it was just what I needed. You and Amelia were just what I needed. There is no place I would rather be than by your side. Where you go, I go. Always and forever. This is my promise. I love you."

I vaguely hear sniffles from the friends encircling us, but my attention is solely focused on Nic and my words, which flow from my heart. "I had a dream, a vision of what I thought my life would be like. When I thought that dream was never going to come true, I made other plans. And then I met you, and my plan came true in the wildest of ways. I am so grateful. I never thought I'd be here like this, never thought we would be here like this, but somehow, by making my plan come true, you did something much more magical. You made my dream come true, and now, I am happier than I'd ever imagined. I'm in love . . . with you and with our family. Where you go, I go. Always and forever. This is my promise. I love you."

We both lean in for a kiss, and I hear the applause, along with some hoots and cheers from our ragtag group of people. Pulling apart, I hold up my sunflowers in victory and I hear Evan call out in a deep voice, "Nice job, now let's eat!"

Laughingly, we all head to the single table set up to hold our small group for a wedding version of a picnic. I smile at the simple white cotton tablecloth and set my bouquet in the middle as a centerpiece.

Ana pulls out a huge cooler and starts to pass around bowls of delicious chicken salad, fruit, and tomato-mozzarella salad. It might still be a picnic, but we aimed for a slightly fancy one.

Devon hands out small glass flutes and Nic pops the cork on a bottle of sparkling cider amid cheers. We thought of champagne, but this way, Amelia can have some too, carefully given to her from her still uncertain sippy cup.

Once everyone's glass is full, we raise a toast, Brad leading. "To Nicolas and Rose Broadmoor. I'm going to make at least a thousand jokes about her unfortunate choice of last name."

"He's being honest," McKayla says. "It took me three months to get him to shut up about McKayla Hardwick."

"Hardwick, that's just too easy." Brad snorts, and I'm glad he hasn't taken a sip of his cider yet or it might shoot out of his nose. He sees Evan giving him a dirty look, obviously not too pleased with anyone making fun of his name, and Brad smirks back, happy to poke at the still occasionally grumpy man. "Anyway, to Nic and Rose!"

Everyone parrots it back happily before sipping their cider, Amelia's reaction earning her a round of laughs as she sputters at first in surprise before grabbing at the cup and giggling madly while downing more. "Whoo, you'd better watch that child," Ana jokes. "She's going to be a handful when she figures out what the good stuff is."

Everyone chats and celebrates and enjoys the rustic picnic, knowing that the celebration isn't over yet. McKayla, who's looking a bit extra glowy, seemingly more from within than from a highlighter blush, comes over at one point, and I wonder if she might have a little secret too. "Where are you going for your honeymoon again? Getting lost in some forest like we are now?"

I laugh, shaking my head. "Not exactly. Nic has clients— friends, really, Sam and Susan who live way out in the woods in Oregon, off-grid. We're going out there for a few weeks. Nic will get to check on their equipment, Devon is gonna take care of the shop for me here, and Nic's parents are driving their RV out to meet us for a little bit, too. We'll get to stay in a small cabin on the property and they said they'd happily watch Amelia for us so we can hike, ride ATVs, or uh. . . whatever."

She smirks at me, obviously knowing what *'whatever'* means. I know that a lot of times when she and Evan go rolling past the boutique on his Harley, her hair streaming out behind her, they're going off to do 'whatever'. "ATVs. Interesting."

"But they'll be close by so we can take care of Amelia," I continue with a roll of my eyes, "feed her and even take her with us out to the woods a bit. It sounds perfect . . . active, outdoors, and remote. Fun for all of us."

She wrinkles her nose at me, probably imagining the forest funk of what we're going to smell like in a week. "Ew, better you than me, but whatever floats your boat, gets your motor running, and turns your crank."

"Speaking of turning cranks—"

Before I can ask, Nic stands up, pulling me up beside him and wrapping an arm around my shoulder. McKayla, I think, knows what I want to ask her, and she knows I won't forget.

Nic raises his glass for a final toast. "To each and every one of you, thank you for coming. This has been a wild and unexpected journey but one I wouldn't change for anything. You are all a part of how we got here and I'm proud to call you all friends." Everyone claps, raising their glass, as he continues, "And on that note, Trey, my current favorite person, has offered to watch Amelia for a few hours till her dinnertime, so if you don't mind, I'm taking my bride home."

Before I can say a thing, he swoops me up and moves quickly down the path to the cars. Behind me, I hear laughter and applause and Trey yelling a promise to knock before he comes in with Amelia. Yeah, he's definitely gonna need to knock, because looking at Nic right now, his eyes flashing with fire as he looks at me and my dress already creeping up my thighs from the hold he has on me, we're gonna need every minute to celebrate . . . as husband and wife.

Thank you for reading, I hope you enjoyed it!

Have you read all the current books in this series?

Irresistible Bachelor Series (Interconnecting standalones):
Anaconda || Mr. Fiance || Heartstopper
Stud Muffin || Mr. Fixit || Matchmaker
Motorhead || Baby Daddy

Join my mailing list and receive 2 FREE ebooks! You'll
also be the first to know of new releases, sales, and
giveaways. If you're on Facebook, come join my Reader
Group!

EXCERPT: DIRTY TALK

BY LAUREN LANDISH

He makes dirty sound so good. So right.

The moment I heard his velvety voice growl that I'm his 'Kitty Kat', I knew I was in trouble.

Derrick 'The Love Whisperer' King gives out relationship and sex advice on the radio to everyone, but he's giving me something a bit more personal. Nobody's ever talked to me the way he does. Daring, Demanding, Sexy... and oh so **Dirty**.

Maybe we started this whole thing a little backwards. Sex first and getting to know each other after. But as we get closer, he's healing the cracks in my untrusting heart and making me believe that maybe fairy tales do come true.

I feel beautiful and hopeful when he worships my body. I feel dirty and naughty when he whispers filthy things in my ear.

But is it real? Can something so bad **really** be good for me?

And more importantly, against all odds, can it last... **forever**?

—

KATRINA

"Checkmate, bitch," I exclaim as I do a victory dance that's comprised of fist pumps and ass wiggles in my chair while my best friend Elise laughs at me. I turn in my seat and start doing a little half-stepping Rockettes dance. "Can-can, I just kicked some can-can, I so am the wo-man, and I rule this place!"

Elise does a little finger dance herself, cheering along with me. "You go, girl. Winner, winner, chicken dinner. Now let's eat!"

I laugh with her, joyful in celebrating my new promotion at work, regardless of the dirty looks the snooty ladies at the next table are shooting our way. I get their looks. I mean, we are in the best restaurant in the city. While East Robinsville isn't New York or Miami, we're more of a Northeastern suburb of . . . well, everything in between. This just isn't the sort of restaurant where five-foot-two-inch women in work clothes go shaking their ass while chanting something akin to a high school cheer.

But right now, I give exactly zero fucks. "Damn right, we can eat! I'm the youngest person in the company to ever be promoted to Senior Developer and the first woman at that level. Glass ceiling? Boom, busting through! Boys' club? Infiltrated." I mime like I'm sneaking in, shoulders hunched and hands pressed tightly in front of me before splaying my arms wide with a huge grin. "Before they know it, I'm gonna have that boys' club watching chick flicks and the whole damn office is going to be painted pink!"

Elise snorts, shaking her head again. "I still don't have a

fucking clue what you actually do, but even I understand the words *promotion* and *raise*. So huge congrats, honey."

She's right, no one really understands when I talk about my job. My brain has a tendency to talk in streams of binary zeroes and ones that make perfect sense to me, but not so much to the average person. When I was in high school, I even dreamed in Java.

And even I don't really understand what my promotion means. Senior Developer? Other than the fact that I get updated business cards with my fancy new title next week, I'm not sure what's changed. I'm still doing my own coding and my own work, just with a slightly higher pay grade. And when I say slightly, I mean barely a bump after taxes. Just enough for a bonus cocktail at a swanky club on Friday maybe. *Maybe* more at year end, they'd said. Ah, well, I'm excited anyway. It's a first step and an acknowledgement of my work.

The part people do get is when my company turns my strings of code into apps that go viral. After my last app went number one, they were forced to give me a promotion or risk losing my skills to another development company. They might not understand the zeroes and ones, but everyone can grasp dollars and cents, and that's what my apps bring in.

I might be young at only twenty-six, and female, as evidenced by my long honey-blonde hair and curvy figure, but as much as I don't fit the stereotypical profile of a computer nerd, they had to respect that my brain creates things that no one else does. I think it's my female point of view that really helps. While a chunk of the other people in the programming field fit the stereotype of being slightly repressed geeks who are more comfortable watching animated 'girlfriends' than talking to an actual woman, I'm different. I understand that merely slapping a pink font on things or adding sparkly shit and giving more pre-loaded shopping options doesn't make technology more 'female-friendly.'

It's insulting, honestly. But it gives me an edge in that I know how to actually create apps that women like and want to use. Not just women, either, based on sales. I'm getting a lot of men downloading my apps too, especially men who aren't into tech-geeking out every damn thing they own.

And so I celebrate with Elise, holding up our glasses of wine and clinking them together in a toast. Elise sips her wine and nods in appreciation, making me glad we went with the waiter's recommendation. "So you're killing it on the job front. What else is going on? How are things with you and Kevin?"

Elise has been my best friend since we met at a college recruiting event. She's all knockout looks and sass, and I'm short, nervous, and shy in professional situations, but we clicked. She knows I've been through the wringer with some previous boyfriends, and even though Kevin is fine—well-mannered, ambitious, and treats me right—she just doesn't care for him for some reason. So my joyful buzz is instantly dulled, knowing that she doesn't like Kevin.

"He's fine," I reply, knowing it's not a great answer, but I also know she's going to roast me anyway. "He's been working a lot of hours so I haven't even seen him in a few days, but he texts me every morning and night. We're supposed to go out for dinner this weekend to celebrate."

Elise sighs, giving me that look that makes her normally very cute face look sort of like a sarcastic basset hound. "I'm glad, I guess. Not to beat a dead horse," —*too late*— "but you really can do better. Kevin is just so . . . meh. There's no spark, no fire between you two. It's like you're friends who fuck."

I duck my chin, not wanting her to read on my face the woeful lack of fucking that has been happening, but I'm too transparent.

"Wait . . . you two *do* fuck, right?" Elise asks, flabbergasted. "I figured that was why you were staying with him. I was sure he must be great in the sack or you'd have dumped his boring ass a long time ago."

I bite my lip, not wanting to get into this with her . . . again. But one of Elise's greatest strengths is also one of her most annoying traits as well. She's like a dog with a bone and isn't going to let this go.

"Look, he's fine," I finally reply, trying to figure out how much I need to feed Elise before she gives me a measure of peace. "He's handsome, treats me well, and when we have sex, it's good . . . I guess. I don't believe in some Prince Charming who is going to sweep me off my feet to a castle where we'll have romantic candlelit dinners, brilliant conversation, and bed-breaking sexcapades. I just want someone to share the good and bad times with, some companionship."

Elise holds back as long as she can before she explodes, her snort and guffaw of derision getting even more looks in our direction. "Then get a fucking Golden Retriever and a rabbit. The buzzing kind that uses rechargeable batteries."

One of the ladies at the next table huffs, seemingly aghast at Elise's outburst, and they stand to move toward the bar on the other side of the restaurant, far away from us. "Well, if this is the sort of trash that passes for dinner conversation," the older one says as she sticks her nose far enough into the air I wonder if it's going to be clipped by the ceiling fans, "no wonder the country's going to hell under these Millennials!"

She storms off before Elise or I can respond, but the second lady pauses slightly and talks out of the side of her mouth. "Sweetie, you do deserve more than *fine*."

With a wink, she scurries off after her friend, leaving behind a grinning Elise. "See? Even snooty old biddies know that you deserve more than *meh*."

"I know. We've had this conversation on more than one occasion, so can we drop it?" I plead between clenched teeth before calming slightly. "I want to celebrate and catch up, not argue about my love life."

Always needing the last word, Elise drops her voice, muttering under her breath. "What love life?"

"That's low."

Elise holds her hands up, and I know I've at least gotten a temporary reprieve. "Okay then, if we're sticking to work, I got a new scoop that I'm running with. I'm writing a piece about a certain famous someone who got caught sending dick pics to a social media princess. Don't ask me who because I can't divulge that yet. But it'll be all there in black and white by next week's column."

Elise is an investigative journalist, a rather fantastic one whose talents are largely being wasted on celebrity news gossip for the tabloid paper she writes for. I can't even call it a paper, really. With the downfall of actual print news, most of her stuff ends up in cyberspace, where it's digested, Tweeted, hashtagged, and churned out for the two-minute attention span types to gloat over for a moment before they move on to . . . well, whatever the next sound bite happens to be.

Every once in awhile, she'll get to do something much more newsworthy, but mostly it's fact-checking and ass-covering before the paper publishes stories celebrities would rather see disappear. I know what burns her ass even more is when she has to cover the stories where some downward-trending celebrity manufactures a scandal just to get some social media buzz going before their latest attempt at rejuvenating a career that peaked about five years ago.

This one at least sounds halfway interesting, and frankly, better than my love life, so I laugh. "Why would he send a dick pic to someone on social media? Wouldn't he assume she'd post it? What a dumbass!"

"No, it's usually close-ups and they're posted anonymously," Elise says with a snort. "Of course, she knows because she sees the user name on their direct message, but she cuts it out so that it's posted to her page as an anonymous flash of flesh. Look."

She pulls out her phone, clicking around to open an app, one I didn't design but damn sure wish I had. It's got one hell of a sweet interface, and Elise is using it to organize her web pages better than anything the normal apps have. It takes Elise only a moment to find the page she wants.

"See?" she says, showing me her phone. "People send her messages with dick pics, tit pics, whatever. If she deems them sexy enough, she posts them with little blurbs and people can comment. She also does Q-and-As with followers, shows faceless pics of herself, and gives little shows sometimes. Kinda like porn but more 'real people' instead of silicone-stuffed, pump-sucked, fake moan scenes."

She scrolls through, showing me one image after another of body part close-ups. Some of them . . . well damn, I gotta say that while they might not be professionals or anything, it's a hell of a lot hotter than anything I'm getting right now. "Wow. That's uhh . . . quite something. I don't get it, but I guess lots of folks are into it. Wait."

She stops scrolling at my near-shout, smirking. "What? See something you like?"

My mouth feels dry and my voice papery. "Go back up a couple."

She scrolls back up and I read the blurb above a collage of pics. *Little titty fuck with my new boy toy today. Look at my hungry tits and his thick cock. After this, things got a little deeper, if you know what I mean. Sorry, no pics of that, but I'll just say that he was insatiable and I definitely had a very good morning. ;)*

The pictures show a close-up of her full cleavage, a guy's dick from above, and then a few pictures of him stroking in and out of her pressed-together breasts. I'm not afraid to say the girl's got a nice rack that would probably have most of my co-workers drooling and the blood rushing from their brains to their dicks, but that's not what's causing my stomach to drop through the floor.

I know that dick.

It's the same, thick with a little curve to the right, and I can even see a sort of donut-shaped mole high on the man's thigh, right above the shaved area above the base of his cock.

Yes, that mole seals it.

That's Kevin.

His cock with another woman, fucking her for social media,

thinking I'd probably never even know. He has barely touched me lately, but he's willing to do it almost publicly with some social media slut?

I realize Elise is staring at me, her previous good-natured look long gone to be replaced by an expression of concern. "Kat, are you okay? You look pale."

I point at her phone, trying my best to keep my voice level. "That post? The one right there?"

"Oh, Titty Fuck Girl?" Elise asks. "She's on here at least once a month with a new set of pics. Apparently, she loves her rack. I still think they're fake. Why?"

"She's talking about Kevin. That's him."

She gasps, turning the phone to look closer. "Holy shit, honey. Are you sure?"

I nod, tears already pooling in my eyes. "I'm sure."

She puts her phone down on the table and comes around the table to hug me. "Shit. Shit. Shit. I am so sorry. I told you that douchebag doesn't deserve someone like you. You're too fucking good for him."

I sniffle, nodding, but deep inside, I know that this is always how it goes. Every single boyfriend I've ever had ended up cheating on me. I've tried playing hard to get. I've tried being the good little go-along girlfriend. I've even tried being myself, which seems to be somewhere in between, once I figured out who I actually was.

It's even worse in bed, where I've tried being vanilla, being aggressive, and being submissive. And again, being myself, somewhere in the middle, when I figured out what I enjoyed from the experimentation.

But honestly, I've never been satisfied. No matter what, I just can't seem to find that 'sweet spot' that makes me happy and fulfilled in a relationship. And while I've tried everything, depending on the guy, it never works out. The boyfriends I've had, while few in number considering I can count them on one hand, all eventually cheated, saying that they just wanted something different. Something that's *not* me.

Apparently, Kevin's no different. My mood shifts wildly from self-pity to anger to finally, a numb acceptance. "What a fucking jerk. I hope he likes being a boy toy for a social media slut, because he's damn sure not my boyfriend anymore."

"That's the spirit," Elise says, refilling my wine glass. "Now, how about you and I finish off this bottle, get another, and by the time you're done, you'll have forgotten all about that loser while we take a cab back to your place?"

"Maybe I will just get a dog, and I sure as hell already have a buzzing rabbit. Several of them, in fact," I mutter. "You know what? They're better than he ever was by a damn country mile."

"Rabbits . . . they just keep going and going and going," Elise jokes, trying to keep me in good spirits. She twirls her hands in the air like the famous commercial bunny and signals for another bottle of wine.

She's right. Fuck Kevin.

DERRICK

My black leather office chair creaks, an annoying little trend it's developed over the past six months that's the primary reason I don't use it in the studio. Admittedly, that's probably for the better because if I had a chair this comfortable in the studio, I'd be too relaxed to really be on point for my shows. Still, it's helpful to have something nice like this office since it's a hell of a big step up from the days when my office was also the station's break room. "All right, hit me. What's on the agenda for today's show?"

My co-star, Susannah, checks her papers, making little checkmarks as she goes through each item. She's an incessant checkmarker, and I have no idea how the fuck she can read her sheets by the end of the day. "The overall theme for today is cheaters, and I've got several emails pulled for that so we can stay on track. We'll field calls, of course, and some will be on topic and some off, like always. I'll try and screen them as best I can, and we should be all set."

I nod, trying to mentally prep myself for another three-hour stint behind the mic, offering music, advice, hope, and sometimes a swift kick in the pants to our listeners. Two years ago, I never would've believed that I'd be known as the 'Love Whisperer' on a radio talk segment called the same thing. Part Howard Stern, part Dr. Phil, part DJ Love Below, I've found a niche that's just . . . unique.

I started out many years ago as a jock, playing football on my high school team with dreams of college ball. A seemingly short derailment after an injury led me to do sports reporting for my high school's news and I fell in love.

After that, my scholarships to play football never came, but it didn't bother me as much as I thought it would. I decided to chase after a sports broadcast degree instead, marrying my passion for football and my love of reporting.

I spent four years after graduation doing daily sports talks from three to six as the afternoon drive-home DJ. It wasn't a big station, just one of the half-dozen stations that existed as an alternative for people who didn't want to listen to corporate pop, hip-hop, or country. It was there I received that fateful call.

Looking back, it's kind of crazy, but a guy had called in bitching and moaning about his wife not understanding his need to follow all these wild superstitions to help his team win.

"I'm telling you D, I went to church and asked God himself. I said, if you can bless the Bandits with a win, I'll show myself true and wear those ugly ass socks my pastor gave me for Christmas the year before and never wash them again. You know what happened?"

Of course, everyone could figure out what happened. Still, I respectfully told him that I didn't think his unwashed socks were doing a damn thing for his beloved team on the basketball court, but if he didn't put those fuckers in the washing machine, they were sure going to land him in divorce court.

He sighed and eventually gave in when I told him to wash the socks, thank his wife for putting up with his shit, and full-out romance her to bed and do his damndest to make up for his selfish ways.

And that was that. A new show and a new me were born. After a few marketing tweaks, I've been the so-called 'Love Whisperer' for almost a year now, helping people who ask for advice to get the happily ever after they want.

Ironically, I'm single. Funny how that works out, but all the good advice I try to give stems from my parents who were happily married for over forty years before my mom passed. I won't settle for less than the real thing, and I try to advise my listeners to do the same.

And then there's the sex aspect of my job.

Talking about relationships obviously involves discussing sex with people, as that's one of the major areas that cause problems for folks. At first, talking about all the crazy shit people want to do even made me blush a little, but eventually, it's just gotten to be second nature.

Want to talk about how to get your wife to massage your prostate? Can do. Want to talk about how your girlfriend wants you to wear Underoos and call her Mommy? Can do. Want to talk about your husband never washing the dishes, and how you can get him to help? I can do that too.

All-in-one, real relationships at your service. Live from six to nine, five days a week, or available for download on various podcast sites and clip shows on the weekends. Hell of a lot for a guy who figured *making it* would involve becoming the voice of some college football team.

So I want to do a good job. And that means working well with Susannah, who is the control-freak yin to my laissez-faire yang. "Thanks. I know this week's topics from our show planning meeting, but I spaced on tonight's focus."

Susannah nods, unflappable. "No problem. Do you want to scan the emails or just do your thing?"

I smile at her. She already knows the answer. "Same as always, spontaneous. You know that even though I was a Boy Scout, being prepared for this doesn't do us any favors. I sound robotic when I read ahead. First read, real reactions work better and give the listeners knee-jerk common sense."

She shrugs, scribbling on her papers. "I know, just checking."

It's probably one of the reasons we work so well together, our totally different approaches to the show. Joining me from day one, she's the one who keeps our show running behind the scenes and keeps me on track on-air, serving as both producer and co-host. Luckily, her almost anal-retentive penchant for prep totally doesn't come across on the air, where she's the playful, comedic counter to my gruff, tell-it-like-it-is style.

"Then let's rock," I tell her. "Got your drinks ready?"

Susannah nods as we head toward the studio. Settling into my broadcast chair, a much less comfortable but totally silent one, I survey my normal spread of one water, one coffee, and one green tea, one for every hour we're gonna be on the air. With the top of the hour news breaks and spaced out music jams, I've gotten used to using the exactly four minute and thirty second breaks to run next door and drain my bladder if I need to.

Everything ready, we smile and settle in for another show. "Gooooood evening! It's your favorite 'Love Whisperer,' Derrick King here with my lovely assistant, Miss Susannah Jameson. We're ready for an evening of love, sex, betrayal, and lust, if you're willing to share. Our focus tonight is on cheaters and cheating. Are you being cheated on? Maybe *you* are the cheater? Call in and we'll talk."

The red glow from the holding calls is instant, but I traditionally go to an email first so that I can roll right in. "While Susannah is grabbing our first caller, I'll start with an email. Here's one from P. 'Dear Love Whisperer,' it says, 'my husband travels extensively for work, leaving me home and so lonely. I don't know if he's cheating while he's gone, but I always wonder. I've started to develop feelings for my personal trainer, and I think I'm falling in love with him. What should I do?' "

I *tsk-tsk* into the microphone, making my displeasure clear. "Well, P, first things first. Your marriage is your priority because you made a vow. For better or worse, remember? It's simple. Talk to your husband. Maybe he's cheating, maybe he isn't. Maybe he's working his ass off so his bored wife can even *have* a trainer and you're looking for excuses to justify your own bad behavior. But talking to him is your first step. You need to explain your feelings and that you need him more than perhaps you need the money. Second, you need to get a life beyond your husband and trainer. I get the sense you need some attention and your trainer is giving it to you, so you think you're in love with him. Newsflash—he's being paid to give you attention. By your husband, it sounds like. That's not a healthy foundation for a relationship even if he is your soulmate, which I doubt."

I sigh and lower my voice a little. I don't want to cut this woman's guts out. I want to help her. "P, let's be honest. A good trainer is going to be personable. They're in a sales profession. They're not going to make it in the industry without either being the best in the world at what they do or having a good personality. And a lot of them have good bodies. Their bodies are their business cards. So it's natural to feel some attraction to your trainer. But that doesn't mean he's going to stick by you. Here's a challenge—tell your trainer you can't pay him for the next three months and see how available he is to just give you his time."

Susannah snickers and hits her mic button. "That's why I do group yoga classes. Only thing that happens there is sweaty tantric orgies. Ohmm . . . my . . ." Her initial yoga-esque ohm dissolves into a pleasure-induced moan that she fakes exceedingly well.

I roll my eyes, knowing that she does nothing of the sort. "To the point, though, fire your trainer because of your weakness and tell him why. He's a pro. He needs to know that his services were not the reason you're leaving. Next, get a hobby that fulfills you beyond a man and talk to your husband."

I click a button and a sound effect of a cheering audience plays through my headset. It goes on like this for a while, call after call, email after email of helping people.

Well, I hope I'm helping them. They seem to think I am, and I'm certainly giving it my best shot. In between, I mix in music and a hodgepodge of stuff that fits the daily themes. Tonight I've got some Taylor Swift, a little Carrie Under-wood, some old-school TLC. I even, as a joke, worked in Bobby Brown at Susannah's insistence.

Coming back from that last one, I see Susannah gesture from her mini-booth and give the airspace over to her, letting her introduce the next caller. "Okay, Susannah's giving me the big foam finger, so what've we got?"

"You wish I had a big finger for you," Susannah teases like she always does on air—it's part of our act. "The next caller would like to discuss some rather incriminating photos she's come across. Apparently, Mr. Right was Mr. Everybody?"

I click the button, taking the call live on-air. "This is the 'Love Whisperer', who am I speaking with?"

The caller stutters, obviously nervous, and in my mind I know I have to treat this one gently. Some of the callers just want to laugh, maybe have their fifteen seconds of fame or get their pound of proverbial flesh by exposing their part-ner's misdeeds. But there are also callers like this, who I suspect really needs help. "This is Katrina . . . Kat."

Whoa, a first name. And from the sound of it, a real one. She's not making a thing up. I need to lighten the mood a little, or else she's gonna clam up and freak out on me. "Hello, Kitty Kat. What seems to be the problem today?"

I hear her sigh, and it touches me for some reason. "Well . . . I can't believe I actually got through, first of all. I worked up the nerve to dial the numbers but didn't expect an answer. I'm just . . . I don't even know what I am. I'm just a little lost and in need of some advice, I guess." She huffs out a humorless laugh.

I can hear the pain in her voice, mixed with nerves. "Advice? That I can do. That's what I'm here for, in fact. What's going on, Kat?"

"It's my boyfriend, or my soon-to-be ex-boyfriend, I guess. I found out today that he slept with someone else." She sounds like she's found a bit of steel as she speaks this time, and it makes her previous vulnerability all the more touching.

"Ouch," I say, truly wincing at the fresh wound. A day of cheat call? I'm sure the advertisers are rubbing their hands in glee, but I'm feeling for this girl. "I'm so sorry. I know that hurts and it's wrong no matter what. I heard something about compromising pics. Please tell me he didn't send you pics of him screwing someone else?"

She laughs but it's not in humor. "No, I guess that would've been worse, but he had sex with someone kind of Internet famous and she posted faceless pics of them together. But I recognized his . . . uhm . . . his . . ."

Let's just get the schlong out in the open, why don't we? "You recognized his penis? Is that the word you're looking for?"

"Yeah, I guess so," Kat says, her voice cutting through the gap created by the phone line. "He has a mole, so I know it's him."

There's something about her voice, all sweet and breathy that stirs me inside like I rarely have happen. It's not just her tone, either. She's in pain, but she's mad as fuck too, and I want to help her, protect her. She seems innocent, and something deep inside me wants to make her a little bit dirty.

"Okay, first, repeat after me. Penis, dick, cock." I wait, unsure if she'll do it but holding my breath in the hopes that she will.

"Uh, what?"

I feel a small smile come to my lips, and it's my turn to be a little playful. "Penis, dick, cock. Trust me, this is important for you. You can do it, Kitty Kat."

I hear her intake of breath, but she does what I demanded, more clearly than the shyness I expected. "Penis, dick, cock."

"Good girl," I growl into the mic, and through the window connecting our booths, I can see Susannah giving me a raised eyebrow. "Now say . . . I recognized his cock fucking her."

I say a silent prayer of thanks that my radio show is on satellite. I can say whatever I want and the FCC doesn't care.

I can tell Kat is with me now, and her voice is stronger, still sexy as fuck but without the lost kitten loneliness to it. "I recognized his cock fucking her tits."

My own cock twitches a little, and I lean in, smirking. "Ah, so the plot thickens. So Kat, how does it feel to say that?"

She sighs, pulling me back a little. "The words don't bother me. I'm just not used to being on the radio. But saying that about my boyfriend pisses me off. I can't believe he'd do that."

"So, what do you think you should do about it?" I ask, leaning back in my chair and pulling my mic toward me. "Is this a 'talk it through and our relationship will be stronger on the other side of this' type situation, or is this a 'hit the road, motherfucker, and take Miss Slippy-Grippy Tits with you?' Do you want my opinion or do you already know?"

"You're right," Kat says, chuckling and sounding stronger again. "I already know I'm done. He's been a wham-bam-doesn't even say thank you, ma'am guy all along, and I've been hanging on because I didn't think I deserved better. But I don't deserve this. I'm better off alone."

Whoa, now, only half right there, Kat with the sexy voice. "You don't deserve this. You should have someone who treats you so well you never question their love, their commitment to you. Everyone deserves that. Hey, Kitty Kat? One more thing. Can you say 'cock' for me one more time? Just for . . . entertainment."

I'm pushing the line here, both for her and for the show, but I ask her to do it anyway because I want, no need, to hear her say it.

She laughs, her voice lighter even as I know the serious conversation had to hurt. "Of course, Love Whisperer. Anything for you. You ready? Cock." She draws the word out, the k a bit harsher, and I can hear the sass, almost an invitation, as she speaks.

"Ooh, thanks so much, Kitty Kat. Hold on the line just a second." My cock is now fully hard in my pants, and I'm not sure if my upcoming bathroom break is going to be to piss or to take care of that.

I click some buttons, sending the show to a song, Shaggy's *It*

Wasn't Me coming over the airwaves to keep the cheating theme rolling. "Susannah?"

"Yeah?"

"Handle the next call or so after the commercial break," I tell her. "Pick something . . . funny after that one."

"Gotcha," Susannah says, and I'm glad she's able to handle things like that. It's part of our system too that when I get a call that needs more than on-air can handle, she fills the gap. Usually with less serious questions or listener stories that always make for great laughs.

Checking my board, I click the line back, glad that Susannah can't hear me now. "Kat? You still there?"

"Yes?" she says, and I feel another little thrill go down my cock just at her word. God, this woman's got a sexy voice, soft and sweet with a little undercurrent of sassiness . . . or maybe I really, really need to get laid.

"Hey, it's Derrick. I just wanted to say thanks for being such a good sport with all of that."

"No problem," she says as I make a picture in my head of her. I can't fill in the details, but I definitely want to. "Thanks for helping me realize I need to walk away. I already knew it, but some inspiration never hurts."

"I really would like to hear the rest of the story if you don't mind calling me back. I want to hear how he grovels when he finds out what he's lost. Would you call me?"

I don't know what I'm doing. This is so not like me. I never talk to the callers after they're on air unless I think they're going to hurt themselves or others, and I certainly never invite them to call back. But something about her voice calls to me like a siren. I just hope she's not pulling me into the rocky shore to crash.

"You mean the show?" Kat asks, uncertain and confused. "Like . . . I dunno, like a guest or something?"

"Well, probably not, to be honest," I reply, crossing my fingers even as my cock says I need to take this risk. "We'll be done with the cheating theme tonight and it probably won't come back up for a couple of weeks. I meant . . . call me. I want to make sure you're okay afterward and standing strong."

"Okay."

Before she can take it back, I rattle off my personal cell number to her, half of my brain telling me this is brilliant and the other half saying it's the stupidest thing I've ever done. I might not have the FCC looking over my shoulder, but the satellite network is and my advertisers for damn sure are. Still . . . "Got it?"

"I've got it," Kat says. "I'll get back to you after I break up with Kevin. It's been a weird night and I guess it's going to get even weirder. Guess I gotta go tell Kevin his dick busted him on the internet and he can get fucked elsewhere . . . permanently. I can do this."

"Damn right, you can," I tell her. "You can do this, Kitty Kat. Remember, you deserve better. I'll be waiting for your report."

Kat laughs and we hang up. I don't know what just happened but my body feels light, bubbly inside as I take a big breath to get ready for the next segment of tonight's show.

KAT

I knock on the door to Kevin's apartment, the voice of Derrick the Love Whisperer still running around in my head. I deserve better than to be cheated on.

"Hey, babe," Kevin says when he opens his door. He's still wearing his 'work clothes,' a black tank top with *KH Nutrition* emblazoned on it along with track pants that are just a little tight and normally worn just a little low on his hips when he works out. I've never really understood why he does it, but it's part of his 'thang.' Every Instagram pic and video he does, he whips off the tank, adjusts his track pants in a way that highlights the Adonis belt V-cut of his abs, then flexes and sort of makes a hooting grunt before finishing the show with "KH, Bay-bay!"

I used to think it was sexy, in a musclehead, caveman-ish sort of way. No longer. "Don't 'hey, babe' me," I growl, looking up into his eyes. I'm not in work clothes, so I'm missing the extra inches of height my heels normally give me. But I'm a legit five-two of fury right now, so I don't care if he's nearly a foot taller. "How long have you been fucking her behind my back?"

"Huh?" Kevin asks, but in his eyes I can see he has a damn good idea what I'm talking about.

"Don't act stupid, you son of a bitch!" I hiss, poking him in the chest. "You know exactly what I'm talking about. Titty Fuck Girl. Where'd you meet her, the gym? When you went out shopping for a new smartphone with the money I gave you because you swore you needed the better camera for your Instagram page? How long has it been going on, Kevin?"

Kevin looks up and down the hallway. For a guy whose

Internet presence makes him look like a big baller, he's living in a cracker box POS apartment building, and I know he's worried about his neighbors hearing me blab his private business. "Come on inside. We can talk—"

"If you don't tell me how long it's been going on, I'm going to put my knee right in your nuts," I growl. "This isn't a negotiation, Kevin." It really doesn't matter at this point. It's most likely just going to make me angrier, but I can't stop myself.

He looks like he's about to run but sighs. "Fine. I met her a couple of months ago when she came into the gym. I was filming a squat."

"What? So she just walked up behind you to compliment your form and suddenly, you're in bed?" I laugh, realizing just how short I sold myself. He's fake—the tan, the persona, the entire image. Just to get more followers.

Kevin looks sheepish but nods. "She said she'd promote my supps, do some spots on her Instagram feed, and let me shoot some selfies with her wearing a KH tank top."

"So you titty fucked her?" I hiss, shaking my head. Seriously, what the fuck? I can hardly take it as I stare at his chiseled face, wanting so badly to slap him. "Do you realize how ridiculous you sound right now? How stupid do you think I am?"

Kevin looks pouty, the same look he used when he hit me up for four hundred bucks for his new smartphone. "You never believe in me, never think I can be successful even though I work so hard."

It's in this moment that I see it. Though his face is schooled into a puppy dog look, his eyes are alight as he turns the blame back on me, thinking he's pulled one over on me once again. And all the fire leaves me. I'm mad he cheated, but I don't even really like him right now, and honestly, I haven't for a long time but was too afraid to do anything about it.

My voice takes a parental, lecturing tone. "You're not working. You're a lazy ass who spends hours at the gym bullshitting with the bros and thinking some scam is going to magically make you money without your having to actually do anything. But you know what? I looked the other way for too long even though everyone told me you were no good. None of that even matters now. You cheated on me. Done. Game over."

Kevin inhales, trying to stand at his tallest, most imposing. His forearms clench and his biceps start to strain as he puffs up. It strikes me that once upon a time, he'd stand over me like this and I'd find it so damn sexy I'd be instantly wet, but now, his attempt at intimidating me is just ridiculous. "You'll be sorry. You'll never find someone who treats you like I do, who satisfies you like I do."

God, how could I have been so blind? "Like you do? You know, I hope you're right because you treat me like an afterthought, using me as an ATM when you're a little short, screwing around, and blaming me for your lack of success when it's your own fault," I reply, keeping my voice calm but firm, not letting him get an inch on me. I'm not going to raise my voice, to yell or let him think that he's gotten to me, because for some reason, honestly, he hasn't. "And as for satisfied in bed, I have literally never had a single orgasm with you. Ever. I'm not gonna lie, your dick is nice to look at and photographs well, apparently, but you don't even know what to do with it. Sticking it in and out for two minutes before blowing into a condom and then rolling over to gasp while staring at the ceiling doesn't quite cut it, Kev. So yeah, I hope I never find someone who treats me like you do. I thought I could settle for content, just float along and not rock the boat, but I deserve so much more."

Before Kevin can reply, I turn and walk toward the stairs, not wanting to lose my nerve in front of him. It's not until I'm halfway down that the shakes start as the adrenaline leaves me, but I keep it cool until I get to my car.

***

One Week Later

A week since the blow-up with Kevin and I'm surprisingly not upset. Disappointed, sure, but if you end a one-year relationship with someone, shouldn't you feel sad? I've felt a lot of other emotions, anger mostly, but they've faded too. Instead, I'm just left with this . . . I guess more than anything, lack of things to do. I've got more free time on my hands, but I'm not sad or upset.

I guess the lack of depression goes to show how far apart we'd drifted and how unattached I was from him without even realizing it. Really, the most annoying part of this whole thing has been that I've had to change my gym membership because I didn't want drama or to limit myself to when I could or couldn't go based on his haunting the place.

Maybe I never really was in love with him. We'd met at the gym, and he'd been charming and admittedly hot, so when he asked me out, I said yes. Our dating just naturally progressed, and somewhere along the way, we started calling it a relationship, but who knows if he was ever really committed? I was faithful, but that was more out of habit and the fact that I would never cheat than any obvious commitment we had. It's not like he ever put a ring on it.

Even though it had been over a month since we'd been intimate, I'd gone to the doctor for a checkup just to be safe, and luckily, everything was clear. I can't believe he'd put me at risk, but I guess I should've seen it coming considering guys always cheat.

Taking the opportunity to do a purge on everything in my life, I've got the radio turned up and I'm cleaning my apartment like a mad woman when I hear the voice. *His* voice.

It's like velvet-covered gravel, and just a few words make me breathless and hot. "Good evening, listeners. Derrick King here, aka the 'Love Whisperer'. What's happening in your love life? Our focus tonight is on pushing boundaries in the bedroom. What's encouraging and fun? What's demanding and over the line? Call in if you've got something to discuss."

I've gone stock-still, my cleaning completely forgotten as his voice washes over me. I turn it up a little more as I finish sweeping, deciding everything else can wait as I listen.

Over the next few hours, Derrick is surprisingly simple in his answers to callers, who want to try a variety of things sexually but for whatever reason haven't discussed it with their partners. It's almost comical how every call gets into a groove, and it sort of goes like this:

I want to do this crazy thing.

Have you asked your partner?

No.

Talk to them. Maybe they're into it.

But I'm not sure they want to.

How could you know if you don't talk with them? If they are, great. If not, decide if it's a deal breaker and move forward according to your answer. Chances are it's not a deal-breaker if you're not doing it now.

It's funny and spiced up with plenty of little anecdotes and witticisms that leave me grinning, while his voice turns me on even as I'm comforted. I listen to his no-nonsense approach as he advocates conversation and honesty at every turn, and I only wish I had a man like that who'd actually talk and be honest with me.

As the show wraps up, I remember his request for me to call him back and tell him what happened with Kevin. He was probably just being nice and doesn't actually expect me to call, but something about it felt real.

I wait for a bit after the show ends to give him time to get out of the studio and wherever it is he goes after work, and then I call. I'm heading out anyway. I've got a late-night rumbling tummy that can only be satisfied by something cheesy and takeout.

The phone rings several times and I'm about to hang up, mad at myself for being stupidly excited about talking to *The Love Whisperer* again, when he answers.

"Talk to me."

It's the same purring growl. That panty-melting voice of his isn't an act.

"Hey, Love Whisperer. It's your Kitty Kat."

There's a throaty chuckle on the other end, but there's concern in it too, which helps me feel better. "*My* Kitty Kat now?" he asks, and I can hear the smile in his voice. "After a week went by, I wasn't sure if I was going to get that return call. I was starting to doubt whether I had an effect at all."

"You set me straight. Hold on. Let me put you on speaker. I've got this technogeek wonder phone that I love to use speaker on."

"Well, I'm in my office, so this isn't private . . . but tell me, how'd it go?"

I plug my phone into the charging dock in my dash and slip my Bluetooth earpiece in as I fire up my car. "First off, I can't believe I didn't listen to anyone."

Derrick

"I can't believe you're the type to settle for anyone," I reply, relaxing back in my office chair. It's late. Almost nobody is around the studio right now. It's one of the benefits of satellite radio, I guess. You can run a lot more shows prerecorded. "So he fessed up?"

"He gave me the most ridiculous line of shit ever," Kat says, her breathy voice causing a stir in my pants. What the fuck is wrong with me? "He said that he did it because she was willing to pimp his line of supplements on her Instagram page."

"You're shitting me," I say, rolling my eyes. "What a stupid asshole."

"You're right there. Honestly, I waited a week to call because I wanted to get a clear head."

"I can understand that. So he fed you a line of bullshit, and you chucked his ass out on the street. That's what I wanted to hear."

"Not quite," Kat says. "I went to his apartment to give him the news. No waiting around."

"Good for you," I tell her. "So, that's it? I mean, I like it, but sounds a bit easy, don't you think?"

"Well, he did try to puff his chest out and tell me no man would ever treat me like he did or satisfy me like him. I took a little delight in telling him that I sure as hell hoped not since he's a cheater whom I had to fake it with because he'd never even made me . . ." Kat says with spunkiness before stopping herself short. "Uhm, I mean—"

"Wait, seriously?" I ask in a sputtering laugh. "Is that true? You weren't just busting his balls? Damn, Kat . . . for how long?"

"It's okay," she says, seemingly comfortable talking to me. "My best friend told me to get a dog or a new rabbit. Or both. She's probably right."

"A rabbit?" I ask, my brain half-buzzed from her voice. Fuck me, I need to get laid.

"Well, um, not a bunny rabbit," she replies, her voice becoming even a little breathier. "You know . . . a rabbit."

She makes a buzzing sound, and all of a sudden, it hits me. She's making me seem like an amateur. I talk about sex for a living. I shouldn't be caught off guard like this. Trying to maintain at least a veneer of professionalism, I clear my throat. "Yeah, I can see where that'd come in handy. Take matters into your own hands, so to speak. I've done that myself more than a few times."

What I just said sinks in for both of us, and the tension between us can be felt even over the phone lines. If I could see her right now, I'd swear we'd just crossed a line. And I'd probably see how far I could push to make a move.

Kat can feel it too. "So, uh, yeah, anyway. That was probably an overshare on my part. Sorry about that."

Fuck it. I don't know why I'm doing this, but I'm just gonna go for it. Her sweet voice is doing something magically delicious to me, something about her intriguing me in a way I haven't felt in a long while. Time to jump in the pool and see if she's willing to swim with me. I look around the studio, not seeing Susannah. "Not an overshare at all. I'm just in the middle of picturing you with your new pet bunny, what you would look like spread wide open with your tits pearled up, pussy pulsing around a little toy that can't fill it, and what you'd sound like when you come."

I know my voice has gotten deeper, lust making it even rougher than my usual smooth radio sound, but I can't stop it. I adjust myself in my jeans, glad she can't see the effect she's having on me right now.

There's a slight hitch in her voice as she adjusts to what I just said. "Derrick, wow. I don't know what to say to that. Fuck."

She's all but whispering by the end of her sentence and I wonder if she's touching herself to let out some tension. I don't even know what she looks like, but I don't care. I want to see her just like I said, maybe in a little skirt that's hiked up so she can show me as I inhale her scent. "You don't have to say anything unless you want me to stop."

I pause, hoping she doesn't say stop because I damn sure don't want to. I barely know this woman, this voice coming through my phone, but she's got me rock hard and on the edge with barely a word. I reach down and undo the button on my jeans, giving myself at least a little room to breathe.

"I think I need to—"

I interrupt, hoping to give her what she wants and needing my own release as well. "What do you need, Kitty Kat? I'll give it to you."

Kat pauses, and I can feel her trembling on the edge before she lets out another deep breath, half moan, half sigh of regret. "I think I need to go. I'm sorry. This is all new to me and I wasn't expecting this tonight. And . . . well, I'm driving. Gotta stay safe. Good night, Derrick."

Before I can say a single thing to stop her, she hangs up. *Damn it, Derrick! You pushed her too far, too fast.* I literally just did a show about listening, not going beyond your partner's limits, and I just blasted past Kat's, lost in my own desire.

My brain is yelling at me, disappointed that she hung up, but my cock is still at full attention, begging for release. I let the image of Kat take over my mind, not even knowing what she actually looks like, but imagining her pink pussy dripping as she rubs a vibrator across her clit.

I reach into my briefs, taking my cock out and grabbing it in one fist, then stroke up and down my shaft, giving me instant relief as I groan. To hell with it. As hot as I am, this will be fast, so the odds of anyone catching me are slim. And if they do, well, they're in for a sight because I can't stop.

I imagine Kat holding the vibe to herself as she slips two fingers into her pussy, thrusting them in and out in time to my own strokes, her eyes hooded with lust and watching my every breath.

In my head, I talk to her, telling her to fuck herself with her fingers. To show me how much she wishes it were my cock filling her tight pussy, how she wants to squeeze and milk me until I fill her up with so much cum that it spills out of her, too much for her little cunt to hold.

The combination of memories of her voice and my own mind filling the gaps and imagining dirty talking to Kat sends me over the edge. I explode, my come coating my hand as I jerk, getting every last shudder from the orgasm as I picture Kat screaming my name as she's lost in her own pleasure.

I glance around my office again, seeing the box of tissues on the corner of my desk. I grab a handful, glad there's something to help clean up this particular spill . . . and damn glad nobody's around to see the mess I've made.

KAT

"Yo, Kat!"

"You already spent that new bonus check?"

I huff, wishing I got a bonus check, but I play along anyway. I give a wave to Harry and Larry, two of my co-workers. "You'll see when the pizzas come in at lunch!" I joke back.

Harry rubs his Monday shirt, a stretched and faded *Pizza The Hut* custom job he got off the Internet. "Just remember, no sausage!"

"That's not what I've heard," I tease, and Harry snorts. He claims to be a ladies-man love machine, but I have more than a sneaking suspicion that's all talk and some serious next-level self-aggrandizing. He's a good guy, though, and he doesn't take anything too seriously.

"Yeah, well, hope you've got another doozy cooked up," Larry says. "My latest game's gonna have me taking your shine soon enough."

I laugh and head to my cubicle. I've finally gotten it exactly the way I want, with triple screens that allow me to code, visualize, and debug all at the same time.

I immediately pull up my next project, an ambitious attempt at totally integrating calendars, social media, and office apps that could turn the whole damn system on its head.

I need to focus because the coding on this is going to be tricky. Integrating all these systems is easy. Doing it without turning someone's smartphone into a brick that works at the speed of a turtle? That's tricky.

As I work, I know I should be focusing on code. Every line has to be correct and every phrase has to be perfect. I can't have any mistakes or any clogs. But instead, my mind keeps wandering back to my phone conversation with Derrick.

The conversation had been nice until it got a little too heated. I mean, he had me half moaning even before he said what he did. I can't believe I just bailed like that.

Sure, I know I was a total coward, but I truly wasn't expecting it and I didn't know what to say. Especially since all of my blood was rushing to my neglected pussy, making me squirm around in my seat and tempting me to pull over right then to take matters into my own hands once again. I was this close to telling him exactly what I needed.

Face it, Kat, you wanted to, my mind tells me. *In fact, you wanted him to be there, his silky voice telling you what to do, talking you through every action as his eyes watched you with rapt attention.*

Shaking my head, I try to get back to work, putting in hour after hour of work and making little progress. Coding is a lot like speaking a foreign language. For some people, those folks who get paid big bucks, they can translate on the fly, able to listen in one language and talk in another almost instantaneously.

Others, like me, might be just as fluent in both languages but can't operate in both at the same time. So for me, coding means I have to put my brain in 'code mode' to really get in the groove.

Just as my left-hand monitor flashes me a signal that it's noon and time for lunch, my phone rings. It's my sister Jessie, who's learned to never, ever call me during my work hours unless someone important is dying.

Jessie's always been like a second mom to me. Eight years older, we never really had that period when she was a teen where she thought taking care of her little sister was a pain in the ass. Instead, she looked out for me, making sure I got my schoolwork done and never letting me veer too far off the path into crazy.

She's not some stick in the mud though. Actually, the first time I ever got drunk was with Jessie, and we both have had plenty of good laughs along the way. With hair two shades darker than mine and another three inches on me, she's beautiful and a stellar wife and mom, all the while holding down a full-time job as a risk management specialist for an insurance company.

She's truly Super Woman and everything I want to be when I grow up, whenever that'll be. With my new promotion, I'm at least *halfway* there, the professional success coming more readily than the personal. "What's up in the land of vehicle recall calculations?" I ask her. "Got anything that'll blow up in my face?"

"Very funny," Jess says with a laugh. "Actually, I called to say congrats on work and your promotion. Good job, Sis. I knew you could do it. Acing it at work, and on the home front too? How's Kevin?"

I wonder for a split second if she can read my mind, the professional-personal discrepancy coming out of her mouth just a beat after it crossed my mind. I can tell she doesn't care but feels like she should ask.

"What about Kevin?" I ask, trying to not sound snippy. Hell, maybe I should listen to her more because she was spot-on with him and has been right before about boyfriends too. "There *is* no more Kevin."

"What do you mean?" she asks, and I tell her about our breakup, leaving out the issues with our sex life and focusing on his cheating and my not putting up with it.

When I finish, Jess gives me a little cheer. "Good for you, girl. You're beautiful *and* smart, and there's no reason you should have to put up with any man who can't see that."

"Well, I don't want to be a downer, but not everyone finds a fairytale Prince Charming who loves you like Liam does you. Gonna be honest here. He's the only thing giving me hope that such a man exists in the real world, because all the ones I run into are cheaters, liars, and users looking for a booty call and nothing else."

Jess knows my experience with men so she gives me a pass. "He's out there," she tells me reassuringly. "You'll find him soon. Probably when you least expect it."

Unbidden, my mind jumps to Derrick and how that was so unexpected. But I don't even know him. Not really, just his radio persona, although he did seem genuine and real when he was listening to my drama about breaking up with Kevin.

Of course, he seems to have a bad boy side too. Good guys don't start talking about how they want to watch me toy my pussy on a second conversation unless they've got at least a decent naughty streak running through them.

There's a part of me that wants to get my own bad girl vibe going . . . kind of. I mean, I want to, but my wild child streak is sadly narrow, but maybe I could learn a few things from Derrick.

"Yeah, well," I finally say, not wanting to go down that particular rabbit hole at the moment, pun intended, "either way, I'm single now."

"Sexy and single," Jess replies. "Whatcha gonna do with all that ass inside them jeans?"

"I'm wearing a skirt today, actually," I retort. "But I do need to get some lunch."

"I gotcha," Jess says, letting it drop. "Listen, don't let any of those cretins you work with have a heart attack because your beautiful ass goes walking by, okay? And if anyone tries to grab anything, you break their wrist with one hand and slap a sexual harassment lawsuit on them with the other."

"I will," I promise her, smiling. "See you later, Jess."

"Will do. Call me tonight. We can catch up on Mom," Jess says. "Love ya, Kat."

"Love you too. Bye."

Getting home tonight, I can't help it. I find myself listening to Derrick's radio show.

"Good evening, listeners, your Love Whisperer Derrick King here, and tonight, our topic is something that seems mysterious to most men. Some men say it doesn't even exist."

"The stupid bastards," Susannah says with an exaggeratedly venomous tone of disdain, making me chuckle.

"I wouldn't say stupid, just . . . uneducated and in need of some enlightenment," Derrick purrs, making the muscles on the insides of my thighs tremble. Oh, what this man could educate me on.

"So tonight, our topic is The Female Orgasm. We're going to start off with an email. This is from . . . H. H writes that she and her girlfriend have sex often, but she is frustrated that her girlfriend can only climax from a dildo or a strap-on. H feels like that's off limits. What can she do?"

I lift an eyebrow. Derrick's chosen a doozy to start the night. "Sounds like someone needs some dick," I murmur to myself before my body whispers back that yes, it does need some dick.

"H," Derrick says, his voice sure and slightly stern, making my mouth go dry, "first, penetration has nothing to do with sexual orientation. What your girlfriend needs is what she needs. There's nothing wrong with her body saying that's what it likes best. It has nothing to do with how she feels about you as a person or her attraction to you. I'm just going to be straight with you. What your email tells me is that you might need to deal with your own insecurities. Talk to your girlfriend. I'm sure you two will be just fine."

I'm hanging on to his every word, and I idly wonder if perhaps my confession to him last week inspired this topic.

"Susannah's got us another caller, Z. Z, go ahead."

"Yeah, D, listen . . . I'm trying my best with my lady, but it seems like no matter what I do, she just doesn't get there. Like, we have sex and stuff, and she says she enjoys it, but she rarely has an orgasm. It's messing with my head and I really want to please her."

In his velvety voice, Derrick tells the caller to take his time and he's gotta build up to the main event with foreplay, not just dive in and pound her and think that'll do it.

"It starts in the mind, talking to her and telling her how sexy she is, what you want to do to her," he purrs. I can't take it anymore. I can feel my nipples tightening in my t-shirt and I cup my left breast, imagining Derrick telling me this face-to-face.

"Cup her face in your hands and kiss her gently at first, then devour her. Move down her neck, maybe tease a little nibble to see if she's into that, and lick along her collarbone. Make it down to her breasts which by now should be full and heavy," he says, and I echo him, massaging both of my breasts. It feels so good I have to sit down on my couch, leaning back and my legs spreading slowly.

"Tease her nipples, palm them and circle your hands, cradle her breasts and lick the nipples until they tighten up, then suck them deeply. If she liked the neck nibbles, maybe light bites or easy pinches here too. Your mileage may vary with that because everyone is different. Make your way down her body, layering kisses with licks and sucks along the way."

"Fuck," I moan, my eyes rolling up as my pussy quivers in anticipation. I let my left hand slide down, cupping myself through my shorts, the heat making me gasp at the first touch. The whole world swims away and all I can hear is Derrick's sexy growling.

"Compliment her pussy and let your hot breath warm her as you let the anticipation build. Then lick her with a flat tongue from slit to clit several times before focusing on her clit for circles. I've heard writing the alphabet with your tongue can be good, and when you find a letter that makes her moan, do that one over and over, but if that's too much, just trace patterns and rhythms. Flat tongue, pointed tongue, fast, slow to see what she responds to best. The answer's easy really, just pay attention to her. Take your time. Take as much time as you need to help her get into it. You'll be able to tell. She's not gonna be shy about it and you'll know. She'll open up like a flower."

I can't take this anymore. I slide a hand inside my panties, rubbing at my lips and wishing it were Derrick. I bet he's got strong fingers that could leave me dripping with desire and a tongue that could write poetry on my clit.

"Eventually," Derrick continues, "slip a finger inside slowly and pull it out, teasing her opening and stretching her. Hell, who knows, maybe two or three fingers or more. Like I said, just pay attention. Curl them toward her front wall to slide across her G-spot if you can find hers."

I follow his words, slipping two fingers inside my soaking pussy and pumping them slowly before finding my G-spot. Derrick's got me so turned on that finding the spot is easy, and each intense stroke leaves my toes curling on the carpet.

"All the while, you finger bang her and you lick and suck her clit like a starving man. It might take a few minutes, it might take a lot longer, but you do what she likes and stick with it until she comes. It'll be the best reward ever, trust me. After that, well, you see what it takes. She'll be open to you. Just listen to her body and be creative. No wham-bam, thank you, ma'am. Most women are more complex than that, all right?"

Susannah interrupts, and I can hear it in her voice that she's turned on too. "Wow, Derrick. That was rather . . . descriptive. Fellas, from a female perspective, let me tell you . . . hell yes to all of that. Hell. Yes."

They laugh, sending the show over to a song, and Mazzy Star's *Fade Into You* comes grooving out of my radio. I keep my fingers going, pumping them in and out and finding all the ways that my body likes it, grinding the heel of my hand against my clit before easing up and brushing it with my thumb.

The whole time, I can only imagine that Derrick's there doing it. I don't even know what he looks like, but holy fuck, I don't know if it matters when a man knows what he knows. My pussy clenches around my two fingers as I strum my clit with my thumb, and I cry out, pushing myself over the edge and coating my hand in my sweet slickness. The orgasm's intense, and I bite my lip hard, moaning his name. "Derrick."

Fuck me. God, I want him to fuck me so badly. When I come back to reality again, I realize the commercial break's over, and I take my hand out of my soaked panties, panting shakily.

Holy Shit, Derrick's cohort is right. Hell yes to all of that. Listening to his voice describe how he gets a woman to come, giving but always in control . . . it's worshipful mastery and I want it.

I want it so badly.

I definitely should not have hung up last night. Kicking myself for my cowardice and the missed opportunity, I click off the radio as Derrick moves on to another caller who apparently wants to know why his girlfriend can't come from anal.

I can't take another answer from Derrick. Not if I want to get any sleep.

DERRICK

The restaurant is full, but not too busy as I scan the tables. It doesn't take long to find my target. After all, there aren't too many six-foot-five, two hundred and eighty-five pound men who have a build like my best friend.

"Jacob!" I call, seeing my friend turn. He's so massive, I didn't even see that he was talking to someone, a petite blonde girl who's looking up at him with one purpose in her eyes. Jacob gives me a nod and turns back, scribbling a signature along with something else on the piece of paper the girl's holding before sending her on her way.

"Good to see you, Derrick!" Jacob says as we embrace like we did back when we were roommates in college. It was a pure chance pairing, two jocks, one on the football team and one moving away from the sport, but it clicked.

"You too. How's the shoulder treating you?" I ask.

"Not as bad as the sportswriters made it out to be. Mostly it was just one hell of a bruise. I've been resting it for two weeks now since we've got a bye week. I'm good heading into the rest of the season. Then, of course, contract talks."

Contract talks. Big money. Jacob's coming off two All-Pro years, and if he's going to stay with his current team, they're going to have to pony up some top-flight money this offseason to do it. Everyone's saying the team would be smart to try and sign him to an extension before crunch time.

"Big contract so you can pay for all of your groupies," I joke. "What is it, thirty-two girls for thirty-two cities now?"

"Don't hate the player, hate the game," Jacob jokes. "Green ain't your color, bro. You ain't a Notre Dame fan. Besides, I know that when I find the right girl, I'll settle down. Until then, fuck it. What about you?"

"Not my thing," I admit, sitting down at the table across from him. The waitress comes over, taking our orders, and then I continue. "I'm not gonna hate on you, but that's just not what I'm looking for right now."

"You never were," Jacob admits. "No matter how many times I tried to bring you to the dark side."

"What can I say? I saw the real thing with my parents, and I've never been able to settle for less. Besides, it's not like I don't get out there at all."

"We all heard that. Lookin' for that perfect freak in the sheets, lady in the streets, I guess. Anyway, I won't bust your balls. How's work?"

"Fine. Been busy, more folks calling in and we can't even get to them all in a three-hour show. But the show seems to be helping people and the ratings are through the roof."

Jacob laughs, sipping his sparkling water. "Yeah, I'm not surprised. I heard last night's show. You probably caused every woman listening to come right then and there. Shit, I'm good, never get complaints for damn sure, but hell, even I was taking notes. Never hurts to up your game a little bit."

We laugh, and I remember what Jacob told me last time we got together. Apparently, more and more of his teammates are listening in to my show as well. It seems odd that celebs and people I know would be listening to the show, but I do majorly appreciate the support. Somehow, when I'm on the mic, it feels more anonymous. The 'Love Whisperer' is just more of an amped-up facet of my personality, not exactly the real everyday version of me.

"You ever miss ball?" he asks me after we finish our food. "I mean, you helped me train during the offseasons. I know you still had the skills back in college."

I shake my head, leaning back. I remember those days, sweating it out in the winter weight room, the summers running wind sprints with Jacob up and down the steps of the stadium. Even though I'm ninety pounds lighter than him, there were too many times I was a step behind or busting my ass just to keep pace. I had the love of the game, but not that one in ten thousand talent like him. "No, not really. I miss the teamwork, the brotherhood. But it wasn't meant for me. I'm happy where I landed. You?"

He nods, rolling his shoulder unconsciously, and I wonder how much of what he told me about his injury being just a bruise was bullshit. If it is an injury, his season's going to be a lot harder than he's letting on. "Definitely happy. It's a crazy amount of work and I already feel like an old man on some days, but it's all I ever dreamed of."

"I'm glad," I reply honestly. "You think you'll make All-Pro again?"

"Pretty sure," Jacob says with a smile. "You coming to the game tomorrow? Season kick-off."

I nod, grinning. "It's a hell of a drive, but no way I'm missing it. Already pre-recorded my show for tomorrow. It'll be an all-write-in show so that I can watch my boy get his ass whooped."

Jacob laughs. "Fuck you, man. You know I'm going to be having a party in the backfield."

"I hope you party all fucking night long. I'll be partying right with you if you do."

One of the benefits of being a radio celebrity is that my face isn't as well-known as my name. So as I sit in prime seats, fifty yard line, two rows up, right behind the players, I'm pretty anonymous. If I yelled, Jacob could probably hear me, but I won't distract him like that because he's at work.

The game is close coming out of halftime, and the tension strums through the stadium. I can see Jacob stretching his shoulder subtly as he leans low to keep his hamstrings warm and loose. He'll be going out with the defense to start the second half and there's a bounce in his step that reminds me how much I loved playing ball.

It started when I was only four years old, throwing a miniball around with my dad, watching games, or at least highlights, since what four year old can sit through a three-hour football game when there were cartoons around, but I loved pretending I was one of the guys on the big TV in our living room.

When I was six, Dad started me with peewee flag ball, the ball damn-near the size of my head. In some ways, I was lucky. Spending four years playing flag allowed me to learn and understand the movements of the game without taking hits. Not that it started that way. For my first year, it seemed every snap the play turned into everyone being directionless ants, running around the field and sometimes generally toward someone who had the ball.

Once I got into sixth grade, he let me play a year of Pop Warner ball before junior high started, and the games got more serious. I learned to appreciate the smell of sweaty plastic and to listen for the sound of my parents in the stands, cheering for me. They never, ever missed a game.

It was during the last game of my junior year that I jacked up my knee. I was playing fullback and linebacker for my team —we were that sort of small school. A chop block on my blind side, two pops, and I was down on the grass with a lot of my dreams strained but not yet shattered.

The surgery wasn't much, a quick repair to my meniscus,

some therapy, and I would've been good to go for my senior year. But while it healed, I reported on the playoffs for the little in-school TV program, and I was gone, hook, line, and sinker.

Sure, I played my senior year. I'd put too much into the team and too much time with my boys to just let it go like that. But I didn't eat, sleep, and breathe football like I did before. Dad was disappointed at first, but I'd shown him how serious I was, even interning the summer after I graduated with our local news station as a gopher guy, running for coffees and making copies just so I could be in the excitement of the whole process.

Sitting in my seat, enjoying the late summer breeze and sunshine, watching Jacob and his team fight for victory, pushing their bodies to the limits . . . there's a part of me that wants to be out there. But knowing that they'll be traveling in a few days just to do it all again doesn't make me miss playing.

Maybe I miss reporting sports, but not the actual playing. It was fun to be able to get to know and to watch the athletes, and hell, it was a lot of fun to be paid to watch. Then again, I had a lot of late nights trying to cram a story in to meet a deadline. The job I've got now is a pretty sweet gig, and I can always watch the game without playing or reporting on them. I can be casual and have fun with it now.

The second half kickoff soars through the air, and I sit forward, cheering as Jacob snugs his chinstrap tight. He jogs out onto the field, ready to defend his house.

In this instance, better him than me.

KAT

I pick up my phone for what feels like the hundredth time, my thumb hovering over Derrick's name in my contacts. Since last night's show, all I can do is think about how much I want all the things he described, want to experience them with his silky voice making me putty in his arms.

But even as I'm about to call, I know deep down that although it felt like he was speaking directly to me, that's just his shtick. It's his *job* to answer the relationship and sex questions, use his sexy voice to get all the female listeners hot and bothered, and maybe add a little shock factor to keep folks tuning in day after day, week after week.

I was able to hold out for hours simply because of the announcement at the top of his show that he wasn't taking calls. It's a recorded show, so he may not even be around.

But as the evening's worn on, I can't help but think that

maybe he'd *want* to take a call from me. Even as I admit it's a stupid move, sure to end in disappointment, I just have to find out. I'm curious if he used our conversation as inspiration for his show, if he was talking to me, maybe even just a little bit subconsciously.

It rings a few times and I'm on the edge of losing my nerve and hanging up when he picks up the line, his smooth voice instantly putting me at ease. "Kitty Kat. I was hoping I'd hear from you again."

I notice that he knew who I was before I even said anything. That must mean he programmed my number into his phone, right?

I take a second to calm myself so I can sound casual and cool, even as my brain keeps jumping to conclusions that he must have really wanted to hear from me. I clear my throat before answering. "Hey, Derrick. I wanted to apologize for freaking out on you the other night. I wasn't expecting that and I handled it like a jumpy virgin instead of the smooth, mature seductress I am."

I hope he hears the sarcasm in my voice because I'm so far from smooth and mature, it's actually laughable. Despite having a sex drive that I think is pretty respectable, I'm no queen of the bedroom either, even if I have desires to the contrary. Hell, the last time I gave Kevin a blowjob was months ago, and he nearly put my eye out when I jumped back because he came without warning me first.

I'm good with swallowing, but it's considered polite to give a girl a little head tap as a warning so she can catch a breath first. Instead, I ended up sputtering, my left eye burning from a blast right in the eyeball and a rug burn on my ass that stuck around for a week. So yeah, I'm totally smooth and mature. Not. I mentally sigh at my lack of game.

Derrick's chuckle is deep and rumbly, and it makes me feel like not only does he see through my sarcasm, but he's ready to have fun with it. "I feel like you're making fun of yourself here, but I'd be willing to bet that's more true than you realize. You just need a partner you feel safe with to explore how smooth . . . or rough . . . you'd like to be."

Two sentences. Just two sentences, and hearing the implied challenge, my body's instant response is a resounding 'yes, yes, yes.' I decide to be coy, adding a flirty tone to my voice. "Perhaps you're right. Maybe I do just need the right guy. Do you happen to know anyone?"

There's flirty and then there's jumping in the deep end, and I'm definitely jackknifing about two inches above the surface as I wait with bated breath to see if this really is as deep as he's letting on or if I'm going to crack my head open and have to back out in total shame.

I hear him swallow, the gulp audible through the line in the prolonged moment before he growls in my ear, turning my knees to jelly and my nipples to diamonds. "Where are you right now, Kitty Kat?"

I stammer, shocked that I'm brave enough, horny enough, or stupid enough to be doing this. But fuck, I need him like I need air right now, even if all I really know is his voice. "At home. I–I worked from home today."

I have a flash of a thought that maybe he's going to demand to come over, and that seems a little too real even as my pussy flutters in excitement at the idea. Still, my nerves are screaming, waiting for his response. "Good, good," he says, making me lick my lips. "I just got home too. Go to your bedroom for me."

With a tinge of regret mixed with excitement, I realize that I've never told him my address. He *can't* come over unless I tell him. This is something different, something I've never done before, but as much as I want him and need him, I'm completely on board even if I am feeling in over my head a bit already.

I try to reassure myself. I'm a grown ass woman and this isn't all that unusual, if Elise can be believed. I can do this. Worst-case scenario, I make a fool of myself, hang up, and never talk to him again. Best-case, this could be just what I need. There's no worries about a relationship here. Intimate, but totally secure because it's casual. There's no concerns of whether he's going to cheat on me because there's no commitment to be more than just this. Faceless, no strings, just his velvet voice softening all the anger and disappointment from the last few weeks, getting me off and making my pussy throb in the best of ways. Resolving myself to go through with this, I feel a thrill of excitement rush through me.

Walking quickly down the hall to my room, I sink into the fluffiness of my soft white comforter, perching on the edge of the bed. "I'm here. What about you? Where are you?"

There's a sound in the background of someone walking, then a settling sound before Derrick replies. "I'm in my bedroom. I'm lying back on my bed, propped up on the pillows. What are you wearing?"

I look down at my dowdy work-from-home outfit of a tank top and Winnie the Pooh pajama pants that's decidedly unsexy, and I decide to lie. I don't want to kill the mood. "I'm wearing a sexy pajama set with little boy shorts and a crop top. The boy shorts keep riding up, showing more and more of my ass."

Derrick laughs a bit, and I can hear the grin in his voice. "Kitty Kat, I don't want you to create some fake story about what you think is sexy. Right here in this moment, all I'm thinking about is you and what's real. What do you *really* have on?"

I smirk, knowing I'm busted but somehow, the fact that he wants the truth puts me at ease and sends another little flutter through my belly. "Loose pajama pants and a black tank top. But . . ." I bite my lip, letting the tease build for a split second before continuing, "I don't have a bra on. The girls are free, perky under my favorite black tank."

"Mmm, that's more like it. A natural woman is always better than some fantasy," Derrick says, making my breath catch. Does he understand that he's a fantasy himself right now? If he does, he's not letting on. "How big are your tits? Small little handfuls, medium ripe melons, or large mouthfuls I can bury my face in and feast upon until my lips ache? Be real."

I look down, knowing that I'm curvy in all the right places, but I want to do this right, whatever the hell that means. "They're definitely more than a handful. I wouldn't say they're huge, but I'd love for you take in a mouthful and suck and lick them."

I can hear the tension in Derrick's voice at my little secret, and he hums for a moment. I can imagine him adjusting himself, picturing me in his head. "Take your shirt off and tease your nipples so they're stiff and achy for me."

As I do what he asks, a small sigh escapes my mouth, and I know he heard it. "That's it, Kitty Kat. Imagine your hands are mine, running through your cleavage and pinching those needy nipples." I whimper, rolling my left nipple between my fingers and watching the dark pink nub turn almost red. "Soothe the shock of pain away. You're not gonna hurt yourself. Just enough to let the sensations mix."

I keep rubbing, arching my back into my own hands as I flip it on him. I love feeling the warm touch of fingers on my skin, but I want more. "Your turn. Take your shirt off."

He chuckles, adjusting himself by the sound of it. "Already done, Kitty Kat. I took my shirt off when I told you to."

Feeling bold, I follow up, my knees parting on their own as I undo the bow tie at the waistband of my pants. "All right, move your hands down your chest and belly to your waist. What kind of pants do you have on?"

There's the sound of a belt buckle being released, and in my mind's eye, I can see it, black leather and shiny as it dangles from the belt loops. "Black denim Levi's."

Black denim? Holy shit, he knows just what to say. "Slip them down and off."

There's a rustle on his end of the line, then his voice comes back strong. "Kat, I'd ask if I should take my underwear off too, but it seems that the same way you were letting your tits free, I'm commando over here too."

The thought of him lying naked in his bed is doing crazy things to my head and especially to my body. I smile to myself, knowing I want to push him the way he pushed me with his questions about my breasts. My pussy flutters in my panties as I mewl like a kitten, hungry for him.

"Is your cock just enough to fill me up, maybe more than I can handle, or a monster I'm gonna choke on?"

I know I hit my mark when he groans, and I can almost imagine him reaching down, holding himself and trying not to stroke. "I bet you could handle me. I'd stuff you so full of cock you'd feel places touched that you never even knew existed . . . but something tells me you could handle everything I could dish out. Am I right?"

"I'm no extra-small, teeny tiny thing," I admit. "Is that a problem?"

Derrick purrs, and when he speaks up, his voice is raspy, thick with desire. "No, I like a woman with some curves, hips I can dig in and hold on to. I'm stroking it for you now, up and down my shaft, spreading out my precum and thinking about your pink pussy, imagining how wet you are right now. Slide those pajama pants off for me, Kat."

I do as he says, settling back against the pillows as he tells me to spread my legs wide and trace my fingers across my heated pussy.

"God, Derrick, I'm already so wet. My panties are . . . fuck, you've got me soaked. Your words, your voice . . ." I trail off as the pleasure gets too intense for my brain to multitask, my focus gathering on the slide of my fingers across the drenched cotton.

"Slide your panties to the side. Let me help you make that beautiful pussy feel good. That's the way your whole body should feel, Kitty Kat. So good and ready . . . ready for more. Rub from top to bottom. Let your fingers spread your honey all over your lips and up to your clit. Tell me how that feels, Kat."

When my fingers find the bundle of nerves, I can't hold back the moan, which rises until I can barely breathe. "Mmm, right there. Derrick, what are you doing to me? How does it feel so good with your voice washing over me, telling me what to do? Are you touching yourself still? I want you to feel this with me. Stroke your cock slow and tight."

Derrick's moan is deep, rumbling and making my fingers speed up a little. "Fuck, yes, I'm touching myself. Your breathy sighs and moans are so damn sexy. I'm imagining it's your hand stroking me. I don't know how much longer I can hold out when I know your needy pussy wants me to fill it up. Is that what you want? You want me to fill you up?"

Incoherent, I moan, but he hears my meaning loud and clear, and I can hear his breath quicken. "Slip your fingers inside for me. Imagine it's my cock thrusting into you, every thick inch stretching you and taking you right to the edge."

I do as instructed, my palm grinding on my clit with every press of my fingers inside. "Fuck, Derrick . . . yes, fuck me just like that."

My hips are bucking, helping my hand, and I ride so close to the edge. I know the sounds I'm making are guttural, but they're out of my control and Derrick is echoing them back in my ear, taking his pleasure as I find mine.

"Faster, Derrick. Fuck your hand like you'd fuck my pussy, pounding into me hard, bottoming out deep inside me." I pant, barely holding on. "I'm about to come, and I want you to come with me."

I can hear the smile in his voice and the tension in his breathing. "Kitty Kat, I've been holding back as much as I can, letting you get there. As soon as I hear the sounds of you coming, I'm a fuckin' goner. I'm gonna nut all over my hand an instant after you come on yours. Together."

In my mind, I picture him pumping his hard cock, his eyes

squeezed tight and tension through every muscle as he holds onto the edge for me. I can see him shiny with precum dripping down his shaft and wanting me, and his stomach muscles are tensed, ridged under his skin with the repressed power inside him.

I hear him growl at me. "Kat . . ." And it feels like a warning that he's reached his threshold. When I imagine his come coating his hand as it rushes out of his cock, it's all I can take. The orgasm crashes over me in waves, the cries loud even to my own ears.

Faintly in the background of my climax, I hear Derrick's grunts and know he's coming with me. I tease it out as long as I can, eventually forced into taking a big breath to settle my body from the intense release.

"Wow," I half whisper in total wonder. That was the most intense orgasm of my life, to the point I can almost feel a cramp developing somewhere in my hips because I was bucking so hard and squeezing so tightly. "That was . . . you're fucking amazing."

Derrick laughs, and I'd feel bad except . . . he's out of breath just like me, and I know he's just as shaken as I am. "Mmm, yes it was. You sound surprised. Have you ever had phone sex before?"

I shake my head before remembering that he can't see me, and I giggle lightly. "No. Never. But definitely checking that off my bucket list now."

"How about you don't mark it off, and maybe we can do that again?" Derrick asks.

"I might take you up on that," I reply, biting my lip. Late-night sessions with the Love Whisperer? Lucky me.

There's a moment of comfortable silence before my brain kicks in and I remember why I called in the first place. Well, I remember the excuse I used to justify calling. "Hey, can I ask you something?"

"Shoot," Derrick replies easily, and I feel another notch of comfort with him. He's not trying to cut the call short now that he's gotten a little action. No wham-bam, thank you, ma'am here. Vaguely, I wonder if he's the rare type that actually likes to cuddle. He might be an actual freaking unicorn . . . sexy, sweet, and dare I say it, nice. "What's up?"

"This is silly, but . . . I listened to the shows this week. The female orgasm topic seemed rather on point."

Derrick laughs softly, and another little tremble goes through my belly. I could listen to that throaty rumble all fucking day. "Yeah, you got me. You mentioned that in our conversation, and it made me think about how many women are not getting what they need. If I can help one guy be a better, more considerate lover and one woman have the orgasm she deserves, I'm calling that a successful show. Thank you for the inspiration. And I'm sure that somewhere out there in the city, there's at least one woman thanking you too."

Me, an inspiration and a muse? He knows how to make me feel even sexier. "See, and here I was thinking you just wanted to get all of us ladies turned on. I bet power companies all over had to fire up an extra reactor for the electrical surge from all the vibrators turned on as soon as you finished that bit. Hell, it sounded like your cohort had to run to the bathroom to rub one out before continuing the next call."

He laughs in that way that tells me something else. Whoever

his coworker may be, he's not interested in her. He's not calling her up late at night and causing her to come her brains out. "Susannah? Definitely not. Most of the time, she barely puts up with me, but she does a great job of keeping the show on track. She's the real backbone. I'm just the pretty voice. As for the rest of the listeners, I don't know. I just hope to help, I guess."

I smile, realizing he does seem like a truly nice guy, with a sexy voice and an unabashed sex drive. I feel a shot of warmth through my cynical heart, a drop of hope for mankind taking hold before I remember that Kevin was like that once too. Actually, several of my boyfriends were.

Too many men in my life start off charming and kind, on their best behavior to get you to relax around them. They made me laugh, they were warm and built trust until I let my guard down, and they found purchase in my heart. I didn't mind, of course. I thought everything was cool until they used that foothold to rip my life to shreds, leaving me spinning, wondering what happened.

My mood darkens, even as my body still hums with satisfaction. Trying not to let the change show in my voice, I try to lighten the vibe. "Ah, noble Sir Sex-a-Lot, riding in on his steed to save the citizens from a woeful lack of romance."

He laughs at my comment, and I can tell at least this one time, I fooled him. "Well, maybe not quite that dramatic, but something like that. Hey, you asked a question. You mind if I ask you one?"

"Sounds fair. I keep the bodies in the attic."

Derrick laughs, sending another thrill through me. "I'll be sure to remember that. But . . . would you mind if I texted you during the days too? I mean, I've got your number, after all."

I smile, lying back on my pillows. "I'd like that."

DERRICK

I'm floating, trying not to get too far ahead of myself. But the mere fact that Kat called me back and was equally engaged in our phone proclivities makes me smile.

Part of me can't believe it really. It's been so long since I found a woman interesting, and I was beginning to wonder if my work had made me jaded. I've certainly had several serious relationships, in college and after, but for one reason or another, they weren't the one.

All except one were good women. I tend to be a decent judge of character, but things never really clicked. I couldn't picture myself with them decades from now, happily hanging out and still chasing each other around the room to get frisky.

I don't even really know Kat yet, but something tells me that she's worth getting to know to see if she has potential to be the one.

There's a shy sweetness to her, even as she stands strong against a shitty boyfriend and says dirty things to me. It's an intoxicating combination. It's been a few days since our late-night session, but even with our conflicting schedules that have her working days and me working well into the evening, we've found time to text. A lot.

There's an anonymity to sitting behind a small screen, a disconnect that somehow lets you feel like you really know someone while simultaneously making it easier to spill your guts because there's no eye contact. There's always that built-in safety net of stopping the texting.

But we've never stopped, and sitting at my desk now, I've got my phone out, tapping away.

Hey KK, I text, my shorthand for Kitty Kat. *What are you doing?*

It's only moments before the reply pops up, making me feel good. *Work stuff. Nothing fun like you.*

I smirk, dipping into the naughtiness that's become a regular for us. *Oh, you want to do me?*

Funny . . . I meant your work is fun. She sends back after a moment. *Mine's dry & I'm rushing to my latest deadline.*

Dry, huh? Well . . . I bet I can change that. *I could distract u. Maybe make things a little less . . . dry. Maybe even slick and wet.*

So tempting . . . so very tempting, but I need to get this done. What's tonight's topic? Should I tune in?

Message received. You want to talk but can't afford to get naughty. That's okay, there's later. *Always. I like knowing you're listening. I don't remember what the show is about tonight. We do the whole week's schedule at once & I forget. Languages of love? BDSM kink? One of those.*

LOL . . . those are very different topics.

Almost as if she were here, I shrug as I type out my reply. *Not really. Both about open communication & respecting ur partner's wishes.*

If you say so, Kat sends back. *I guess I'll have to listen.*

I glance up and see the clock, hissing at the time. *Gotta go. Pre-show meeting has probably started without me.*

I see her kissy face emoji as I slip my phone into my pocket, smiling as I enter the conference room. Susannah raises an eyebrow as I sit down. She's always one to dress nice, especially nicer than my usual jeans and t-shirt, but she's dressed even better than usual in a creamy silk blouse with understated gold jewelry at her neck and ears. Wonder what's up with that, who she's trying to impress? This is radio, after all. We could do this in our pjs and listeners would be none the wiser since they can't see us. "Nice of you to join us, Mr. Love Whisperer. Something more pressing than tonight's show?"

She's scolding me like she's my boss. There's even a thinly veiled trace of anger in her voice, and I wonder why she's so upset and behaving like a snarky child. Shit, I'm less than five minutes late for the meeting, and beyond a refresher on the topic, I don't need any more prep. I'm ready to roll like I always am. I attempt to defuse, showing I'm on board. "Nope. Here and ready. What's tonight . . . love language or BDSM?"

She clucks, obviously surprised I knew what was on the agenda and disappointed that she doesn't get to ream me out. Looking down at her checklist, she makes a mark with her pen. "Technically, it's called *Languages of Love* tonight. Remember, we're doing an on-air interview with the psychologist who wrote the book. She's hot shit on the Amazon market and there's talk she might end up on New York Time's Bestselling list by year end. So we're basically a big commercial block for the book without sounding like an infomercial. Here's the monologue for the top of the show explaining it all, along with a background on her so you don't stumble into any issues. I picked emails to highlight each of the points she wants to cover so we need to hit those as a priority over phone calls."

I take her typed notes, skimming the psycho-babble descriptions contained in each section. Boring as fuck, honestly. It takes me fewer than ten seconds to realize that whatever this lady has to say, it could be summed up in two paragraphs written in really little words. Ah well, guess my job's the same. "Emails are the priority. Got it. Hey, Susannah?"

She looks at me, her eyes still flinty. "Yes?"

"Thanks for this. There's more here than usual. I can see you pulled a lot together for tonight's show, and I'll try to do all of your hard work justice," I say, but not just to assuage her hurt feelings. She's a good co-worker and does do a great job of keeping me on track, especially with a fancy topic like this. I'm more of a 'love her well and treat her right' kinda guy, but obviously, some folks need a bit more guidance, and I'm glad Susannah is here to make sure I don't do something stupid like contradict the author.

She really is the glue that keeps the show successful, even if her work is more behind-the-scenes. There've been several times she's had to feed me good advice for a caller when the questions got a little beyond dark and into *whoa* territory. I have a pretty broad 'book knowledge' at least on most things, including some of the darker sides of sexual relationships, but I've always been sort of the 'good guy with an edge.' Nobody's ever accused me of being the bad boy.

That's one of the ways Susannah balances me. She's dabbled in a lot of things I haven't, or at least she comes off as familiar with them in a way I'm not, and she's always focused on making the show the best it can be while I focus on helping the most folks. Without her driving us and scheduling topics, I'd have run out of shit to say months ago.

I see her soften, and I know despite the hard-edged bitch

persona she likes to project, she's got a real side to her too. "Sure thing, Derrick. We've got this. C'mon, Love Whisperer."

There's a teasing note back in her voice, and I know whatever made her mad about my being late is settled, or at least pushed to the back burner. Susannah is an utmost professional, and she's ready to rock this show with me like always. "Good. Now, what's the schedule for the other upcoming shows?"

"Like you ever remember?" Susannah says, and I smirk. She's right.

"Amuse me," I retort. "Imagine that I actually am a professional at this, and forget to remind me that I'm an idiot tomorrow and the rest of the week."

"Don't I always?"

KAT

"And that, ladies, is why you should always tell your man where exactly you want him to bury his tongue. That's what I call 'quality time.' Am I right?"

I was just getting my dinner ready and missed the opening segment of Derrick's show, but now, as he gives advice to a woman who wrote in about her partner's oral skills, I have to set my fork down before I drop it on the floor. The deep intensity in his voice sends a shiver through my body even as he talks to the whole city. It feels like he's talking just to me.

Setting the bowl of pasta down, I hold my breath, not sure if I'm listening to *Languages of Love* so I can get to know Derrick's heart a bit better, or *BDSM* to get to know his sexual leanings better. I've never been into hardcore BDSM, but the way Derrick speaks . . . maybe a little spanking wouldn't be too bad at all.

Of course, there's always a degree of fakeness for the airwaves. Derrick's careful. He's not going to divulge too much personal information, but he always manages to weave enough of himself into the advice he gives that you can't help but get to know him. So I keep listening, mixing in the little tidbits he tosses the listeners with the information he's shared only with me . . . and liking what I'm finding more and more.

"Okay, here's an email from Lexus," Derrick says. "Now, I'd like everyone's opinion on this one. It says, 'Dear Love Whisperer, I've been with my boyfriend for three years now, and I've got a problem. You see, I only really feel like he loves me or gives me attention when he buys me things. For the first two and half years of our relationship, he bought me diamonds, pearls, even a new car for my birthday. Recently, though, he lost his job and he's tried to make up for it with what he calls 'little things' like cooking me breakfast in bed or drawing me pictures, but it doesn't feel the same. What should I do?' "

"I have no idea what *she* should do," Susannah says, "but if I were Lexus's boyfriend, I'd be thinking it's time to trade her in and see if there's a better ride that doesn't cost so much."

"Hold on," Derrick says, barely holding back his laughter.

I snort, thinking Susannah's right. But the special guest tonight butts in. "I disagree," she says in a haughty voice. "It's obvious that Lexus has felt a lack of dialogue with her partner as their situation has changed, and she must take the initiative to make sure both of their needs are being met on a level they agree on—"

Derrick interrupts, his tell-it-like-it-is self not wanting to wait his turn. "Let me put it to Miss Lexus straight. I get that some people feel loved with gifts, surprises that let you know your partner was thinking of you and wanted to give you something to make your day a little brighter. But hell, honey, it sounds like you're venturing into gold digger territory here. It seems like you don't want a boyfriend. That's a relationship of partners, of equal give and take across all areas of your life. That's what it sounds like your boyfriend's tried to do. I'm curious how many late bills he's accumulated to buy you those diamonds and pearls. Unless he happens to play second base for the Red Sox, I would think quite a few."

"Now, hold on—" the guest says, but Derrick is on a roll and wants to finish.

"Sorry, just one second. Lexus, what you want is a sugar daddy, someone who will just take care of you and spoil you. And just so it's clear, there's nothing wrong with that. Just recognize what you really want and set out for that. Find someone who gets his joy from buying you things."

It's surprisingly good advice for a listener who sounded rather unlikeable from the whiny tone of her email. Maybe they were a little harsh, but with an email like that, it's hard not to get a little snappy.

With that, the show goes into a song break, the recognizable beats of Iggy Azalea's "Fancy" blasting out of my speakers. Feeling light and happy, I dance around my apartment a little bit, the song infectious and making me laugh at how decidedly *not* fancy I am.

I'm mid-twerk, dropping it down at the start of the second verse when my phone dings on the table, signaling a text message. I'm surprised to see it's from Derrick.

U listening? Just had a doozy.

Always listening, I text back, smiling. *U kno I'm ur #1 fan. Btw, can you buy me a Benz, Daddy?*

Stop it. I'm on air. Can't laugh yet. Suz is still pissed at me.

Then y r u texting me?

Song break. Was thinking of you.

I smile, the simple idea of him thinking of me while he's supposed to be focused and attentive at work somehow making me feel good.

He's all I think about too, playing and replaying the phone conversations and texts over in my mind. I bite my lip, knowing I shouldn't do what I'm considering. This is going to take things to a whole new level, but it's not too serious.

U want something to really think about?

There's a bit of a delay, and in the back of my mind, I hear the song change over from "Fancy" to "Yeah!" by Usher. Nice transition.

Song says it all.

Fuck it, if a man is willing to send me messages through the radio, I'm doing this. I slip into the kitchen where there's better light and pull my V-neck tee down, revealing the deep line of my cleavage and the pretty floral bra I selected this morning because I was feeling extra sassy.

I snap a pic from above, being smart while doing something totally crazy and making sure nothing else is in the shot. No face, no room, nothing identifiable. Ensuring it's flattering and anonymous, I click *Send,* along with the note, *think about these.*

I've never done this before, but he makes me feel so wanted even though I've never met him face-to-face. And something about the whole thing with Kevin makes me feel like taking this risk, like it's a common cultural phenomenon I've somehow never participated in and am maybe missing out on. This is a fuck you to Kevin, an invitation to Derrick, and a shout from my spirit that I am the head bitch in charge of my destiny. Seems like a lot to ask from one spontaneous shot of my breasts, but I have to admit, they do look great from this angle.

The response comes back so quickly that I know he's watching his phone like a hawk. *Holy shit, KK. So fucking hot. Look at that, they're begging me to taste them and mark them as my own. Bad girl, gonna make it hard for me to focus on the next segment because all my blood is rushing to my cock.*

I smile, glad that it worked. This is a big step for me. And a big step in whatever this is I'm doing with Derrick. Phone calls and texts are not the same as real-life pics, and I'm well aware how quickly a simple pic can send things into a tailspin.

But I'm not cheating like Kevin was, and I'm not trying to get more out of Derrick. I'm just having a bit of fun. I'm single, he's single, and it's all good.

Right?

Give me a call later. Maybe you can see . . . more.

This is only up to Chapter 8 of 28. Want to read the rest? Grab it HERE or visit www.laurenlandish.com

ABOUT THE AUTHOR

Join Landish Landish, my Facebook Reader Group!

Connect with Lauren Landish
www.laurenlandish.com
admin@laurenlandish

Irresistible Bachelor **Series (Interconnecting standalones):**
Anaconda ‖ Mr. Fiance ‖ Heartstopper
Stud Muffin ‖ Mr. Fixit ‖ Matchmaker
Motorhead ‖ Baby Daddy

Made in the USA
Columbia, SC
23 February 2023

12856130R00176